WOULD SHE BE
HIS WIFE IN EVERY WAY?

"If you did not want me here," Alex informed him, grinning, "you should have locked the door."

Hawk closed his eyes, because to see her was to desire her. "I did lock the door."

At her ripple of laughter, he opened them.

"I know." She allowed another salacious giggle to escape without a qualm. "The lock is broken. Everything in this house is." She beamed as she approached the tub.

At the glitter of purpose in her eyes, Hawk reared back.

"Relax," she said. "My intentions are honorable. I plan only to wash your hair, not to ravish you."

Hawk sighed, remembering ravishment with a great deal of wistful fondness, wishing it were possible, wondering what would happen if . . . "Be gentle with me," he said, tired enough to allow the good ship *Alexandra* to stay her course, however fraught with peril the waters.

Rich and honeyed with promise, her only words were, "Oh, I will."

Dear Romance Reader,

In July 2000, we launched the Ballad line with four new series, and each month we present both new and continuing stories set everywhere from medieval England to the American West—the kind of passionate, romantic stories you love best, written by the most gifted authors. At the back of each book, we tell you when you can find subsequent books in the series that have captured your heart.

This month, Alice Duncan concludes her charming *Meet Me at the Fair* series with **A Bicycle Built for Two**. When a young woman with no illusions about love tells fortunes for a living, she's bound to meet some interesting characters—but she never thought she'd meet a handsome city swell who would fall in love with her! Next up, the fabulous Annette Blair introduces the second book in her wonderfully sexy *Rogues Club* series, **An Unforgettable Rogue**. The day of a wedding is no time for the bride's first husband to show up—especially when he's supposed to be deceased! Can a couple who missed their first chance at happiness find it a second time around?

Kate Silver takes us back to the glittering adventure of the Three Musketeers' era with a second book in the *. . . And One for All* series, **A Lady Betrayed**. Can a young woman desperate to prove her father's innocence take vengeance on the young soldier who accused him . . . especially if he's the man she loves? Finally, the always talented Susan Grace concludes the *Reluctant Heroes* with the alluring tale of **The Runaway Duke**. Escaping from someone who wishes him harm, a rebellious nobleman finds that his savior is a most seductive woman . . . and one who harbors dangerous secrets of her own.

These are stories we know you'll love! Why not try them all this month?

Kate Duffy
Editorial Director

The Rogues Club

AN UNFORGETTABLE ROGUE

Annette Blair

ZEBRA BOOKS
Kensington Publishing Corp.
http://www.kensingtonbooks.com

ZEBRA BOOKS are published by

Kensington Publishing Corp.
850 Third Avenue
New York, NY 10022

All Kensington titles, imprints and distributed lines are available at special quantity discounts for bulk purchases for sales
promotion, premiums, fund-raising, educational or institu-
tional use.

Special book excerpts or customized printings can also be created to fit specific needs. For details, write or phone the office
of the Kensington Special Sales Manager: Kensington Publishing Corp., 850 Third Avenue, New York, NY 10022. Attn.
Special Sales Department. Phone: 1-800-221-2647.

Zebra and the Z logo Reg. U.S. Pat. & TM Off.

First Printing: October 2002
10 9 8 7 6 5 4 3 2 1

Printed in the United States of America

This book is dedicated with love,

To Gail Bryson in fond memory
of our many trips,
especially the one to St. Albans.

To the Brothers at Watling House,
St. Albans, England.
Thanks for your friendship and hospitality
in opening your home to us.

Prologue

Hawks Ridge at Devil's Dyke,
St. Albans, England
March 1815

Anton Wakefield, fourth duke of Hawksworth, caught his shallow breath, his zealot's eyes dimmed by a rheumy haze. "In life, I have failed."

The family curse, Bryce thought, though no man should die thinking himself a failure . . . nor live that way, either. "No, Father. Do not imagine so."

His father grasped his hand with more strength than Bryce would have thought possible. "Tell me what worth I leave behind me."

Not surprisingly, his sire voiced no attachment or pride in his son, but neither did he mention any of his litany of disappointments. Still, how did one deal with a parent who had not so much as touched one's hand for all of a lifetime and now clasped it to his heart?

One attempted, Bryce decided, one last time, to invoke some spark of kinship. "You leave *me* behind, Father."

Fervor brightened that normally vexed gaze. "You will make me proud?"

God knew he had tried. "I would like to think I will."

His father struggled for breath, and Bryce felt the panic of waning life in his weakening grip. Hope for approval waned as well, unless . . . "I will. Of course I will. Tell me what I—"

"Go and fight Bonaparte." The familiar flare of obsession shone in the old man's eyes for one last bright moment. "Bring honor to my name. I would be . . . proud."

One

Would that he had died as everyone supposed. Bryceson Wakefield, the fifth duke of Hawksworth, stood at the mouth of hell—not on the field of battle, but in the vestibule of a church, Gothic and empty of guests.

There he saw from afar his wife, a bride with her bridegroom standing before a priest . . . and there, Hawk knew, living again just might kill him.

Thrice on his way to this improbable place, he had ordered the carriage turned around, and thrice he had turned it back.

Even now, he wanted to leave rather than face Alexandra with the dreadful sight of him, but her very presence drew him up that aisle like a beacon in a night-dark storm.

Smile, Alexandra Wakefield told herself as she turned to face her bridegroom. But her attention was captured by a bearded derelict making his lone way up the aisle, the tap of his cane a desolate echo in the vaulted church.

His bearing, tall, sturdy, and wide-shouldered as he took the front pew, and the sharp, intense gaze he directed her way sent a shiver of startled awareness through Alexandra. He made her think, absurdly, of her late husband—not the first time Bryce came to mind that day—but the brooding stranger watching her, as if he might devour her, looked nothing like Bryceson Wakefield, the fifth duke of Hawksworth. A rogue by nature, swarthy, charming, and handsome as sin, he had enraptured every female who beheld him.

Alexandra had been no exception.

"Beauty and his beast," some slyly called them, for Hawk was the beauty. The day he asked for her hand in marriage had been the happiest of Alexandra's life. Then she learned the real reason he married her, and it hurt.

It hurt enough for her to say yes to Chesterfield's proposal of marriage, one year to the day after Hawksworth died at Waterloo.

At the memory, a sob rose in Alex, until the vicar cleared his throat, snapping her back to reality with a hot rush of embarrassment. "Do you, Alexandra Huntington Wakefield," he was forced to repeat, "take Judson Edward Broderick, Viscount Chesterfield, as your lawfully wedded husband?"

Panic gripped Alex—grief, soul-deep—but she had no time to regard it as the brooding stranger stood, his jaw rigidly set, and tapped his cane on the floor. "You will pardon the intrusion," he said, his husky and familiar voice swamping her in a miasma of yesterdays. "But my wife must decline."

"Bryce?" Alex cried, but no sound emerged from her throat, none save the sob that had been trapped there. Then the chapel's ceiling tilted, dipped, and kissed its floor.

Hawk hastened awkwardly to his wife's side and ignored the agony of kneeling, aware that he would have the devil of a time rising again. But at this moment, he cared for nothing, no one, save Alexandra. "Give us a minute," he enjoined the beleaguered vicar, because warning her hovering bridegroom away with even a veneer of civility would be impossible.

"I object," Chesterfield said, revoking the need for civility.

"What?" Hawksworth snapped. "You think I will abduct her from the altar? You would have no say even if I did."

His old adversary hissed and bared his teeth, like a hound after a bone.

"She is my wife," Hawk said, as much to affirm his responsibility as to stake his claim. "Mine."

"Gentlemen, remember where you are," the vicar admonished as he took Chesterfield's arm and urged him up and toward the sanctuary, nodding for the unknown groomsman to follow.

Hawk lifted and supported his wife's head and shoulders, drinking in the sight of her like a man parched, shocked that the vision before him was not the hoyden he remembered. "Ah, my funny-faced minx," he said, a rasp in his voice, "what were you thinking while my back was turned—to go and blossom into a beauty and to accept Chesterfield, of all people?"

Hawk had known for some time that Alexandra deserved better than a broken man like him, that for her own sake, he must set her free. But as he made his way up the aisle, he recognized her bridegroom and faltered in his resolve. Yes, he must seek an annulment as planned, but not just yet, for she also deserved better than the scoundrel standing beside her at the altar.

Hawk smoothed a curl from her brow. "You were such a discerning sprite; you cannot possibly love the knave." Then again, she had married once without love, why not twice?

"Ragamuffin?" Hawk called, less in banter than in challenge, the old nickname certain to ruffle her feathers and bring her around. "I know I am scarred and changed," he said, "but am I so horrid that you cannot bear to look upon the sight of me?"

Even then, Alex did not stir.

With a rush of panic, Hawk called for water, and almost as soon as he did, the vicar was there offering a cup.

Chesterfield, two steps behind, knelt and reached for Alex's hand.

"Do not," Hawksworth snapped with the command of a man who led regiments, halting his wife's accursed bridegroom like a hail of grapeshot. If only he had a weapon to hand now, Hawk thought as he placed the cup to his wife's lips and tipped it upward.

She swallowed involuntarily, coughed, opened her eyes, and swooned again.

Would that she were overcome with joy, he mused facetiously as he stroked her cheek with the back of a hand, rather than frightened to death by the loathsome sight of him.

Hawk wanted to take Alex into his arms, stand and carry her as far from the cruelties of life as he could get her, except that *he* was the ultimate cruelty. Besides, rising at all without revealing his blatant and embarrassing weakness was a feat that he had not yet mastered.

Without choice, but mortified all the same, Hawk gently returned his wife to the mercy of the cool marble floor. Then he stood in one resolute, pain-racked motion, no one save him aware of the cost in sheer willpower, or the shout of anguish trapped behind his firmly-set lips.

Chesterfield impaled him with a look, fists clenched at his sides, malice in both stance and expression.

"Sorry," Hawk said. "I lived." Though he had repeatedly questioned his survival when better men had died, true regret escaped him for the moment. "You may carry my wife to my carriage, or I shall have my man transport her. Either way, you will say your good-byes."

To Hawk's consternation, Alexandra's lock-jawed suitor bent effortlessly to bundle her into his arms, rose as easily, and awaited further instructions.

Moments later, Hawk made his fraudulent, stiff-spined way down the aisle, repudiating pain, his concentration firmly fixed upon his wife, secure in her limber buck's sturdy arms.

Other than his concern that Chesterfield might try to abscond with Alex, him unable to prevent it, Hawk found that he was almost glad of his bride's near bigamy, for it compelled him, if only for a time, to join his life to hers once again.

Still, he detested the thought of imposing his scarred and savage self upon her.

Once upon a time, he had conceived of a naive anticipation to return to her, which grew daily stronger, as did he, until he saw his scarred face in a mirror, attempted to walk, and realized that he might never be a man, in *every* respect, again.

By God, he wished things were different: that *he* were different, whole; that they could go back to the simple and easy friendship between them; that he deserved her.

He wished, most selfishly, that *she* had not changed. She used to be downright plain and all his. Now she was beautiful. Breathtaking. And to whom she belonged remained yet to be determined.

Her very presence infused him with the contentment of his youth, of their youth. Just seeing Alex again uplifted him in an extraordinary, almost abstract way, and it brought him the same overwhelming joy that her calling him from the light had once done, when against all odds the memory of her had brought him back to life. When *she* had brought him back.

Either fate or God must have a sense of humor, Hawk mused. Of a certainty, they had switched places, he and Alex, for she was now one of the most beautiful women he had ever beheld. Exquisite. And him? Well, he was beastlier than anyone could have imagined.

With the reminder, regret swamped Hawk. Guilt. She would have fared better if . . .

But no. No. If he had died, she would be condemned to a life with Chesterfield, a fate Hawk could not conceive of as acceptable under any circumstances.

Look at the strutting, thick-skulled cockscomb: agile, capable, more comfortable in his fit and strapping body than Hawk would ever be in his scarred and broken one again. Hawk wanted to beat the blackguard bloody just for existing, which was nothing to what he wanted to do to the cad for touching Alex, despite the fact that his robust assistance had been required, damn his eyes.

As they approached the church's thick, groaning, gothic doors, held open by an apprehensive vicar, Hawk vowed that the day would soon come when he could carry Alex up a bloody mountain if he pleased. Correction: if *she* pleased. If only he were granted the miracle of time and strength to accomplish it.

A wife should rest secure in her husband's arms, blast it—except that she would not be his wife for very much longer, Hawk reminded himself.

As if his agonizing walk down the aisle, with its sights and insights, were not enough, Hawk was forced to feign perfect agility—and endure perfect hell—once more, as he climbed into his waiting carriage beneath her stalwart swain's vigilant gaze.

Then reward came, for he took excessive satisfaction in accepting Alex in his arms, especially as she was being relinquished by the furious man with whom she had damned near replaced him.

Still, she was his for the moment, and since he was the only one who knew their marriage would end, the moment must be enough. Hawk was tempted, however, to rub salt in her ousted bridegroom's raw wounds just for sport, but Alex was taking so long to awaken, he was becoming increasingly concerned about her. "Alexandra?" He tested her brow for fever, chafed her hands and brought them to his lips. "Ragamuffin, wake up."

Alex floated in a sea of warmth, safe, secure, happy—an unusually blessed experience, since Bryce . . .

Her rare and singular contentment began to trouble her. She remembered dreaming that Bryceson had somehow, impossibly, returned from the dead. Then, as in all dreams, everything shifted and she found herself being carried in a death-grip by Judson for a long, long distance.

Voices had drifted above her, angry one minute, soft the next, hushing and admonishing as well. She remembered a great deal of movement—bouncing, jostling—and being held so tight, she could barely breathe.

As if, within the dream, her deepest, most private

yearnings were being granted, Judson had handed her to Bryceson of all people, and she had become incredulous, then elated.

She loved being held in her husband's arms so much, but hated as much facing Chesterfield with her guilty joy, that she wished she could remain there, asleep, or unconscious, or floating in whatever netherworld she existed, forever.

Did death beckon then, finally, and would she feel as peaceful as she had sometimes imagined?

Would Bryce be there waiting for her?

As much as she wanted to give herself up to the promise of peace, something—someone—called to her.

Alex shivered.

"Myerson, where did you put the lap rug?" That voice, again. Bryceson's, but impossible. Alex was exhilarated and frightened by the sound. It could not be real. 'Twas not Lazarus, after all, she imagined hearing, but Bryceson Wakefield, Duke of Hawksworth, dead this past year and more.

Alex heard herself whimper as warmth covered her like a blanket and she slipped blissfully back into that all-enveloping state of happy oblivion, there, in the only place where Bryceson's arms could possibly remain about her.

"Myerson, Stephen's Hotel, if you please. We will not be going on today, after all."

Alex smiled at the familiar voice and slipped deeper, in search of the place where it dwelled.

Two

Hawk saw a smile curve his wife's pale lips, and he bundled her close as he regarded the two silent men by the open door of his carriage: Chesterfield, vigilant, scowling; the vicar, a study in apprehension.

Hawk nodded. "I'll just take her to bed, shall I?"

The vicar's lips thinned. Chesterfield growled and made to charge, but the vicar stopped his forward surge. "You do not even know her," her discarded bridegroom accused over the struggling vicar's shoulder.

Hawk's heart beat at a frantic pace, for something in the accusation stung deep. He raised a speaking brow. "Not know her? I assure you that no man knows Alexandra better than I do." After today, he no longer believed it, but he would not give her erstwhile suitor the satisfaction of hearing as much.

Someone shut the carriage door, severing Chesterfield from sight, but rather than the exultation he would have expected, Hawk experienced a flash of sympathy for the man. He, too, was about to lose Alex, though not quite so soon.

"She does not want you," the malcontent shouted, negating Hawk's compassion. "She wants me."

Upon the blade-sharp echo of that sobering thrust, Hawk's carriage began to rattle and dip, shiver and clatter, as it crept across the cobbled terrace before Holy Trinity Church.

When at length the vehicle pulled safely into London's Sloane Square traffic, exultation filled Hawk, euphoria, followed by a shot of blind panic.

Yes, he had gotten Alexandra safely away, but Chesterfield's parting volley, echoing in Hawk's brain like a death knell, made him question every decision he had made since his father's death.

Until today, he thought he could not fail Alex any worse than he already had, but suppose he was wrong. Suppose he had just broken her heart by stopping her from marrying the man she loved.

Could she love Chesterfield? It hardly seemed possible, given their dissimilarities. Then again, she might have changed, as he certainly had.

He had all but died and risen from the dead. Dying changed a man. War changed him the more. There were his scars, to begin with; how would Alexandra feel once she saw the likes of them in the light of day?

She might take one look and run screaming into Chesterfield's arms.

He and Alex had certainly switched places, and in more than looks, Hawk feared, for with his return he might now become the thorn in her side.

And what would he do with her now that he had her? Not that he did not know precisely what he wished to do. He was not so broken that he did not want to be her husband in every way, though desire and action were two entirely different matters. As were desire and duty.

Or trust and honor.

Hawk slipped a wisp of his wife's rich nutmeg hair behind her ear and examined her in the fading rays of afternoon light filtering through the uncurtained carriage window.

During her growing-up years, none of Alexandra Huntington's features had seemed to match. Her eyes were too big and too bright for her small, pale face. Her eyebrows, like unmatched wings, appeared drawn by an angry hand, brows one wanted to trace with a fingertip. Hawk did so now, amazed to see how much better they fit nearly two years and one war later.

Her mouth was still too wide, her lips too full, her nose elegant but tip-tilted. Yet the amalgam had become all of a piece, falling into symmetrical and harmonious placement, of a sudden, making of his ill-favored hoyden a beauty—striking, too remarkable not to be kissed.

Like the beast his scars proclaimed him to be, Hawk wanted to awaken the slumbering princess in just that way, or lay siege to her tower fortress. Or was beauty storming the beastly rogue's lair even in sleep?

Difficult to tell which tale fit. Hawk knew only that in this marriage he had created from whole cloth, he must take care not to play the jackal and claim her for himself.

Rogue wolf, after all, was the role for which he had been born and bred. But Alexandra's role—and which of them would maintain the sturdier fortress—remained to be seen.

He already knew that there would be no happily ever after for them.

Still, to Hawk's surprise, something akin to anticipation began to take root deep within him. He looked forward to every minute he would spend in Alexandra's life, for however short a duration.

His decision to give her an annulment and set her free had been difficult. But not consummating their marriage might be easier than he expected, given his physical condition and her penchant for staid, lumbering bridegrooms.

On the other hand, the course upon which he was determined might also be fraught with peril, for he could never tell Alex he was giving her up for her own good. If he did, she would fight him rather than leave him, for she was in the habit of placing the welfare of others before her own. And he could not be so cruel as to pretend dislike, or worse, disinterest.

He could not dispirit so bright a flame.

A low, simmering flame, capable of flaring into blaze at any time, he remembered as he watched her sleep.

Unable to keep from stoking her fire and awakening her, Hawk touched his lips to hers in that age-old mythical rite. But Beauty turned the tale and awoke her astonished beast by deepening the kiss and bringing him to alert and rigid attention. A startling and extraordinary turn of events in every respect, for Alex was exceedingly eager, and he was sexually aroused for the first time since the Battle of Waterloo.

Impatient to prove his prowess and taste her once more, Hawk parted her soft, sweet lips with his own, taking the kiss to a deeper, more intimate level, both testing himself and gauging his wife's reaction.

Alex moaned. She sighed. She moved restlessly against him, enhancing his physical reaction. But rather than rejoice over his unexpected progress, Hawk worried about the "lessons" her blackguard of a bridegroom may have taught her.

He did not remember the imp kissing with such fervor before. Not that he had kissed her above twice, and then in a brotherly fashion, except on the day of their wedding, when he had kissed her with promise before saying good-bye.

How blind he had been; how foolish, kissing scores of others when the flower of his youth could kiss like a dream.

Still, Hawk would give his fortune—if he was still in possession of it—to know the name of the man who had taught his wife this exquisite lesson.

To his delight, Alex sighed; then her lids fluttered, and her eyes, bright and soft as turquoise velvet, opened at last. For a moment, she appeared for all the world as if she were that princess of legend, waking from a years-long sleep, her eyes growing wider and wider as she regarded him.

As if seeking a touchstone to reality, she scanned the interior of the carriage with her gaze, the passing scenery, then his face again, taking in and examining his every flaw.

Hawk watched a range of telling expressions flit

across her amazingly unguarded features, though not one of them revealed her revulsion or disgust.

He supposed she must need to verify what may seem like a dream, but in the verification, her eyes awash with unshed tears, she appeared less certain as the silent seconds passed, but more curious.

Not fearful or pitying, but not well pleased, either.

Then her frown deepened and her eyes turned to blue flames, and she lashed out and struck him square in the jaw. "Dead!" she shouted, her trembling voice a rusty rasp. "We thought you were dead. How dare you let us believe it!"

"Alexandra, Alex. Shh, calm down."

"A year." She smacked his shoulders. "A blasted year. No. Longer than that. How could you?" She slapped his arms as he tried to brace her. "Where the blazes have you been?"

When Alex kicked her dead husband's shin, he winced. But when she smacked his thigh with a fist, all color left his face. Pain etched the harsh angularity of his firm jaw and ashen features, further whitening the new lines carved there. He had suffered—she recognized that now—and her wrath pricked her.

"You lived, while we wept because you died." Broken and elated by the shock of his return, Alex begged to understand. "Why did you not tell us?"

"I was not capable, not for some long time."

"Because you were wounded?"

He nodded.

"Unable to speak?"

"For the most part, no."

"You *could* speak?"

"When I was conscious."

"You were unconscious for a year?" Her voice rose.

He winced.

"You lost your memory, then?"

Denial again.

Alex wanted to strike him every time he refused an offered excuse. "*Someone* should have written to us." She shoved his shoulder. "I am so . . ." Her sob took her by surprise, fast and wild and from the depths of her soul. She grasped his lapels to anchor herself in a careening world. And when that was not enough, she clutched him about the neck, afraid she would shatter if he did not hold her together.

He held tight.

The storm did not last long. Alex was glad, for rage was exhausting. "I am furious with you," she said after a calm moment.

"I know you are. It is no more than I expected."

"And deserve." She accepted his handkerchief.

Hawk nodded. "I do deserve it. Beat me if you will, but mind my left leg . . . and my face." There, he had said it, Hawk thought with relief. He had brought his ugliness into the open.

At once solemn and assessing, Alex reached toward his battered and badly mended face, stopped, and pulled her hand back as if he might burst into flame—as if touching him repulsed her.

Hawk rejected anguish, and an overwhelming need to crush her in his embrace once more, and donned his old devil-may-care mask. "What, Alexandra? Am

I not still a handsome rogue? Does my countenance not please you?"

She frowned and reached again, hesitated again. And after too long a time to be borne, she extended her hand the entire distance between them, to finger a coil of the overlong hair lapping at his shoulders, unadulterated amazement overtaking her.

Hawk braced himself against the grateful quiver that her touch, even on his hair, engendered. "It's beastly," he said. "I know. Uncivilized, like me. If you find it in your heart to forgive me, can you tame me, do you think?" Would she even care to?

"I may never forgive you."

"I guessed as much, but I am the eternal optimist."

"You are the eternal charmer, but you will not charm your way back into my good graces."

"I applaud your perception and your determination."

Alex shrugged and fingered his overlong hair. "You remind me of a cat," she said. "A night-stalking lion, jungle-bred and ravenous, but I am your huntress."

"Odd, you remind me less of a cat's doom than its plaything."

"A mouse?" she said with more than a trace of indignation, her defense at the ready, if he did not miss his guess.

"Catnip," he corrected.

"Oh." Her turquoise eyes widened, making her appear even more beautiful, coy, flirtatious yet naive, unmistakably in need of a good loving, God help him.

The notion brought his body to hard attention once

more. Rejoicing inwardly over the reaction, Hawk settled his delectable wife more intimately against him to enhance and savor the torture, her breasts no more than a stroke and a kiss away.

She moved a lock of his hair from his eyes, her warm breath bathing the scars on his face like a blessing, and Hawk caught her familiar violet scent with a new rush of expectation.

As he sat stunned and entranced, she smoothed his beard, which shrouded the worst of his scars, and all but cupped his face.

In that instant, Hawk ached to turn his head and set his lips to her palm, knowing full well that if he did so, a slap might be his for the taking. Her very touch unmanned him, made him want to rush dangerously forward.

Such a mad turnabout—the wicked-as-sin duke of Hawksworth, moonstruck over the girl he once treated like a pesky pup.

But the paradox was not new. Alexandra herself, the memory of her, laughing, teasing, driving him daft, had kept him going, kept him fighting for his life during those endless, pain-racked months after Waterloo.

And all that time, a world and a war away, a lifetime away, when he still expected to die of his wounds, he was becoming enthralled with his own wife.

"I like it," she said—of his beard, he presumed, for she was stroking it—but he was too taken with her touch to focus on anything else. "It makes you look a danger," she said, catching his attention as she fingered his scar.

"I am a danger, make no mistake—jungle-bred and rapacious, as you say. And well you should remember and keep a safe distance."

But before he could garner her promise, Hawk was forced to close his eyes, as he entered hell—or heaven—for she had begun to trace the red, uneven welt with a gentle touch, from beside his eye, along its raised and puckered surface, down his cheek and into the depths of his beard, where it disappeared near his chin.

At the wonder of her touch, remorse rose in him, chiding him and ordering him to make amends. He could not keep her—he must not—for she merited better than a battered hulk for husband, a man who would walk away with no glance back. An undeserving fool who knew not what he had but sought instead what he could never have—his father's approval.

Why did he not appreciate the people in his life who cared about him, until he all but lost them? His nieces, Beatrix and Claudia, his uncle Giff, Alex's aunt Hildy, and Alexandra herself.

They were his family, though all of them, especially Alex, might have done better to remember him as he was rather than see what he had become. A beast. Ugly. Disfigured.

"For your sake," Alex said, "I am sorry your scars forced you to join the flawed human race, but you are still the Bryceson I hero-worshipped." With a fingertip, she soothed the hideous knot of discolored flesh nearest his brow. "Does it pain you—other than when you are rightfully beaten for your thoughtlessness?"

Hawk opened his eyes and feasted upon her, struck anew by her beauty, but more by her words. He had not felt like "Bryceson" for a long, long time. Neither had he felt anything near human.

Would she understand if he said his inhumanity was the reason he had not contacted her?

He covered her hand against his face with his own. "At this moment," he said, "even the memory of pain escapes me."

"Your leg?"

Hawk shook his head, denying weakness until the end. But she gave him a disbelieving look, and he knew that with Alex, prevarication was useless. He shrugged. "On occasion."

She tried to move from his lap then, but he held her in place, his hands at her hips. "No, stay. I am becoming fond of the ache; it is far better than feeling nothing, and I like you here."

Her incredible blue-green eyes widened, swam, and Hawk scolded himself for the admission even as he agonized over what she must be thinking.

Three

Alexandra was in a fair way to screaming as emotions bombarded her from every quarter.

Joy—for here, miraculously, sat her husband, back from the dead, the man she had been unable to forget even during her wedding to another.

Sadness—for the time they had lost and the pain she had glimpsed, deep and abiding, behind his winking jest. Yes, his legendary perfection had been startlingly altered, but he had survived, for which she would remain forever grateful.

But fury hardened her heart as well. She had taken a great deal of satisfaction in pummeling the arrogant, marble-hearted rogue to pudding, though she had not expected to hurt him—which in turn hurt her.

So many people had mourned him—the very family he had all but deserted. Alex sighed. Yes, he had married her for mercenary reasons and left her at the church, yet her anguish was nothing to theirs.

But he was alive after all, and perhaps the future could be set to rights, though a loveless marriage had never been her intent—not with Bryce, at any rate. She had once naively thought that her love for him would be enough to carry them through life, but now, more than ever, she was uncertain. Despite the fact that he had kept his survival from her for far too long, she could think only, against all hope, that he was alive.

To prove she was not dreaming, Alex placed her hand on the coarse fabric of his frock coat to feel his warm, thickly-muscled arm beneath, and her heart leaped as her spirit rejoiced. Alive. Her husband was alive and holding her in a way she had always imagined in her deepest, most secret dreams, except . . .

Chesterfield would not take kindly to being set aside, especially after the bargain they had struck. This time, she had been willing to marry without love in order to support the family she and Bryce had all but failed.

But Judson Broderick, Viscount Chesterfield was a powerful and persuasive man. For agreeing to wed him, she had accepted a favor in advance, thereby granting him a hold over her, the stronger for her having cast him aside.

Bryce would not appreciate the irony. But there was nothing she could do if he did not. She had thought he was dead, after all. Besides, he might never find out, if luck remained with her.

"Other than your justified anger at my, er, tardiness, you have not said how you feel about this unexpected turn," Bryce said, asking for what she dared not give—a glimpse into her heart.

If he knew how she really felt, how much she loved him, had always loved him, he would flee in panic, bad leg or no. She knew him that well. "Despite my anger, I am glad you survived. Of course I am."

"Of course." His scowl still had the power to set flame to tinder. "I suppose I do not blame you," he said, "for preferring to be a new and beloved bride rather than a reclaimed and convenient wife."

Convenient. Ouch. So, it was laid bare. In the open. Irrefutable. Theirs had been a marriage of convenience. It hurt more to hear from his own lips than to suspect or hear secondhand.

Alexandra sat straighter, hurt overriding embarrassment, but before long ire replaced pain and she was grateful. "Do you think to take me for granted as you have done for the past year and a half, ever since we wed and you fled?" His turn to wince. Good. "As you tolerated me when we were growing up, while I trod in your wake, a devoted pup after its master? If such is the case, then you are right: I *had* rather be Chesterfield's cherished bride."

With as much dignity as she could muster, given the tardiness of her move, Alex shifted from her husband's lap to the seat opposite, folding her arms before her and allowing several silent moments to pass, until she remembered that she should not show her hand.

She sighed and forced herself to relax. "We are married for good or ill," she said, setting herself and her clothes to rights. "And neither of us has a choice in the matter. If we held sway over life, we would be God." *What a foolish statement,* she thought. With Hawk's return, God had granted her everything.

Nevertheless, she pinned her wayward husband with a look of steely regard. "I will not be overlooked or underappreciated. Not by you or anyone. Do so at your peril."

"If I do, will you beat me?"

Behind the jest, Alex saw an easing of his anguish, though she dared not let down her guard. "If you force my hand, Bryceson Wakefield, I will . . . go and live in sin with Chesterfield."

"The devil, you say!" The very demon flared of a sudden in the fire of Hawk's eyes. *Jealousy,* she would name it, green and sizzling to a turn. "I see you have not changed your rule-breaking ways," he said, as close to a sulk as one could imagine on a heartless rogue.

Alex shivered with the elation of success. "In case you have not noticed," she said, adjusting the blond lace on her low-cut cream satin bodice, "I am a big girl now. A woman. Chesterfield wants me."

That devil in Hawk's eyes leaped. "So you *do* love him?"

How dare he. Alex refused to cater to her husband's fittingly overburdened conscience. She would not give him the satisfaction of revealing her true feelings. He did not deserve to know them. Not yet. Perhaps, not ever. "I said I was glad you lived."

"Being glad I lived and glad I took you away from the man you love are not one and the same thing."

"They are not, but Chesterfield is strong; he will recover."

Hawk sighed, feeling the sharp bite of his wife's pointed though silent censure. As she would not recover, she did not need to say . . . because she loved the man. Her omission spoke louder than her words ever could, and even Hawk could not utter them, for to do so would surely give them credence. "Chesterfield loves you, then?"

"He adores me." Alex raised her chin. "It has been a delightful change." She quirked a brow. "And an exhilarating experience."

Hawksworth winced at the bald statement, feeling remorse and possessiveness, both new and uncomfortable sensations for a rogue like him. Positively disconcerting for a man bound not to touch his wife.

"Poor Alexandra," he said, running headlong into the subject with which he had been toying for weeks. "Would you rather we lived apart?" Even as the words left his lips, Hawk's heart nearly stopped.

Alex paled to the color of flour paste. "That will not be possible."

His heart caught the beats it had missed and continued on its palpitating way, albeit a bit faster than normal, for he was as taken aback by her answer as he was relieved by it. Though he should not be, he reminded himself, for they *must* part in the not too distant future. "No?"

"Do not be foolish."

"I am never foolish, Alexandra. I am occasionally blind, I have come to understand in hindsight, but never knowingly foolish. I should think that someone who cares naught for the rules and loves another might consider separation a solution."

"Only an annulment would serve as a solution, as far as my alliance with Chesterfield is concerned, and well you know it. But the fact remains that neither an annulment nor a separation is possible, for your wards need no family skeletons further littering their rock-strewn paths in life."

That she wanted an annulment at all, whether possible in her mind or not, damn near broke Hawk. And still, she had given no elaboration as to whether she did or did not love the man she had been about to marry.

Hawk found the lack more than frustrating. He found it ill-mannered, evasive, and downright exasperating. "My wards?"

"Your nieces, Claudia and Beatrix."

"I know who you mean. I simply cannot imagine how two little girls can have any bearing on the matter."

"You have been gone for nearly two years, Hawksworth. You must realize that Beatrix is now six, and Claudia, I will have you know, is due a season this year. She has some funds but more beauty. With so small a dowry to her name, however, even something so simple as a separation in the family could be infamous enough an excuse for an ambitious mama to thwart a titled son's unsanctioned attachment."

"Then I take it that you will not be living in sin with Chesterfield . . . until after Claudia marries?"

"Do not push me, Bryceson."

Feeling immeasurably uplifted of a sudden, Hawk nodded. "If Claudia is due a season, then so must you be. You cannot be more than two years older than she." *And stuck with a beast.* The intrusive thought sent Hawk's spirits plummeting.

"Claudia is seventeen, and I am an old married woman of twenty," Alex said. "There are many things

I do need, but a season in London is not one of them, thank you very much."

Hawk wanted to ask what it was she did need, but he might not like her answer.

Adoration, obviously—Chesterfield's, at least—but what about him? Would she accept his worship if he were so foolish as to offer it?

At one time, he had thought she might.

And should he check himself into Bedlam today, or tomorrow, for having the idiocy to imagine it? Especially now.

The angel of death must surely scramble one's brain, Hawk mused, hoping that rest and further recovery would set his bedeviled mind to rights. Until it did, however, he would tread warily and guard his heart. "I hope you do not expect *me* to adore you."

Her easy laugh made Hawk see crimson. Was he still not good enough for her, then? Was the exalted Chesterfield an unexceptionable rogue? More attentive? Never more practiced?

"The family will be in bliss," she said, dismissing his ire if she even noticed it. "In veritable transports, to learn that you lived. I am sorry to say that Jud is not much liked by any of them, except Claudia."

"Jud," Hawk said, giving the name a harsh, dull sound, "should be playing a crude musical instrument with his unshod feet in the remote reaches of America."

Alexandra's grin broke before she could stop it, and when she did, it was too late. She had warmed Hawk's cold rogue's heart in a way that organ had not been warm since he left her. Unfortunately, the thaw made him deuced uncomfortable. "Wait a minute," he said, pinning her with his look. "I would have expected you to try and defend your swain."

To his entertainment, Alexandra raised that obstinate chin of hers, impaling him with narrowed eyes and glaring ire. She examined him so thoroughly that Hawk began to chafe with a disturbing need to hide his scars. Instead, he lay his head against the squabs and closed his eyes. Let her look her fill, and let him get on with being an object of horrified fascination. And there, her reason for preferring Chesterfield came clear, for the knave stood handsome and unscathed.

Be damned! Hawk cursed inwardly. Would his father not have a good laugh at this turn of events?

Once upon a fleeting time, Hawk's many dalliances, a source of rare swaggering braggadocio to his father, had been legion and widely known.

If not for his sire's deathbed promise of true pride, Hawk would not have gone to fight Boney, though it turned out to be an idiotic reason to support a patriotic and worthy cause. Despite his injuries, Hawk was glad he had fought for England.

Before the war, however, he had not needed to walk with the aid of a cane. He had stood proud and strong, as prepossessing as any of the rogues in the Wakefield portrait gallery, as any London buck, including Chesterfield.

He had stood handsome, as well. A heartbreaker, women had once called him. A rogue, a lady-killer. He had been all that and more. Even Alex had been fond of him then.

But he would slay the ladies no longer, not unless the women he gazed upon died of fright, as Alex had nearly done upon sight of him.

The doctors in Belgium had said that one of his bayonet wounds sat so close to his eye that only a miracle could save his sight.

Only a miracle could have saved his life as well.

Yes, he got his miracles, both of them, and for that he must give something back.

He must give Alexandra her future.

"Here we are," he said, loath to continue his painful reverie. "Bond Street. I have rooms at Stephen's Hotel until the end of the month. I think it best we spend the night here and travel on to St. Albans in the morning."

Home in the morning. Alex could hardly believe it. With Hawksworth, her husband. To begin their life together. Finally. Though the bigger part of her rejoiced, a goodly part was still angry. He had used her . . . as she had used him, she must admit.

In the way he had needed a caretaker for his family, she had needed a home and medical attention for her aunt. Besides which, she loved him and had foolishly thought he cared for her. But the fact remained that if he had baldly told her his true reason for marrying her, she would likely have married him anyway. God knew, if she had known she would lose him, she certainly would have agreed to be his wife. Though then, she would have demanded to be a wife in deed as well as name.

Lord, she was a love-struck fool, an idiot, a detestable weakling who deserved what she got, because despite all of it, she was deliriously happy to have him back.

She loved him that much.

She only wished he loved her a fraction as much. She particularly wished that he had kept the fact that he did not love her to himself.

Four

Disgusted with her calf-eyed self, Alex gazed out at Bond Street, a jumble of tall brick buildings with few courtyards or alleyways to separate them. Signs proclaimed establishments such as John Jackson, Boxing Salon, better known to the sporting set as Gentleman Jackson's. They passed Yardley of London; Smith Adam & Charles, Linen Drapers; and Mr. Weston, the tailor Bryceson had once frequented.

Alex's heart sank as they passed Stedman & Vardon, Goldsmiths & Jewelers, which she and Bryce had visited on the day they wed, the day after he buried his father. As they passed, she wondered if he remembered the plain gold band he purchased for her that morning, and the wider one he had chosen for himself.

She had worn hers until she arrived at Holy Trinity Church to marry Chesterfield earlier, removing it in the carriage before going inside. Even now, the precious symbol of her marriage to her one true love sat tucked in a velvet box inside her reticule. What fate had befallen his wedding band? she wondered as she regarded his unadorned hand.

Once they arrived at Stephen's Hotel, Bryce

seemed to struggle as he stepped from the carriage, though he did so in the same way his man helped him—without being obvious. Once he was down, Bryce turned to offer Alex a hand, and she took it, though she made certain not to burden him with her weight and quickly let go. She no more wanted him to lose his balance than to guess at her undying love.

The impressive hotel stood taller and less soot-stained than most of the Bond Street shops. On the Clifford Street side, there waited a score or more saddle horses and half as many tilburies. A six-horse dray—*Barclay's Brewery* lettered in red on the side—was being unloaded of its delivery of wooden casks.

In the front of the five-story structure, men milled about in groups, talking, laughing raucously, several reeling from overindulgence. Some of them were obviously dandies, but most wore the red or blue of the military.

"Am I allowed inside?" Alex queried, stepping closer to her husband's side as they walked arm in arm toward the black-lacquered double front doors.

He patted her hand on his arm. "Stephen's is mostly frequented by officers of the Guards—the Life Guards in red and the Royal Horse Guards in blue—but you are my wife and will not be turned away. Though as the rare female among us, you will be much admired, I daresay."

That surprised her. "Admired? Me?"

Bryce shook his head, as if she had made a poor jest. Alex wanted to call him to task for it, but they stepped inside the hotel and her attention was taken with the bustling activity and gentlemanly ambiance.

"You will be safe from the crush beside the stairs," he said. "Wait there while I fight my way to the desk to claim my key."

Feeling at sea, Alex kept her gaze trained on him while several men in uniform saluted as he made his way toward the front. She wished she could hear what he said that relaxed his subordinates and made them smile.

Closer by, a military man in the red of the Life Guards mentioned Hawksworth by name, catching her attention. "Excellent commander," the handsome officer said. "Had the full respect of his men." The speaker went on to say that Hawksworth was brave, forthright, and had saved his men's hides a time or two.

One soldier shook his head, as if disbelieving. "How was it, then, that he was so carelessly given up for dead?"

Since awakening in his arms, Alex had wondered about that, as well.

"Hawk told me that he was so near death as to be incapable of correcting the medic—dodging grapeshot—who pronounced him dead. So Hawk was painfully tossed on the body heap. Minutes or hours later, Hawk said, a peasant boy leaned over him to snatch the gold buttons from his coat, and Hawk did the only thing he was capable of doing; he bit the blighter's hand.

"The boy took him to the Waterloo Inn, but the doctors there, scrambling to save those more like to survive, said they could do nothing for Hawk. When our man was given up for dead that second time, the lad went looking for a dray and went back for him. Took Hawk home and his family nursed him back to health."

"Good God!"

"Good *lad*."

A body heap? Alex wished she had not eavesdropped, for she felt as boneless and light of head as she had at the church when she heard Hawk's voice for the first time. But despite the dip in the room, she was determined to remain upright.

When Bryce called her name, the storyteller noticed her and must have realized what she heard, for he stepped forward, appalled, and lifted her into his arms. Despite her argument that she had not been about to swoon, the repentant officer carried her all the way up the stairs at Hawk's direction. Mortified to have made a spectacle of herself for the second time that day, Alex wished she could shrink from sight.

The man sat her down in a leather chair in the sitting room of a small apartment that looked very much like a gentleman's study, while Bryce poured her a brandy. After she sipped it, while her husband stoked a fire in the hearth to "warm her and take the damp from the room," Alex turned her attention to her rescuer. "Thank you for becoming my chariot."

"If not for my thoughtless story," he said, "you would not have needed a conveyance."

"But it was a true story?"

He grimaced. "Indeed."

Bryce looked from one of them to the other, silently questioning, but when neither of them enlightened him, he cleared his throat. "Alexandra, may I present Squadron Corporal Major Reed Gilbride of the Life Guards, and a charter member of The Rogues Club. Reed, my wife."

"Your wife? Congratulations are in order, then?" The officer bowed and kissed her hand.

Bryceson waved his friend's congratulations away, as if their marriage meant nothing, and Alex's heart sank. He must have removed his ring and never mentioned having a wife the whole time they served together. Alex swallowed the rising lump in her throat. "We married shortly before Bryceson joined the Guards," she said to explain why congratulations were unnecessary, and to keep her husband from seeing her hurt. "Tell me about this Rogues Club."

"We were bored playing at war, Your Grace," her rescuer said, charming her out of countenance, for she had not been courted by a gallant for longer than she could remember. "So in our dreary tent, we formed an unofficial club."

"But exclusive," her husband said.

"Oh, very," her rescuer replied with a chuckle, regarding Alex. "My true identity is something of a mystery, you see, even to me." He said it with a wink, and Alex was doubly taken.

She smiled. "What must one do to become a member of this Rogues Club?"

"Why, be a rogue, of course," Bryce said with a shrug and a wink of his own.

"He means we are all scamps," the charmer explained, "who banded together against Boney and in support of Mother England."

"Sounds like a worthy club, then," she said. "I am pleased to make your acquaintance, C.S.M. Gilbride."

"The honor is all mine, I assure you." He bowed. "I shall leave you to recover, and hope that I may see you again in the near future."

Alex said her good-byes and Bryce walked his friend out, shutting the door, leaving her alone inside. When he did not return for fully fifteen minutes, she began to think he had deserted her again. But he finally returned, followed by a succession of servants bearing a table, linen, everything necessary for an intimate supper. Other servants brought up the rear with her bags, which Hawk's man must have taken from Chesterfield's carriage at the church.

Dinner looked and smelled divine, but Alex was in a fair way to dozing off after such a taxing day. The joint of roast pork and the fried sole were simple but delicious fare. She was just too tired to eat much beyond a nibble.

Hawksworth waited until everything to do with supper had been collected before suggesting they retire early, which woke her right up. Was this, then, to be the first night of their marriage? Finally?

Since this was supposed to have been her wedding day, Alex thought it fitting for the wedding night denied her nearly two years before.

This man leading her into the bedroom was Bryceson, after all—her friend first, now her husband, her love.

Hawksworth, his friends now called him. Hawk. She liked it.

Hawk, taking the pins from her hair, turning her

in circles until he found the hooks beneath the rose-buds marching down the front of her cream satin wedding gown.

Hawk, opening and sliding her wedding dress off to bare her to her stays and petticoats.

And this was Alexandra, not only allowing such intimate attention but reveling in it, flattered and amazed to have so much of her husband's focus directed upon herself.

He sat her on the bed and left her then. And like a bisque doll on a nursery shelf, Alex sat unmoving, waiting to be redressed, or undressed, or dropped and shattered, at whim.

Far in the back of her mind, she knew she was acting lovesick and calf-eyed again. But at this moment, she cared not a whit.

When Hawksworth returned, he laid her portmanteau beside her on the bed and extracted the gossamer gown she was supposed to have worn for her wedding night with Judson, one of several he had dared to purchase for her.

Hawk's brow rose as he regarded it, then he set it aside and extracted the wrap that went with it. When he was finished, he lifted her foot to his knee, removing first one cream kid slipper, then the other.

As if she floated outside her body and watched from afar, Alexandra wondered what or who had taken over her more sensible self and why she was letting it happen. But the only answer that came was love, or lovesickness, as she thought.

Why neither of them spoke, Alex did not know. Perhaps Bryceson was too busy concentrating on his task, while she was too busy appreciating and noticing everything about him. She knew only that his topaz eyes were warm, kind, loving. Here stood the gentle boy who'd tended scraped knees, extracted slivers from small hands, and dried a lifetime of silly tears. She saw that his shoulders were broader, his arms stronger, his huge hands callused, his sable hair prematurely silver-gilt.

His demeanor no longer bore the mark of a young god, perfect of feature and seeking admiration, but of a soldier home from war, wounded and scarred, though striking still, and virile. So potently male that Alex lost her breath just watching him. As opposed to his former chiseled perfection, Hawk's face now bore a hard, flawed quality, which gave him an aura of jeopardy, a provocation that would draw women like moths to a flame.

He was definitely older, though she could not yet vouch for *wiser,* but after overhearing his amazing story earlier, she surmised that he could hardly have escaped some degree of wisdom. She did know that he must have survived a great deal more than he would ever willingly reveal. "Your father would be proud of you," she said without thinking.

"If I had died fighting Boney, perhaps, but I expect that he would have considered any man mustered home, broken, as a failure."

"But you were not mustered home because you were wounded. The war ended."

"Gideon guarded Napoleon all the way to St. Helena, and Reed is still one of Wellington's aides."

When put that way, Alex knew he was right about his fanatical father, but what could she say?

She was embarrassed that she had mentioned the man, but she was even more embarrassed when Bryceson slipped his hands up her leg to unhook her garters, and she shivered and squeaked because she felt the lightning shock of his touch to her core.

He looked up and quirked a brow. "I am not going to ravish you, Alexandra."

After a stunned, silent moment, she sighed with resignation. "I am sorry to hear that."

Bryce reared back, and after a similar moment, he shook his head. "Stand," he said, and she understood why his men obeyed him, as did she. He untied the laces on her half petticoat, slid his hands down her hips to push it to the floor, and she stepped out. Her second was a full petticoat, and he helped her out of that with entirely too much experience, in the same way he loosened and removed her stays—expertly and efficiently.

At a knock on the outer door, he turned to leave her standing in her new lawn shift, and again like an empty-headed porcelain doll, Alex waited and hoped for more.

When Bryce returned, he slipped her white gossamer nightrail over her head, and her arms into her matching wrap. "You will surely catch your death without both," he said, a hot, hard glint in his eyes. "Or worse."

The tardy promise in those last two words—his gaze piercing—shivered her to her trembling knees.

When she was dressed in the nightrail made for her

trousseau, Bryce neither stepped back to admire her or his handiwork, nor did he comment further on the exquisite finery—a disappointment. He simply peeled back the bedcovers and urged her into its feather-filled warmth. Heart pounding, Alex did as her husband bade, moving toward the center, expecting him to undress and slip in beside her.

Instead, he pulled the covers up to her neck, sat beside her on the bed, and waited with a disapproving frown as she freed her arms. Then he took possession of her hand. "I am afraid that this has been a long, tiring, and shocking day for you," he said. "And I am sorry for all of it. Reed told me what he said. I am especially sorry that you heard, but perhaps it is best you know. Get a good night's sleep now, for we have another long day ahead of us tomorrow, though hopefully a much less alarming one."

"But what about you? Are you not going to sleep?"

"I am having the settee made up as we speak. I will be fine there for one night. I have slept on worse."

Alex sat up and saw by his arrested gaze that the blankets had fallen away and exposed her breasts to his view. She did not cover herself and he did not look away, not for several pulsing beats. She had her husband's full and blatant male attention while she was conscious and could appreciate it, and she was glad.

When he did look away, she sighed. "Bryce, this is your bed. You are too tall for that short sofa. Come, sleep beside me."

Five

Hawk cursed his trembling hands as he tucked Alex back into his bed and admired the cloud of cinnamon waves forming a silken halo upon her pillow. Had any man ever needed such willpower as he was compelled to call upon at this tempting moment?

He regarded the siren for signs of the sprite who had in turn shadowed and vexed him through their growing-up years. While he was grief-struck by the loss of that child, he was intrigued no small bit by the emergence of the woman. His first reaction was natural; his second, both unacceptable and a clear threat to his sanity.

As he rose, he bent to kiss her brow. "Sleep. I command you." Then he stroked her cheek, snuffed her candle, and left the bedchamber, shutting the door behind him.

In the sitting room, Hawk discarded his cane and his frock coat and untied his cravat before pouring himself a brandy with palsied hands. He made an awkward, confined pace about the room, twice or thrice, the better to tire himself to the point of exhaustion.

As he helped Alex from her clothing, he had ached

for her corresponding ministrations, her cool fingers against his heated skin as he had touched her—for her tenderness to be directed toward his comfort, her gaze toward his face, when all the while she had been unable to bear the sight of him and looked away instead.

Why had she said she was disappointed he would not ravish her? Was she teasing? Was she that angry with him?

Perhaps he was making a horrendous mistake in letting her go. . . . Once upon a time, she had liked him enough to marry him. Perhaps she had even wanted him then.

Perhaps she wanted him still.

Hawk damn near laughed. Perhaps delirium had once again set in. . . .

Was she toying with him? Being facetious? She had, after all, liked Chesterfield enough to marry him, as well.

Hawk cursed. Here he was worried about her, trying to do what was best for her, while she was shaking the foundation of his conviction and undermining his altruistic intentions. Why could he not sense what she wanted?

Likely not him. Not anymore. No, he must give her that annulment as soon as may be and free her from his abysmal self, though not so soon that Chesterfield might still be unattached when he did.

That part of his plan, he must alter.

When he had returned to England, weak, scarred, and furious at fate, he assured himself that his family was well. And when he was convinced they were, he delayed notifying them of his return. He could not ask them to endure the daily reminder of his failure—his scars, his very presence.

He had gone to the aid of his sister-in-law, Sabrina, and of Gideon St. Goddard—another rogue of the club, the husband he secured for her when he thought he was dying.

To get himself declared alive again, Hawk petitioned the House of Lords, and parliament in general—even the prince regent and a score of his advisers and friends, Tory and Whig alike. Some that Prinny would have at his side, were it not for the mad king's sane moments, had more influence than perhaps was good for England.

Since Hawk's father's solicitor was unavailable, he sought another to notify Baxter Wakefield, his cousin and heir, that he lived. Hawk did it all, anything and everything he could, to avoid facing his family with his disagreeable self. By then he had concluded that, for Alexandra's sake, he must release her from their marriage.

Then he heard that she was about to remarry.

That she loved someone else was all the more reason to let her go, though he could not allow her to commit bigamy. And so he had gone to stop her wedding.

Now, for the sake of his nieces, he must take up his responsibilities as planned and proceed as if his marriage to Alex would continue. This would give Claudia and Beatrix a chance to get used to having him back. He would encourage them to depend more upon him and less upon Alex.

When the paperwork reinstating him as the duke of Hawksworth bore fruit, and what was left of his wealth, title, and estates reverted to him, he would move his family from Huntington Lodge, Alex's family home, back to Hawks Ridge, his own estate. By then, his nieces would perhaps be dependent upon him again and less destroyed by Alexandra's departure from the bosom of their family.

Also by then, Chesterfield may have married another.

More than anything in this world, Hawk wanted to keep Alexandra for himself. Second to that, he would keep her for his family. But with no choice but to give her up, he must at least keep her safe in their marriage until Judson Broderick, Viscount bloody Chesterfield was absolutely out of the running for her hand.

No matter her seeming indifference to his scars, Hawk would not sit back and let Alexandra's apathy in the face of his appearance turn to valor, which would most assuredly fester into disgust and destroy the entire family.

Alexandra stared at the burgundy brocade bed canopy above her while the scent of the snuffed beeswax candle remained a lingering reminder of one man's penchant—her husband's—for walking away without looking back.

The bridegroom she had thought sacrificed to the wages of war, relinquished to the vaporous vagaries of perpetual rest, had been, quite impossibly, returned to her. A literal miracle, she had discovered upon hearing Reed Gilbride's story. And yet, despite the wonder, Bryceson Wakefield had once again deserted her. He had left her alone in the center of his bed, steeped in hurt, shock, and disappointment.

All the time he undressed her, she had anticipated undressing him the same way. She anticipated more kisses like the one they shared in the carriage. She expected the leisure and the right to kiss her husband whenever and wherever she chose. She ached to kiss the scars on his face, to press her lips to all his scars, to all of him, and she wanted the same intimate attention from him.

After nearly two years of marriage, she was long past due his husbandly ministrations. As his wife, she had fulfilled every single requirement save one, the marriage bed, that lack not having been her choice. She deserved a marriage, signed, sealed, and consummated.

She wanted to go and shake him, scream and rant, but Alex bit her lip and tightened her fists, aware that she must conquer her tendency to be precipitate, else she would rush from the room with admonishment in mind and end up ravishing her husband as he slept.

'Twould not do to let him see how much she wanted and needed him. If she had learned one thing about the male of the species, young or old, it was that if a female's attention was difficult to secure, then a male continued tenaciously in her wake, attempting to secure it, or her. By the same token, she had observed that while males could be encouraged by any sign of interest, however slight or fleeting, they soon lost enthusiasm for the chase if the female appeared easy or eager to be caught.

Well Bryceson Wakefield, Duke of Hawksworth—her husband, by God—would not be losing interest in her any day soon; she would see to that. She was due a wedding night, Alex mused, and she would have one—despite her bridegroom's detestable reason for marrying her.

When she had learned the truth of it, she had nearly expired herself, of sorrow. 'Twas not said to her face, of course, but behind her back by some of his friends, after Bryce had first left for the war.

She could have stepped away when she heard her name, of course, as she might have done downstairs when she heard Hawk's, but she had not. That first time she eavesdropped, she learned that Bryce married her so she would care for his family while he went to war. One of his cronies said she would do anything for her husband's pat on the head, "which is all poor old 'Bry' could bear to give her." They said it was too bad he had not lived long enough "to bed the beauty" she had become.

To the devil with beauty. What did looks have to say to anything? 'Twas Hawk's love she wanted, plain and simple.

Unlike the scores of women who had always flocked to the proud, handsome-as-sin Bryceson Wakefield, Alex had loved him despite his magnificence. All the while he had been trying to prove his worth to his father—and to himself, if he but knew it—Alex had loved the kind and gentle soul who dwelled inside the quintessential rogue.

Was she the only one who glimpsed that gentle man? Or had she been as blind to his faults as others were blinded by his beauty?

She wished she knew.

She was sorry, for Hawk's sake, that his legendary good looks had been marred, but she hoped that without the outer trappings of perfection, he would discover and come to appreciate the good and gentle man he was.

That man, she yearned for, body, heart and soul.

That man, she loved.

Though her concern over Chesterfield's reaction to their cancelled nuptials, and her anger at her husband, went a long way toward dampening Alex's inclination toward celebration, she still wanted, more than her next breath, to walk into the sitting room, slip into Hawk's embrace, and weep with unmitigated joy at his return.

But she could not, she thought, swallowing her gathering tears. Not yet.

Hawk found himself standing outside a ruin of a manse, a dreamlike fog shrouding the night in ashen vapor, a ponderous regret cutting deep in his belly, for he bore the horrific sense that he had arrived too late.

At the sound of carriage wheels on cobbles, he turned to see Alexandra and Chesterfield driving away.

"No," Hawk shouted. "No." He could not allow them to live in sin together. Alex belonged to him, not to Chesterfield.

Hawk mounted his horse—miracle of miracles, he could do so without pain—and he chased the carriage for hours, it seemed, catching up only when the vehicle stopped at a lavish estate in the heart of the mist.

"Alex," Hawk called. "Alex, I am here. No need to do this. Come, love. Come home with me."

But she continued walking away, as Chesterfield stepped forward to block his path and keep him from following. "You gave her up," the knave said. "Your marriage was annulled, at your behest, and now Alexandra is *my* wife. Mine."

The blackguard laughed. He laughed until Alex called to him from an upper window, in that white diaphanous gown, her nutmeg hair flowing free and barely covering her sweet, lush breasts.

Alex, calling Chesterfield to her bed.

As if clamped in irons, Hawksworth struggled, unable to escape his invisible fetters, while Chesterfield entered the stately structure on his way to—

"No!" Despite his struggle, Hawk could not free himself from immobility. Neither could he reach Alex.

Soon it would be too late. "No!"

As if doom had risen from the depths of hell, his father began to laugh.

Alex awoke to a mournful cry and bolted from the bed. Bryceson was sitting up, trembling, elbows on knees, scrubbing his face with the flat of his hands, his shirt and trousers, even his bedding, drenched with perspiration.

She knelt before him and tried to take his icy hands to warm them between her own, but he grasped hers instead and brought them to his brow, as if nothing but her touch could soothe him.

"Bryce, what is wrong? Are you in pain? What can I do for you?"

"It was only a dream," he said. "A bloody nightmare, like a fretful three-year-old."

"Of the war?" she asked. "Was it terrible?"

He relinquished her hands. "Light a candle, will you?"

Alex did as he requested; then she poured him a brandy. *"Was it terrible?"* she asked again, handing him the glass of dark-amber liquid.

He sipped it and laid his head against the back of the sofa. "Horrid."

"Would you like to tell me about it?"

His sigh was heavy. "There was a huge, hulking dragon. . . ." He paused and opened his eyes to regard her. "I believe it was purple. And scaly."

Alex sat back on her heels. "You rat, you are toying with me."

Hawk sat forward and fingered the hair coiled on her shoulder. "Toying with you, am I? If that were true, then I would be satisfied."

Alex frowned. "What are you—"

"Your hair finally grew past your waist," he said, extending the coil its full length. "You waited all your life for this."

"You made fun of me because I made you measure it."

"Daily," he added. "But I teased you more for your

impatience, because it never grew fast enough. Nothing ever happened fast enough for you. You were so certain that one day your husband would adore your hair, long and flowing past your waist.

Alex regarded her hands, splayed on her knees, reluctant to discover what said husband really thought.

An ember snapped in the hearth.

"You were right," Hawk said, thrumming her nerves and speeding her heart. "Go back to bed, Lexy. You will take a chill. Did you bring nothing warmer for sleeping?"

Lexy. No one else had ever called her that. Hawk's tone had gone from gruff to teasing, and she dared to regard him. "I understood," she said, "that a bride wore less, rather than more, to 'sleep' during the honey month—though I have no firsthand knowledge, you understand."

"A pity, that," he said, as if he meant it. "Did Chesterfield realize he was taking a virgin widow to wife?"

Alex bristled and felt cornered once again, as if a misstatement now might carry a price she could not fathom. "We thought you dead for more than a year, Bryce. What makes you so certain that I remain untouched?"

Hawk's jaw set; the fire in his eyes leaped, and under her hand, the pulse at his wrist trebled. "Are you saying . . ." He shook his head. "I dreamed . . ." After a long moment of expectation, he nodded and said nothing more.

Alex rose and went to open his portmanteau, regarding its contents, rather than her husband, as she answered. "I am saying, in all fairness to me, that what I did after you 'died' is not your concern—especially given the length of time between the 'event' and your return." She extracted a fresh shirt and went to offer her hand. "Come, sleep in the bed. You cannot stay here. The covers are soaked."

"No, I am fine," Hawk said, but he rose anyway—a measure of his nightmare-muddled senses, Alex thought, as he allowed her to lead him, much as he had led her earlier, into the bedroom. By her guess, the time must be going on two in the morning.

With the only light in the bedchamber coming from a candle left to drown in its own wax, and a scuttle's worth of glowing embers, she sat Bryce on the edge of the bed and went for his shirt studs.

Stud by stud, Alex divested her husband of his damp shirt and replaced it with the dry one, though neither of them sought to replace the studs.

Somehow they communicated without words that he would retain his trousers, though Alex ascertained, with a sweep of her hand along one tensely muscled thigh, that they were not as damp as his shirt had been. Then he allowed her to tuck him into the bed, and after she went around to climb in on the opposite side, he even accepted her warmth beside him.

"Cold, are you?" he asked after a silence, more in derision than question. "I warned you."

"Um-hmm." Alex sought his hand, clenched tight at his side, and cupped the hard fist despite his resistance, taking a good deal of satisfaction in stroking his knuckles with her thumb.

He sighed then, either in relaxation or resignation—Alex could not be certain which—as she kissed his temple.

"Be still and let a man sleep," he said.

Before long, Alex heard the soft rumble of his deepened breathing, and she reveled in the beauty of the moment.

Some time near dawn, during that sweet drifting time between sleep and wakefulness, Alex thought she felt a hand in her hair, someone's breath upon her brow, a butterfly-soft kiss, but before she could ascertain whether it was a dream or not, her husband left the bed.

Pleased to believe she had not been dreaming, Alex slipped back into the waiting arms of Morpheus.

Hawk woke her hours later, close to noon, gruff and impersonal once more. They departed Stephen's Hotel before breaking their fast, with his promise that they would stop soon.

Alex surmised that his sullen, somber mood must have to do with his nightmare.

Six

After traveling for nearly an hour, in the throes of a need to drive himself beyond endurance, Hawk ordered a stop at the Old Welsh Harp Inn, along the Broadway in West Hendon. Alex needed to stretch her legs and refresh herself, and Myerson needed as badly to water the horses.

Hawk realized that this was not a war game he was playing, that slogging on would not catch the enemy unawares. Neither would it drive them—or *him,* he should say—beyond the enemy's reach, for in his weaker moments, Hawk very much feared that his worst enemy lived inside himself.

He secured a bedchamber where he and Alex might both freshen up, but as soon as they entered, the great four-poster in its center loomed large, bright, and boldly inviting in counterpoint to the future, which loomed dark, narrow, and depressingly bleak.

Alex did not love him, Hawk reminded himself, and she deserved better, at any rate. He excused himself and stepped outside on the pretext that she could refresh herself at her leisure and in peace and privacy.

When she came down, he seated her in the private

dining parlor he had secured, and took his turn upstairs. By the time he returned, the future seemed so
grim that any appetite he might once have imagined
no longer existed.

While they waited to be served, Alex caught him
up on his sister Rose's daughters, now his wards, all
the while keeping her aversion to his scars from her
expression, even in the well-lit parlor, where his every
imperfection must appear obtrusive and hideous.

Beatrix had been four and her sister, Claudia, fifteen, when their widowed mother died of consump-
tion. Among the few remaining members of Hawk's
family—besides his sister-in-law, Sabrina, and her
children—Claude and Bea had been his wards for a
year, and Alexandra's for nearly twice as long.

Alex regaled him with homely tales that revealed
just how much she had come to love his nieces, prov-
ing he had been right in his decision to go to war.
They *had* been better off with her than they would
ever have been with him. If only they could all remain
together now that he was back.

But he owed Alex such a debt of gratitude, the least
he could do was set her free.

"Bea has so vivid an imagination," Alex said, "that
we never know what she will fabricate next. Last
month, she told us she was a fairy. And what must we
do before every meal but carefully fold her invisible
wings for all of ten minutes so she could sit properly
back against her chair to take sustenance. Claudia informed her in exasperation one evening that everyone
knew fairy wings were supposed to fold flat without
help, but Bea replied sadly that hers were defective."

As the meal progressed, Hawk actually felt the knots ease from his shoulders, and the heaviness of dejection lift from his spirits.

"At one point," Alex continued, "the imp insisted for weeks that she had been turned into a mermaid, though her tail fin was suspiciously invisible. She reminded us, of course, that mermaids have no need of baths."

"Devil take it, you did not allow her to go without bathing for all of that time, did you?"

"Oh, yes, but not without the requisite 'swims' to keep her scales shiny and magical."

Guilt halted his laugh somewhere deep in his throat, where it sat like a lump of stone. So many of his comrades had died, and Hawk knew, more than most, how they felt at the last, making mirth impossible to sanction. "You have been a good parent to the girls," he said. "Thank you."

Some time while they talked, the inn's specialty, turkey-and-ham pie with Cumberland sauce, oyster creams, and assorted savories, had been placed before them, hot and well-spiced. The service had been quick, the serving-ware and servers clean, and the ale smooth and dark. And despite himself, Hawk relaxed and ate the entire meal, even the orange fool—a dessert recipe likely filched from Boodle's.

By the time they were ready to leave, the rain, which had barely begun when they arrived, was coming down in torrents.

"A good thing we are no more than an hour or so from Devil's Dyke," Hawk said, standing beneath the Welsh Harp's small front overhang, watching their carriage shudder beneath the furor of the windy downpour.

"With the muddy roads," Alexandra said, "that hour may very well turn into two or three."

"Right. Shall we make a run for it, then?" They dashed toward the carriage, running between the raindrops, as the young Alex used to say.

After they set off again, they fell into a rather uneasy silence, Hawk dividing his time between trying not to stare at the agreeable sight of his wife and gazing out the window. He no longer took any of the sights for granted, however, given the fact that he never expected to see her, or the town where they grew up, again.

"Nothing changes here," Alex said, as if to cut the tension, as they drove through the center of St. Albans. "The old curfew tower stands yet."

"As if in welcome. As it has done for centuries."

"Remember the day I talked you into following that poor keening sheepdog up to the top?"

"I remember every one of those ninety-three steps," Hawk said with a grimace. "I remember that somehow I got locked in at the top with her while she delivered six squealing pups."

"While I had to go for help."

"The pups were amazing," Hawk admitted, "though I still shudder over the scrapes you got me into."

"I?" Alex said, using the same innocent tone that saved her satin skin that very day, though back then he had not pondered her skin's texture with such morbid and single-minded preoccupation as he had been wont to do today, Hawk mused.

"And there," she said with the excitement of a first-time visitor, "is a piece of the old Roman wall. My father said every other generation wanted to clean up those ruins."

"Destroy them, more like."

"But somebody always managed to save the old city enclosure for succeeding generations."

"I clearly recall the day a certain brat climbed that particular section when she ought not, me at the bottom shouting for her to come down."

"I *told* you there was a mewling kitten up there, and it *was* stuck, and I saved it, but you were such a scold, you made me fall."

Hawk scoffed. "Did I also make you tell your father that nothing hurt, until your wrist swelled like a hot-air balloon, and a doctor needed to be fetched."

Alex grinned.

Hawk shook his head. "As always happened, you charmed a chuckle from your father while mine thrashed me with a birch cane for encouraging you."

Drawn by the combination of sympathy and mischief in her eyes, Hawk was shocked anew by the desirable woman his bride had become, and discomfited anew by the tension churning in the pit of his belly because of it. Which made it doubly surprising to him that any of the old ease in her presence existed, particularly with a war and two weddings now standing between them—never mind a future annulment, if she but knew it.

This burgeoning physical awareness, however, was

something new, and as enticing as it was frightening. "How old were we?" he asked, "the first time you lured me into trouble?"

"I was three and stuck at the bottom of the dyke. You were eight and tried to rescue me."

"Slipping down a forty-foot slope of mud was easy, as I recall; getting back up, impossible." When he spotted her, his clothes had been, as always, pristine. Her knees had been scraped bloody, her dress torn, and mud had caked her short, curly hair.

When they were rescued, after the most fun ever, they were in the same sorry state. That had been the first time his father warned him away from Alexandra Huntington.

"It only took being stranded together that day for us to become fast friends," she said. "If I remember correctly, we were inseparable after that."

"Because, no matter how hard I tried, I could not shake my tenacious shadow—a bit of a sprite, but more of a spitfire. So small, I thought you might break, though I soon discovered that you were sturdy as a tree trunk and thrice as stubborn as its roots."

"And I made you laugh, you said. You loved having me around. Do not pretend otherwise. Stubborn, did you say? Me?"

Hawk shook his head, looking back. "In my arrogant maleness, I did not, for the most part, mind keeping in tow a female who venerated the ground upon which I walked, until I learned that you had been warning other girls away."

Alex covered her mouth with a hand, but the bright

light in her eyes revealed not one whit of remorse. "You knew and did not try to thrash me?"

"By the time my indignation took hold, I was off to Oxford and it no longer mattered. What drove me most to distraction was your goading me into some lark or other that broke a corresponding rule, for which I, not you, would be punished. I suffered mightily for that penchant in you. Why were you always after breaking rules, Alexandra?"

"I only broke a rule when I had good reason to do so. Besides, you made up half the blasted rules yourself, as if rules and the following of them were the be-all and end-all of existence."

"They are more than that. Rules, whether written or unwritten, like honor and ethics, are the very backbone of a civilized society."

Alex closed her eyes and laid her head back, as if overtaken at once by weariness. "Pity you did not follow any rules where your family was concerned."

Hawk winced, for her blade struck bone. Having come from a long line of privileged rogues, he had always attempted to act more civilized than his less-than-exemplary ancestors. He had prided himself on following a code of ethical conduct that would keep him from wreaking the kind of havoc his father and grandfather and scores of other male ancestors had perpetrated before him.

He had treated his tenants with generosity and respect, bedded only those women who wanted bedding—lucky for him, a great many had back then. He had gambled only with rich, greedy, bird-witted men who seemed to want to lose, Chesterfield prime among them.

Against his father's exhortations that he owed more to his name than to marry the penniless Alexandra Huntington, he had married his maddening hoyden of a neighbor, the plague and nuisance of his growing-up years. Because she had no other chance for marriage, or so he thought, and would have a better future as a rich and titled widow. And because she was prudent, trustworthy, resourceful, and penniless, and would appreciate the favor he did her.

He had married her because she would take better care of his family than he, while he was off fighting Boney—a glory for which his father had offered everything a son could ever hope to have.

Glory be damned. His father be damned. Waterloo had been worse than hell. He had gotten what he deserved, going off to war, but Alexandra had not deserved what she got, yet her life had been altered as well.

Hawk would never forget the look on her face when he bade her farewell at the church immediately following their wedding ceremony. God's teeth, he had used her ill.

As if that had not been bad enough, he was so eager to fare off to glory that he married her and shipped off to France before the reading of his father's will. He had known that all Hawksworth brides were well provided for at the time of their husband's deaths. He had known it and counted upon it.

He still did not know what had gone wrong in the case of *his* bride, for his father's old solicitor had also passed away, leaving everything in the hands of his nephew, who had been traveling since Hawk returned.

He had not known that he left his family to be cast off by his heir, without a farthing to their names or a roof over their heads. Or that they had been forced to take up residence in Alexandra's ramshackle manor, between St. Albans and Wheathampstead. But devil take it, she was right; he had not followed his own code of conduct where his family was concerned. God knew how they had managed, though he would learn soon enough.

Alex opened her eyes of a sudden, in something of a panic, as if to ascertain whether he was actually there.

"Did you fall asleep and think you dreamed me?" Hawk asked. "Or would that have been more of a nightmare?"

"I dreamed, but I did not sleep," Alex said enigmatically. "And as to whether you might be a dream or a nightmare, if you do not already know that answer, then you do not deserve to know it."

And what did that mean? With that faraway look in her eyes, Hawk had feared she was dreaming of Chesterfield, the bloody knave, but now he was not so certain.

"Tell me," Hawk said, to turn her thoughts, "how stands the 'house that Jack built'?"

"It stands."

"Always a promising beginning."

Alex nodded. "It is improved in some respects," she said. "And worse in others."

"I regret that I did not make provisions for you all," Hawk said. "You were right. I ought to be drawn and quartered."

Alex tilted her head consideringly, as if perhaps he ought, and Hawk felt that old need to suffer for his failures. What better did he deserve? "You must have wanted to trounce me when you found out."

"When you believe someone has died, your thoughts do not usually run toward vengeance," she said. "But you should have realized, Bryce, that you could die in the war and that your heir might inherit. What were you thinking?"

He could offer no excuse, damn his eyes. He thought only of pleasing his dead father, but if he told her so, she would despise him the more, which he would deserve.

"What did faring off to glory get you, anyway?" she asked, "but dead—which might more easily be true than not."

"You are not telling me something I have not told myself a score of times. Now I have to undo the whole blasted mess, and my countenance does not help. Few people, if any, recognize me, though my voice in some cases saves the day."

"Your voice frightened *me* witless, coming from a derelict off the street, or so I thought you."

Hawk paled and sat straighter. "My sincere apologies, madam, but my physiognomy is not something that can be altered. God knows, I would if I could."

Alex sighed. "I have no aversion to your appearance, Bryce, which is not entirely unpleasing, you may not know. You were simply unknown to me at the time."

"A derelict, Alex?"

"Look at your hair," she said. "Did you ever, in your stylishly groomed life, wear it wild and flowing away from your face, for all the world as if it were a lion's mane? Though it is too devilish dark to be any such thing, of course. And those clothes. They are not even yours."

Hawk fingered the frock coat he might have tossed on the flames a war and a lifetime before. "Do you not appreciate my stylish attire? Is the weave of the fabric not fine enough for you?"

"As if clothes ever mattered a jot to me."

"These clothes were a gift from the peasant family who nursed me back to health, I will have you know." Hawk shook his head, but he could not help looking back. "I remember that they were as pleased to present them as I was to receive them. I have nothing else to wear, as things stand, and by the time Sabrina told me of your upcoming nuptials, I had less than an hour to stop you. I could think of no better way than to go myself, my destitute appearance notwithstanding."

His words furrowed Alex's brow. "Had you been in London long? And Sabrina knew you were there?"

Seven

Hawk could not precisely say why he had been back so long without contacting Alex, because he could no more explain it to himself than to her; but knowing the length of time would only hurt her, so he decided on a temporary half-truth. "I have been back long enough to discover that you were no longer living in my London house and that you did, in fact, sell it, for which I planned to teach you some vengeful lesson."

"I most certainly did not sell your house. What kind of lesson?"

"I learned the truth before your lesson was ever devised." He shrugged. "I soon discovered that my heir tossed you out and later disposed of the town house, that you were living at Huntington Lodge and taking excellent care of the family. Again, thank you."

"It was my pleasure," she said. "I love them."

Hawk grew uncomfortable with his inability to say how much his family loved her, without including himself in the declaration. He cleared his throat. "For all my dastardly ancestors' rule-breaking, I doubt any of them ever found themselves in the incongruous position of trying to wrest, or should I say, rescue, what little was left of their fortunes and estates from the greedy hands of their improvident, globe-trotting heirs. Nor did any of them ever have to stop their wives from marrying another."

Alex knew Bryce was probing for the details of her alliance with Chesterfield again, but if he thought she would reveal them, he had another thought coming.

Even now, he regarded her in such a way as to invite her to take up his verbal gauntlet, but she firmed her spine and her resolve and remained adamantly silent.

"Tell me," he said, giving up, "how is your Aunt Hildegarde? She was always my biggest fan. Did she mourn me for long?"

"Aunt Hildy did not mourn you at all."

Hawk's arrested shock at her response made Alex chuckle. "She did not mourn you, because she refused to believe that you had been killed. We tried to tell her, but doing so was like speaking to a stone, so we gave up.

"On the rare occasions she still asks for you, we tell her that you are on a hunting trip, or taking care of business in London. I thought that perhaps my marrying Judson and moving everyone to his house might bring her around, but none of that matters now, does it?"

Hawk looked away, unable to tell how Alex really felt about the turn of events. However it was, they were nearing the lodge, and the thought of seeing his family, and of their seeing him, knotted his stomach and slicked his palms. The arrogant rogue of Devil's

Dyke, as frightened as a schoolboy who forgot his lessons.

The carriage climbed Gorhambury Hill, along the River Ver, toward Devil's Dyke and the house where Alex grew up. With the placement of their family homes, fate had merged their lives at so early an age, Hawk could not remember his life without Alex in it.

Hawks Ridge, the home of his birth— temporarily his heir's—sat at the opposite summit overlooking Devil's Dyke, which formed the valley between. Hawk gazed westward to catch sight of his estate, but nearly a mile separated the houses, and he had forgotten that, other than in the dead of winter, the very woodland they had romped in grew too lush to allow for even a glimpse from the hill.

Besides, night had long since fallen, and Alex's looming lodge claimed his full attention. A few windows shone with light, but the rest remained dark. And though a half-moon shone, he could not tell whether the house was still as much a leaking, tumbling pile as he remembered, or worse.

"Should I go in alone first and break the news?" Alex asked as the carriage came to a stop before a set of weather-beaten granite steps. "I would not want your Uncle Gifford to have a seizure."

"You think my scars will come as that bad a shock to him?" Hawk asked. Apoplexy was very near what he expected the first time people who knew him caught sight of him.

Alexandra regarded him as if he were daft. "Of course not. But I think the ghost of his dearly beloved nephew walking through the door, more than a year after his death, might do the trick."

Hawk felt himself flush.

"I perceive that your scars are a great deal more of a difficulty for you," Alex said, "than for the people who must look upon you."

"Therein lies the crux of the problem. They *must* look upon me, but they would not if they could help it."

Alexandra sighed and shook her head, as if she might argue the point, but the carriage door was thrown open and Claudia and Beatrix scrambled inside, out of the rain.

Even as the interior grew bright with the light from their lantern, they began tossing rice in the air. "Hurrah for the bride and groom. Hurrah, hurr—"

Sound stopped as if severed by a blade.

Hawk braced himself even as he consumed the blessed sight of them: Bea bigger, but still a halfling, Claudia nearly a woman, but sadder somehow.

When Bea focused on his face, she gasped and stepped back, regarding him fixedly, her curly little saffron head tipped in concentration. "Do I know you?" she asked, her small voice wobbling.

"Do not be afraid," Hawk said.

To his horror, she began to cry as she climbed into Alex's lap.

Hawk felt the blood drain from him and went stone cold, inside and out.

Alex wrapped Bea in love and soothing words. The little one had taken one look at him and was frightened to death. His worst nightmare come true—or one of his worst.

"Muffin?" Alex coaxed. "What is it, love? Why are you crying?"

"That man made me sad. I miss my Uncle Bryce."

Claudia's gaze shot to his face then, as if the scales had slipped from her eyes, and she saw him true and understood the reason for Bea's confusion.

Hawk gave her a half nod, and as quickly as he did, Claude covered her mouth with a hand and her eyes filled to brimming—not for the first time that day, if he did not miss his guess. Her tears overflowed and spilled onto her cheeks.

Hawk wished he knew whether she wept with happiness or horror, or both. At least he understood the little one's tears. "Come," he said, lifting Beatrix away from Alex. "Come, pup, I am Uncle Bryce." He hugged her close and smoothed her hair. "No more tears for missing me. I am here, sweet. I am here."

Bea looked up at him, taking her lip between her teeth, her eyes wide, sobs escaping at odd moments, her expression moving from doubt to wonder. "Uncle Bryce?"

"Bumble Bea?"

"Uncle Bryce!" she screamed, throwing her arms around his neck. Then Claudia was laughing and hugging him too, and all his girls, Alex included, wept openly, laughing through their tears.

And as Alex reached for his hand, and the little one kissed him all over his face, scars and all, Hawk felt, amazingly, as if he had come home—for the first time in his life.

Beatrix had so much to tell him that they did not move from the carriage for fully three quarters of an hour, and even then Alex kept telling her that she would have the rest of her life to catch him up.

"Hello the carriage," came a gruff, old, curmudgeonly shout from the darkness. "Where has everyone got to?"

"In here, Uncle Giff," Alexandra said. "Come in, out of the rain."

Hawk shrugged at Alex as his stodgy old uncle squeezed into the seat opposite, so busy ordering Claudia aside that he had not yet regarded the seat across from him. And when, at length, he did, he simply furrowed his grizzled brow in bewilderment.

Hawk kissed Bea's little head, firm against his chest. "I am Hawk, Uncle. I survived, after all."

"No."

"Truly, though I am a little the worse for wear, as you see."

"No."

Alexandra laughed. "Quiz him, Giff. You will discover that he knows all our atrocious middle names, including the most ridiculous of our secrets. No doubt about it. He is Hawksworth."

"No."

The girls burst into laughter and began talking at once, and Beatrix practically fell from the carriage, she was so excited; then she dashed for the house.

In the foyer's dim light, Hawk noted that his uncle's hair had turned the color of pewter in the intervening time, and that his manly physique may have thickened and shifted somewhat. But all in all, the old boy looked fit and spry and seemed much less a curmudgeon than Hawk remembered.

"Well what do you know!" his uncle said, quite belatedly slapping him on the back, at long last accepting the truth before him. "The dotty old magpie isn't five feathers short a tail, after all, but wise as an owl." Giff grinned. "Hildy," he called, striding to the bottom of the stairs. "Hildy, you will never guess."

"Alex?" Claudia asked, stepping near. "Did you find Uncle Bryce *today?* Or yesterday?"

Alex smiled. "He found me . . . before I married Ch—"

"Hurrah," Claudia exclaimed twirling away from Alex and into her uncle's arms. "I love you, Uncle Bryce."

Hawk knew he had missed some pertinent component in that exchange; then he heard Alexandra's aunt Hildegard reproaching his uncle from somewhere on the upper floor.

Nothing had changed.

When Aunt Hildy started down the stairs, Hawk saw her focus on him right away. And she did not miss a beat, not even when she took his uncle's arm halfway down. "Bryceson, you stayed away too long this time," she chided, beaming, as if he had not changed a jot, as if she had been expecting him all along.

"But we forgive you, do we not, Alexandra? I am so glad you are back." She stood on the bottom step, and still she barely reached his chin. "Though why your letters stopped more than a year ago, I cannot imagine. And it was too bad of the war office to ship you out a mere week after your wedding. Poor Alex wept for months about not even having your child with which to remember you. Now you have another chance; you can get on with having that family of yours while you are still young. I shall put in my order, now, shall I, for a big, noisy brood?"

His uncle Gifford's sudden paroxysm of coughing turned into a strangled laugh.

"Er, good to see you, too, Aunt Hildegarde," Hawk said, feeling the tightening of his cravat.

The dear old lady bussed his cheek, but when she did, and he placed an arm about her shoulders, he realized from the degree of her trembling that she was a great deal more shaken than she was letting on. And when he bent nearer, he saw tears hovering on her lashes.

"Praise be," she whispered.

"My sentiments exactly," Hawk said, for her ears alone, kissing her cheek in turn. "Especially now that I have seen my best girl."

Hildegarde swatted his arm but preened anyway. "Are you hungry?" she asked, stepping off that last step and composing herself. "Thirsty? Have you dined?"

"I am fine," Alex said. "How about you, Hawksworth?"

"Nothing for me." Hawk felt all the nervousness of an imposter. Alex was treating him like Hawksworth, the stranger, rather than Bryce, the friend. His family believed good of him when no good existed.

He had chosen to ship out immediately after their wedding rather than risk leaving Alex with the child of a man she did not love. And he had not written, not to anyone, to sever their ties early in hopes that, when he was killed—which he daily expected—their shock and grief would be diminished.

Had Alex stayed somewhere else in London, alone for a time, to shore up a pretense of wedded bliss? Had she passed them news that *supposedly* came from him? Considering what her aunt had said, had Alex even pretended for a time that she might be carrying his child?

"Why has little Miss Beatrix not been sent up to bed, I would like to know?" Alex asked, cutting the tense silence, looking as uncomfortable as he, as she ruffled Bea's curls. "It is gone past ten."

"Because of your wed—because these are special days," his uncle said. "Though we expected you yesterday."

"Very special days, more than you can imagine," Hawk said. To his mind, stopping Alex's nuptials to Judson Broderick, Viscount blasted Chesterfield, offered a great deal more to celebrate than her marrying him might have done.

"Exhausting days, all the same," Alex said. "And it is very late, past time for little girls to be tucked into their beds."

"Time for all of us to go up," Aunt Hildegarde said.

"But there is no bedchamber for Uncle Bryce," Beatrix wailed in distress.

"Of course there is," Alex said. "He shall have the master bedchamber."

"But that is your b—"

Claudia had clapped a hand over her sister's mouth.

"You heard Alex, Miss Mischief: time for little people to be in their beds."

"Big people, too," Giff said, taking Aunt Hildy's arm. "Let us all go up and allow Hawk and Alex the opportunity to, er, settle everything."

That fast, Alex and Bryce were left standing at the base of the main staircase to regard each other. Alex wished the foyer did not seem so drab for his homecoming, while he appeared for all the world like a raw boy with his first girl, the way she was certain he had never appeared in the whole of his life.

"I do not want to put you out," he said, wrapping dignity about him like a shield, much as he had done the evening before. "As you know, I do not sleep well these days. Any bedchamber will do."

Plague take it, Alex thought. Was not a husband expected to sleep with his wife? They were home now. She was no longer in shock. And if she did not begin the way she intended to go on, then she would deserve the consequences. "There *is* no other bedchamber," she snapped.

"There must be a dozen at least."

"If they have beds, they have no mattresses."

"Why ever not?"

Alex gave a long-suffering sigh. "When we were *forced,*" she stressed, "to return here, the mattresses had been turned into mouse houses, so we turned them out of our house, leaky and dilapidated as it is."

Bryceson clearly bit back an oath, and that old impatient tic worked in his cheek. "The tower room in the attic," he said, seeming to grasp at straws. "Isn't there a chaise longue, or a daybed, that would serve?

When we used to practice our archery up there on rainy days, I am certain we proved the thing indestructible."

"You are able to climb so many stairs, then?" Alex asked, hoping to discourage him.

"I climb better than I descend, it is true, but I can manage. Besides, I am convinced that the more I use my legs, the better they will work."

Myerson cleared his throat from the door of the servants' hall, self-consciously turning his dripping hat in his hands. "Excuse me, Your Grace, but the horses?"

While Bryce oversaw the stabling and feeding of the matched pair he had borrowed with the carriage, Alex carried a candle and bedding up three flights of stairs to the attic tower.

Sure enough, the huge, sparse circular chamber appeared dry as toast and looked exactly as it had the last time they played there, except for the additional dust. Everything as they had left it, including their old archery equipment *and* the dratted daybed.

Thoroughly annoyed by the sight, Alex placed her candle on a table, and the bedding on the longue. She went for a bow and arrow and set them up, crossed the room, and in a fit of pique she let the arrow fly, hitting the target dead center.

"Rotten roof leaks everywhere," she muttered, choosing another arrow. "Wouldn't you just know it would hold above this one blasted room?"

She notched the second arrow but changed her mind about its destination and turned her sights—and her weapon—upward. "Bloody, stupid roof." She sent the missile skyward.

The arrow disappeared into the darkened attic rafters, and almost as it did, a drip hit the floor, then another, and another, until rain dripped down in a rapid, steady rhythm. "Oops," Alex said. "Must have been ready to give at any moment."

Her mind worked and her smile grew as she chose yet another arrow and aimed it unerringly toward the rafters directly above the chaise longue. But when she let it fly, nothing happened, and she could not tell exactly where it disappeared within the shadowed labyrinth of beams closer to the tower's peak. "Drat."

Hearing footsteps on the stairs, she stashed the bow, saw the daybed was dry, and sighed with regret. Doomed to spending another night alone. *Double drat.*

As Hawksworth entered, she beamed a bright smile. "Only one small leak," she said with feigned pleasure. "Your bed is fine. See?"

Even as they regarded the makeshift berth, an arrow dropped, flat on its side, dead center of the bed, and rain poured—literally—down, soaking the bedding and the longue, rendering it completely useless.

Rainwater must have eased the arrow from the rupture where it had struck and stuck, Alex mused as she bit her lip and regarded her husband.

He raised a brow. "Are we under siege?"

"I was . . . practicing," she said by way of feeble explanation. "And I heard . . . something. And I jumped . . . in fright. And accidentally, my shot went wide . . . accidentally."

"Very wide. Accidentally."

Alex swallowed a knot of hysterical laughter, but she could not quite stop it from rushing forward, so she clamped a hand over her mouth.

Hawksworth regarded the source and sorceress of all his dreams, her turquoise eyes wide with trepidation yet brimming with merriment all the same.

He shook his head. Behold the thorn in his side, his hoyden . . . his wife.

Eight

"Sleeping with me will not be as dreadful as you seem to think," Alex promised as they made their plodding way, arm in arm, down the stairs toward the family bedchambers. "My bed is big. You will not even know I am there."

Hawk scoffed, feeling all the restrictions of a cage. "Well, you will bloody well know *I* am there. If it were not so late, and you did not look so tired, I would fight you on this. You will be sorry when I push and kick and trample you in my sleep. You may end up more severely wounded than I."

Alex bit her lip, appearing not the least bit worried or repentant. "Oh, Myerson," she said when they saw his man in the upper hall, "welcome to Huntington Lodge. Do you think you can bring up a tub and some hot water to my—er, our dressing room? His Grace will want a bath before I cut his hair."

"His Grace will not want his hair cut," Hawksworth said. "And you would not be doing the cutting if he did."

"The bath, please, Myerson," Alex said. "And thank you."

Hawk followed Alex into a well-appointed bedchamber. The curtains and counterpane, like the up-holstery on the two wingback chairs by the hearth, were covered in the deep-turquoise velvet of Alex's eyes. Pillows of gold brought the color, the very room, to life.

Upon her dresser sat a Roman pottery vase, one of the childhood treasures they had unearthed near the dyke, though this one had always been Alex's favorite. Colored pale tan to deep blue-gray, and looking as if someone had combed a staff of shallow half-circles in the clay before firing, the vase lent an air of reality to Hawk's illusory sense of home-coming.

Though the bedchamber was not rich by any standard, it was in better condition than he would have expected. "You expected to share this room with your husband, did you not?"

"On occasion," Alex said. "Which is exactly what I am doing."

Hawk nodded, hardly daring to believe it. He could be comfortable in this room, with very few adjustments, if only Alex would not expect him to play the husband—correction: if he had the right, and the confidence in his ability, he would gladly play the husband.

With the manner of an artist evaluating a work of art, Alex regarded him critically. "Your beard is as wild as your mane. I will trim both."

"You will not."

"Hawksworth, do you want me to awaken in the night and scream because I have a beast in my bed?"

"You will have a beast in your bed, make no mistake."

"The one now growling beside me?"

A rather foreign and uncomfortable bubble of mirth caught in Hawk's throat, making it ache, making him angry. "Indeed."

"There are beasts, and there are beasts," Alex said pointedly, shivering as if in anticipation. *Damn.*

"Just a little bit?" she cajoled in the charming way that only Alex could. "I will only cut your hair a little bit. And after traveling all day, I am certain we would benefit from a hot bath."

"We? One at a time, of course."

"In a slipper bath? I should say so. As if there is any other." Her grin shot an arrow of doubt straight to Hawk's conscience. He was not the rogue of old, and he should tell her so.

"There *is* another way, is there not?" she said, her ripple of mirth and sparkling interest speeding Hawk's heart. "Chesterfield promised me," she said consideringly, "that he would teach me all manner of entertaining pastimes in marriage. Now, I expect there will be no one, unless you teach me." She released a sigh, heavy with irony, if only she knew it. Or did she?

Hawksworth began to sweat. He had known she would be like this, even about the marriage bed, eager for new experiences, excited, and exciting, drinking of life in huge, greedy draughts. *Bloody hell.*

To protect her from Chesterfield, he had no choice but to remain her husband, Hawk told himself, which eased the constriction about his chest somewhat and allowed him to breathe again—barely.

A sad day, he thought, when the Rogue of Devil's Dyke became the lesser of evils. Imagine a man of legendary prowess being pleased about that!

Imagine him being grateful.

Lo, how the mighty have fallen.

Part of him was relieved—and pleased and grateful—that he had not broken her spirit by leaving her to bear such burdens, as he might have done with a less "lively" individual, but another part was frightened by the very "liveliness" he admired.

Hawk looked up and caught his breath at the sight of her absently pulling pins from her hair before her mirror—watching him, in the glass, watching her. Her arms raised, her lush and generous breasts all but bared in proud invitation, she presented the ultimate picture of bewitchment and seemed totally oblivious to the fact.

He should be shot for what he was thinking.

Drawn by her mesmerizing, almost-come-hither gaze, her eyes in candlelight the very color and depth of the sunniest south sea, Hawk could not keep from approaching. He moved her hands aside to savor the sensation of his own in her hair, and removed her hairpins himself. He had no sooner buried his fists wrist-deep in the silken bounty than the cinnamon mane tumbled down to her tiny waist and beyond in one long, waving sweep.

Why not make her his in every way? They were married, after all.

To the beat of his speeding heart, Hawk combed

his fingers through the silken treasure, top to tail, literally, stroking her perfect bottom twice or thrice along the way, almost by accident. The satin against his hands enticed him almost as much as those womanly curves beneath, so deliciously near that his palms itched to explore every gentle swell and graceful hollow.

He was in trouble. Big trouble.

He wanted her. He could not have her.

But he would be forced to lie beside her every night. All night. Sweating. Aching, if today was any indication—both a hopeful and a dangerous turn of events.

Alex turned her back on him then and lifted her hair, presumably for him to undo the buttons down the back of her rose silk gown. Hawk closed his eyes, remembering how good she had felt in his arms yesterday in the carriage, how much he had wanted to hold her in the bed last night. He inhaled the scent of her: violets, woman, softness, and need.

Joy. Willingness. Life. Alexandra.

And just as he bent to place his lips against that spot at her nape begging for his kiss, Myerson called from the dressing room that His Grace's bath was ready.

Hawk stilled, cursed himself roundly, and after undoing the last of Alexandra's buttons with all due haste, he took the opportunity to flee.

Once inside the dressing room, he shut the door and locked it, certain he would fail at the goal he had set for himself—to let her go. He hoped beyond hope that he would not, because Alex would pay an awful price for all of a lifetime if he failed.

After Myerson left, Hawk undressed and lowered his awkward and scarred body into the warm, lapping, incredibly soothing water. As heat radiated to his limbs and deep into his marrow, sweet and numbing, his screaming muscles calmed and so, too, did his fast-beating heart.

Alex had been right. A bath was just what he needed.

"I was right, was I not?"

Hawk jumped all of a foot, splashing them both and feeling like an idiot. "How did you get in here?"

"Through the door. How else? I thought you might need my help. I could scrub your back." There she was again, that innocent three-year-old, coaxing him down a forbidden hill with no more than that wide-eyed look.

"Go away."

"Why?"

The string of oaths Hawk released should have turned her face crimson and chased her from the room.

She grinned. "If you did not want me here, you should have locked the door."

Hawk closed his eyes, because to see her was to desire her. "I did lock the door."

At her ripple of laughter, he opened them.

"I know." She allowed another salacious giggle to escape without a qualm. "The lock is broken. Everything in this house is." She beamed as she approached the tub.

At the glitter of purpose in her eyes, Hawk reared back.

"Relax," she said. "My intentions are honorable. I plan only to wash your hair, not to ravish you."

Hawk sighed, remembering ravishment with a great deal of wistful fondness, wishing it were possible, wondering what would happen if . . . "Be gentle with me," he said, tired enough to allow the good ship *Alexandra* to stay her course, however fraught with peril the waters.

"Oh, I will." Like warm, soft toffee, her words melted on her tongue, rich and honeyed with promise.

It was the most glorious experience of his life, Hawk thought, as Alexandra worked his hair in soft soothing strokes, with lots of rich lather, turning the process into a seductive dance.

With her talented soapy fingers, she stroked his neck, his shoulders, a way down his back, a longer way down his front, her slow, creamy, circling strokes teasing his senses and bringing him pleasure with just her touch.

Almost as good as sex, Hawk mused, though after a year and a half, he had about forgotten what that was like. Almost.

When he became aroused, Hawk waited with bated breath to see if his erection would last; but it diminished, or he nodded off—it was difficult to tell which happened first.

Ultimately, he must really have slept, because he awoke to the sound of clipping, except that he was still in the tub, afraid to move lest he lose an ear. "Are you cutting my hair?"

"I think so."

"I would rather you were certain," he said. "How did you go from washing to trimming in one step?"

"You must be exhausted, because you slept as if you had not slept in ages. I rinsed your hair and trimmed your beard a bit, but you never woke."

"I did not get much sleep last night."

"True. Bryceson?"

He was almost afraid to respond. Her very tone made him skittish. "Alexandra?"

"I rather prefer your hair like a lion's mane, albeit a tamer lion. Would you mind if I only just trimmed that as well?"

Hawk released the breath he had been holding. "Fine."

"The longer length fits with your beard, I think, and makes you look wickedly piratical. I expect you are too sleepy to plunder and pillage?"

Hawk bit back a new flurry of mirth. "I *am* sleepy. I do not think I have felt this comfortable or this re-laxed since . . . very."

"Come, let me help you step from the tub, so I can help dry—"

"No, I will step out and dry myself off, after you return to your bedchamber."

"But Bryce . . ."

Hawk pointed toward the door. "Out."

"But we were children together. We swam together. Your scars cannot be that bad."

"They are."

Like a heartbroken pup, Alexandra turned away.

Hawk caught her hand to stop her as she passed. "Lexy, you have seen enough of my ugliness. Leave me some dignity. Please."

Alex sighed and grudgingly recovered her spirits. "Well, if you express it that way, what choice do I have?" She shut the door quietly as she left, and Hawk breathed a heavy sigh.

Never having owned a nightshirt in his life, he prudently donned his dressing gown, thinking that medieval armor might prove worthless with the tenacious Alexandra. He grabbed his cane, snuffed the candles, and made his toe-stubbing way to the bed, cursing as he went.

"Serves you right," Alex said from somewhere across the room. "Am I to bathe in the dark, then?"

Hawk climbed onto the far side of the bed and arranged the covers. "I humbly beg your forgiveness. Relight the candles, if you wish. The light will not disturb my sleep."

He heard her exasperated huff, and when the candles were lit, she, too, wore only a dressing gown— and that not too well fastened. Hawk both raged and salivated as he watched her delightful breasts, more fit to spring free than in her seductive night rail the night before. And as she stepped into her dressing room, she gave him an amazing glimpse of one long and shapely leg, ankle to thigh, almost by accident.

Despite himself, Hawk imagined her dropping her dressing gown and stepping naked about then into the tub in which he had just bathed. If he had not vowed to set her free, he would go and join her, his scars be damned along with her modesty and anything else.

But he did not have the right, and no matter his bride's reassurances, seeing each other through the gauze of wet garments at the age of ten and seeing each other naked now were nothing like.

Her innocence might remain intact, despite her denial to the contrary, but *his* certainly did not.

"I think you should come and wash my hair," she called. "I washed yours."

Hawksworth mentally applauded her tenacity and considered the tower room daybed with longing.

Accidentally, indeed.

He had been right, he mused, as he closed his eyes and drifted toward sleep: living again just might kill him. Then again, for the first time since the Battle of Waterloo, living again felt rather . . . hopeful.

Hawk yawned. For a dead man, he had had a tiring day.

Alex was thoroughly disgruntled by the time she climbed into bed beside her husband. She was no expert, but she did not think that marriage beds were supposed to be tedious or dull as ditch water. Neither did she believe that any of Hawk's former mistresses had found him unconscious when they climbed into bed with him.

Though she was very much tempted to slip the bedcovers off and examine him at her leisure, she supposed that in fairness to his dignity, she should wait until she was invited, if the blasted day ever arrived.

She must also face the fact that Hawksworth had not chosen her as his bride in the truest sense. Which might mean that he did not care to touch her, or could not bear to, which made her want to smack him as he slept, the paper-skulled jackanapes.

To be fair, however, 'twas only a little more than a year ago that he had been so badly wounded that he was taken for dead, and he could still be recovering his strength. Too often to count today, she had caught the pain in his eyes, though he tried to hide it.

She had not seen the damage to his leg—not yet, at any rate—but the limb might very well be festering still. Leg wounds often did.

When all was said and done, however, even though she was not his choice, Hawksworth was her first and only choice. In addition, they were already married— till death do them part. But life could seem a very long time if one was feeling neglected and . . . needy.

If Hawksworth did not plan to seduce her, then perhaps she should try to seduce him.

If only she knew how.

She supposed there were worse schemes than to seduce one's own husband. Though seduction seemed too good for him, considering his reason for marrying her, and the fact that he had waited so blasted long to let her know he lived. Punishment seemed a better choice.

Just thinking about his "offenses" made her angry all over again. And sad, and hurt, and . . . devil it, she wanted him to *know* how much he hurt her. She wanted him to *feel* her pain.

What she should do, Alex thought, turning yet again in her formerly comfortable bed, was make him worship her, as she had always worshipped him, to the point that she might pay him back in kind.

Let him ache to have her and see her walk away.

To do that, she would have to make him think she wanted him, until he wanted her as desperately. Then, when she was certain of his adoration, she could tell him of her coldhearted plan to even the score between them. Better yet, she would get one of her friends, or his, to do the telling.

Let him see how that felt.

Then she could walk away.

Nine

Alex sat up in the bed, for it seemed at once obvious and clear that only after Hawk understood how much he had hurt her would they be free to go forward with their marriage on an equal footing. In which case seducing him just might turn out to be the smartest plan she had ever hatched . . . and she had hatched several noteworthy schemes in her time.

She would do it, she thought, as she lay back against her pillows. As soon as she figured out how one went about conducting a seduction, she would begin a "captivating" campaign.

Alex smiled in the darkness, wishing she knew who she could ask about seductions in general.

When Chesterfield had embraced and kissed her, sometimes at length, he would tremble and close his eyes, as if against pain, and tell her that he wanted her. When she questioned him, he promised that after their wedding he would teach her everything about married love, to set her as afire for him as he was for her.

If she had married him yesterday, she might now be receiving her second lesson.

Alexandra knew from her lack of regret that she

must be in a bad way, for she did not pine for Chesterfield or his lessons. No, she would rather lie needy beside Hawksworth till the end of her days than be set afire in Chesterfield's arms even once.

She rolled to her side to regard her husband, his marred but no less striking features lit by the moon. He may no longer be perfect of face, but no woman capable of drawing breath would be able to resist his air of masculine danger and denied vulnerability. Especially not she, who had been unable to resist him at his arrogant worst, or best, however one considered it.

Then again, had there not always been something of a "hurt boy" vulnerability about him, which had simply risen to prominence with his scars from the war?

Lord, had nothing changed? She loved him. She wanted to protect him, to heal his hurts.

She desired him.

His topaz eyes still shone more than the jewels themselves, especially when he gazed at her pensively or furiously, as if he wanted nothing more than to set her over his knee—the delicious way he appeared when she said she would live in sin with Chesterfield.

Alex shivered.

At the inn along the way, when Bryce left her to go upstairs and refresh himself, she noticed that he was as small of waist, as broad of shoulders, and as firm of bottom as ever—good form for a man, in her estimation. And in his black brocade dressing gown tonight, which formidable sight stole her breath as he snuffed the candle, she could not help thinking him the most tantalizing rogue she ever hoped to make her own.

She tried to touch his leg with her foot just then, but she could not quite reach. Sliding surreptitiously closer so as not to awaken him, she stretched and tried again but encountered only his dressing gown.

Moving closer still, Alex slid her toes beneath the brocade silk and touched his bare foot.

He stirred.

She stilled, her heart beating as fast as a careening carriage.

After a minute, she moved her seeking foot farther upward, a bit past his ankle and toward his calf.

Bryce moaned. Alex warmed. This could work.

Afraid to go farther lest she rouse the self-proclaimed beast, she was cheered nonetheless by the possibility of seduction as a form of vengeance, which came very near, in her mind, to eating one's sweets and keeping them, too.

With a smile on her lips, Alex slipped as near Bryce as she dared, without disturbing him, to savor the simple joy of sleeping beside the man she loved.

She longed for him to hold her again as he had in the carriage, but perhaps her forwardness put him off. Perhaps *he* would rather be the seducer. It was something to think about, she supposed . . . perhaps.

Right now, however, unable to resist temptation, Alex reached over to place her hand against his chest, atop the blanket.

To her surprise, at the contact, Bryce swept her into his arms, clasped her tight, and spoke her name.

With a grin of triumph, her heart singing, head tucked beneath his chin, top to tail against various and sundry parts of his firm torso, Alexandra reveled in her unforgettable rogue's possessive embrace.

Tears filled her eyes for all her years of missing him, and for having him back beyond all imagining. And when she calmed and emotion turned to joy, Alex realized a little something about seduction. It must have to do with figuring out what those various and interesting parts were for, and why one of them seemed actually to be pulsing.

Hawk woke to the light of bright morning, shocked and erect, and clutching a handful of titillating breast. Alexandra's knee was positioned against his naked and vulnerable groin, her hand riding dangerously low inside his dressing gown.

More than anything, he wanted to explore the possibilities, but he had not the right if he planned to let her go—which he must. Besides, since his bride was unused to having a man in her bed—please, God—he was afraid that if he took to exploring, he might surprise her into moving her knee a little too hard and a bit too fast, which could injure him the worse.

While he pondered his precarious situation, Hawk noticed, between the hanks of hair in her face, that Alex was watching him. "Do not move your knee," he said softly, so as not to startle her. But she must have realized just where it rested, because she jumped and did exactly what he had tried to avoid.

"*Oomph.* Ouch! Alex, be careful."

Like a spring-wound toy, she shot up and knelt over him. "Bryce, I am sorry." She tugged on the bedcovers to pull them down. "Did I hurt your leg? Let me see."

Hawk fought for his modesty and won, barely. "My *leg* is fine."

"Are you certain? Because if it is festering, and I bumped it . . ."

"It is not festering, but fully healed and pain-free at the moment."

Alex released her breath and lay back down beside him. "Thank God."

Hawk shuddered at the throbbing soreness in his nether regions. "They should have put you in the bible—pestilence, flood, famine, and Alexandra Huntington."

With a proud, man-slaying smile, his bride turned to face him across the pillow. "Make that pestilence, flood, famine, and Alexandra *Wakefield,* thank you very much."

"Sorry, I forgot."

"You forgot?" Again, she shot up . . . and shoved him from the bed.

Caught off guard, Hawk grasped the blankets and landed with a curse.

Alex rose and stepped right over him. "I am determined to cure you of that."

"Of what?" he snapped, closing his dressing gown beneath the blankets and trying not to stare at her in that appallingly diaphanous night rail.

"Of forgetting that I am your wife."

"Oh." Giving up the fight, Hawk pillowed his head

in his hands and crossed his ankles while his unrepentant bride fluffed her hair into a billowy curtain of cinnamon silk and stretched like a svelte and contented feline.

Like a practiced coquette, mischief in her glance, she watched him as she untied her bodice ribbons, not entirely unaware that the light of morning, behind her, turned her gown to air and revealed every scintillating freckle on her lush and feminine form.

Hawk became aroused just watching—another very good sign, indeed.

He used to worry that the London doctor he visited when he returned to England was offering hope where only despair existed, but the medical man had been right after all. Time and rest did help. Last night had been his best night's sleep in ages, entangled with Alex, as it were, and this morning he felt new again. Not that he should be making a practice of such entanglements in the future, but the novelty of his sexual awakening was worth the risk.

Alex arched a wry brow. "With no more than the hint of a smile lighting your eyes, you still remind me of the proverbial cat that ate the cream," she said. "But you should be hanging your head in shame for forgetting that I am your wife and a woman grown."

Hawk quirked a brow. "You may safely assume that your womanhood has been made abundantly clear to me at this juncture."

She tried to kick off his covers, but Hawk caught her foot and stroked her shapely ankle until she closed her eyes and sighed.

When he made to slide his hand higher, she

squeaked in surprise and Hawk let her go, knowing it was best, but before he realized what she was about, she succeeded in uncovering him.

Her turn to quirk a brow as she regarded the evidence of his manhood, as stark as her womanhood, though better covered. "Care to explain that?" she asked, with feminine satisfaction, of the arousal raising his dressing gown. "It used to happen to Judson all the time. Oh, but . . . where did it go?"

Shot with possessive fury, Hawk sat up. "You distracted me with your nonsensical chatter about your beef-witted suitor. I would have expected *him* to teach you what you wanted to know, though I am pleased I overestimated him." His harsh tone surprised even Hawk, but before he could apologize, he saw that Alex's eyes were no longer bright with mischief, but aglisten with tears.

Even as she stepped away, Hawk wanted to call his words back. "Devil take it," he snapped. Hurting her had not been his intention. "Alex, I did not mean . . ."

A stifled sob escaped her as she ran.

"Wait, come back." Hawk could not stand quickly enough to stop her before her dressing room door shut with finality.

Alex paced, attempting at the same time to catch her breath. What had just happened? What did Hawksworth mean, touching her ankle, her leg, in the way she would allow only a husband—only him— then insinuating that she might have permitted Chesterfield such liberties before their marriage.

She leaned against the door separating them and closed her eyes, tears slipping beneath her lashes despite her attempt to stem the flow, despite her fury at herself for allowing them.

Her breasts ached and that place between her legs pulsed. There she wanted Hawksworth, with a need—nay, a desperation—the likes of which she had not experienced with Chesterfield or anyone.

Had Bryce continued touching her, she suspected that what might have happened could have been the "something wonderful" that Chesterfield had enigmatically promised but, she believed, only Bryce could deliver.

After what he had just implied, however, how could she get close enough again to find out?

Alex turned and touched her brow to the door. "Why did you say such a horrid thing?" she asked, smacking her palm against the shuddering portal as if it were her stubborn husband's chest. "Why?"

"Because I am a weak, jealous bastard," Hawk said as faintly as her words had come to him. He closed his eyes, regret lancing him for causing her pain once more.

Why had he said it? he wondered. Anger? Jealousy? Because he could not make love to her? Because if he consummated their marriage, he would bind her to him without hope for her future, damn it to bloody hell.

She also deserved better than his abuse, which he had not intended.

He should grant her an immediate annulment and leave Huntington Lodge without looking back. He was too jaded for such an innocent. And still he wanted to go to her, now, this minute, and apologize until she granted him forgiveness—except that he must stand before he could take a step to do anything more.

Bracing himself against the agony of rising, Hawk realized that he deserved all the wretchedness God saw fit to give him, so he closed his eyes and pulled himself upright, the pain be damned.

After his anguish, at length, passed, he released his breath and opened his eyes . . . only to find Alexandra on the opposite side of the bed, horror etching her features and paling her skin to flour paste. "Lexy, forgive me. I can be a blackguard sometimes."

"You said you were free of pain, but in pushing you down, I hurt you by making you rise again."

"Not as badly as I hurt you."

"You move always with some difficulty; I noticed that. But rising from so far is . . ."

"Getting easier by the day. Alex, listen. About my unforgivable insinuation . . ."

Alex lowered herself to sit on the bed, keeping her back to him. "I am sorry I pushed you. I meant only to be playful."

"I wish I could say the same." Hawk came around to sit beside her. He tried to take her hand, though it turned out that he ended up fighting her for it and lost. "Damn it, will you not hear me out?"

She looked him full in the face. "Not now. Please, I do not wish to speak of it right now."

"So be it, then. But later you will hear what I have to say, if I have to tie you to the bed."

With the image his promise engendered, life shot

through Hawk once more, and he cursed his fickle body as he rose.

"Breakfast in half an hour, Your Grace," Myerson called from the dressing room.

"Just a minute, man." Hawk handed Alex a more modest dressing gown, and once she donned it, he called his valet into the room. "Since I no longer have bachelor quarters, nor even a separate bedchamber, I will not require your services as valet for the nonce, but I do believe, if it is agreeable to you, that Her Grace has tasks you might perform about the house." He looked to Alex for confirmation.

She had composed herself admirably. "Thank you, Hawksworth. Yes, Myerson, we very much need your services, if you do not mind. Meet me in the kitchen in an hour and I will go over your new duties. Until then, and if you have already broken your fast, you may see if Mrs. Parker can use your help."

"Very Good, Your Grace."

After Myerson left, Alexandra went wordlessly into her dressing room, shutting the door.

Hawk dressed and made his way downstairs. Alex needed time to compose herself, and he required even more time to dislodge his very big foot from his very big mouth.

As he entered the breakfast room, conversation came to an abrupt, uncomfortable halt.

Hawk took the empty chair beside his uncle. "Good morning." He nodded and took to buttering a piece of toast, aware he was cross as a bear. "Do not stop talking on my account," he said, assuming that they must have been discussing his disfigurement, or his overlong absence, or any number of subjects for which he was heartily embarrassed.

"Come, now," he said. "We are family. I am certain you must have questions that have gone unanswered for far too long. Would you not rather ask than conjecture?"

To Claudia's exclamation and Hildegarde's gasp, a hedgehog ran from beneath the table; then Beatrix crawled out from under there and popped up between them. "I have a question, Uncle Bryce."

"Excuse me," he interrupted, "but did I just see a hedgehog cross the room?"

"That's Nanny." Beatrix, the unrepentant eavesdropper, came around to climb on his lap. "Do not worry, she will be back."

"Nanny?" Hawk asked.

Giff chuckled. "Bea wanted to give her hedgehog a name with hog in it, but all she could think of was *Hogmanay,* except that Bea calls it *Hogmananny,* so that's what she named her hedgehog."

"Nanny, for short," Hawk said. "Good name, Bumble Bea. I approve. Have you shown Nanny to your cousins?"

Bea shook her head. "Aunt Bree says Damon and Rafe have a cat and a dog both, so they will not care for her."

"Ah, but I think they will. Hedgehogs are such unique pets, after all."

"Really?" Beatrix beamed, picked up the toast Hawk had just buttered, and took a bite. "When can we move back to the London house, so I can show them?"

Hawk accepted a replacement for his toast from Hildegarde. "Thank you, Aunt," he said, taking a bite to stake his claim. "Why do we not wait, Bumble Bea, until Alexandra joins us before I tell you how things stand with my title and estates?"

"You mean you have not even told *her* yet?" the wide-eyed child asked. "Take care or you will make her cry again."

"Make her . . . cry? What are you talking about?" Could Bea have heard them earlier?

The child of seven-going-on-forty gave a long-suffering sigh. "Before you died—or we thought you did—you wrote to Aunt Sabrina, Damon and Rafferty's mama, remember? They were staying with us then."

Why did everyone suppose that he had forgotten the members of his family while he was away? "I remember."

"You did not write a letter to Alex when you were dying, or even think of her at the last, and that made her cry."

"Devil take it." Hawk rose, taking Beatrix with him, and in silence he deposited her in his chair and left the breakfast room.

Halfway across the hall, he saw Alex coming down the stairs and waited for her at the bottom. "Alexandra, we need to talk."

Ten

"No, Bryceson, I told you, I am not ready to talk."

"This is not about what happened earlier," Hawk said. "This is something I insist we settle, something I can at least explain." He took his stubborn wife's arm and urged her into the library.

"What is it? What is wrong?"

Hawk possessed himself of her hand. Surprisingly callused, it was small and pale, as opposed to her spirit, which shone bright and strong. "I am concerned by something Beatrix said."

"If you let everything Bea says bother you, you will be disquieted for the rest of your days."

"You cried when I wrote to Sabrina, before I supposedly died, because I did not write to you? Is that true?"

Alexandra turned to gaze out the window, except that she did not see the rolling lawn gone to seed, or the home wood overtaken by bracken, but her own life as she had viewed it the day that letter came, stretching barren and pointless before her without Bryceson in it.

"I was emotional, devastated, because I thought I—I thought you had died." She shivered.

Hawk placed his cane on a nearby chair and slipped his hands down her arms to chafe and warm them. "You should have worn a shawl," he said. "This place is as drafty as a dovecote."

Alex closed her eyes, immersing herself in his nearness and his touch.

"I wrote to you first," he said from close behind her, absently stroking her arms. "Or I began to, but I . . . I feared that I would expire at any moment, and I knew that Sabrina's very life depended upon the arrangements I had made for her. So I put your letter aside, unfinished, to write hers before it was too late."

Hawk gazed into the past, at that smoke-hazed, bloody day, the pain and the horror of the Waterloo battlefield, of dead friends and dying comrades. Of lying atop the "heap." He saw the blood in his eyes, tasted it in his mouth, smelled it clogging his nostrils.

He remembered well the stench of death, especially his own.

In many ways, he *had* died that day, or a part of him had, anyway . . . until he beheld Alex from the back of that church, and had begun to come back to life, whether he wanted to or not, minute by minute, piece by lost and broken piece.

"Because I was incapable of writing myself," he said. "An old woman at the Waterloo Inn wrote my final words for me. When I finished dictating Sabrina's letter, I had no strength left, nor did I wish to share with a stranger what I could not seem to find the correct words to express to you. The last I remember, I was being excruciatingly loaded onto a dray for a trip to the country. Your letter was never finished, Alex, and I am more sorry about that than I can say."

"Where is it?" she asked, not turning from the window, almost as if she did not believe him.

"I never saw it again," he admitted. "I lay delirious for weeks, in and out of my mind, despondent for months. Once I returned to London, I looked for your letter among the few meager belongings left to me, but it had disappeared."

"I am sorry," she said. "I would have liked to receive it, even half written. I wish someone had sent it. I would have been comforted to know that you thought of me at all, especially after the way we parted." Her sorrow broke in a sob for their dreadful parting, for his unfinished letter, and for his hurtful words of that morning.

Hawk put his arms around her from behind, placing a hand flat against her abdomen, feeling a need to mark her intimately as his, and pulled her close.

Her head rested against his coat front, his cheek against her hair. He must give her this much, at least, he thought. She deserved some truth. "If not for thinking of you, Lexy, I do not believe I would have survived."

She turned in his arms then, her wide eyes bright. "That is perhaps the nicest thing you have ever said to me."

"In that case, I should be horsewhipped." The temptation to kiss her was strong, stronger than Hawk could resist.

"Your Grace."

They pulled apart.

"Your pardon," Myerson said, red-faced, when he saw what he had interrupted. He held forth a silver salver with a visitor's card upon it.

"Thank you." Hawk took the card, read it, cursed inwardly, firmed his lips, and handed it to his wife. "Myerson, is the, er, gentleman in question still waiting?"

"Viscount Chesterfield is in the drawing room, Your Grace, but he is not asking to see you. He wishes to see Her Grace. He was very specific about that."

"I am certain he was. Thank you. You may go. Alexandra," Hawk said, after the retainer had shut the door. "I shall leave you to greet your lover in private."

"No," Alex said.

Hawk stopped and turned, releasing his breath, clutching at hope. "Am I to understand that you do not wish to see Chesterfield?"

"No. Yes. I wish—I *must* speak with him." She bit her lip.

Hawk shuttered his eyes and closed his expression. He knew he was doing it, but he could not seem to stop.

"I owe Judson a great deal," Alex said, her explanation more accurate than she would wish.

"Then see him, you shall." Hawk bowed. "Good morning to you, madam."

Chesterfield appeared astonished when Alex entered the drawing room, though he did not take a step toward her, for which she was grateful. "I did not think he would let you see me," he said.

Alex remained by the door. "I am so very sorry about our wedding."

Judson firmed his lips, much as Bryce had just done. "What happened was not your fault."

"I deserve your anger and more," Alex said. "Five thousand pounds you gave me in exchange for my promise to wed you, but I failed to fulfill my part of our bargain, and I cannot repay you. Not yet, at any rate."

"Why do you not let Hawksworth worry about repayment?"

"I do not want him to know about the money, Judson, please. He would be angry that I took it. Let me repay you, myself, in time."

"For once in his charmed life, let Hawksworth face his responsibilities. Everything has always come so bloody easy to the rogue. Looks, money, a title, women, all handed to him on a gilded platter."

"You are not being fair. Hawksworth fought for his country and suffered mightily for its cause. His looks are altered irreparably; his title and wealth have gone to another."

"But as for women, he ended with the best." Chesterfield bit off a curse. "You understand, do you not, Alexandra, that he set off to play at war, leaving you to carry his burdens. That is why he was shocked out of countenance and damned near broken. He discovered that war was not devilishly entertaining sport, nor particularly glorious, either."

Chesterfield's words resembled her own often-uncharitable thoughts after Hawksworth had first left. "No, there you are wrong. Do not be angry with him."

"I have lost my bride and my future, yet you do not want me to be angry with the man who took them from me."

"You do not love me, Judson. You wanted a mature wife, and I wanted a secure future for my family. No matter what has passed between us, it is finished now. Let us at least be honest with each other."

Chesterfield nodded. "So be it." He turned to the window. "You are in transports I take it, that your true love has returned from the dead."

True as the words were, Alex did not appreciate the way Chesterfield sullied the sentiment with his caustic tone. "Hawksworth is well liked by everyone," she said. "Why do you dislike him so?"

"For that reason, I suppose. Because everyone else likes and accepts him without question, while I see him as a spoiled boy who takes and takes but never learned to give. The very same reason he despises me. I see him as he really is. Selfish."

Alex had learned long ago that Hawksworth disdained Chesterfield as much as Chesterfield disdained him, and where they were concerned, emotions ran high and animosity had festered too long to give credence to much that one said of the other. But in her mind, it all boiled down to one thing. "You have always been jealous of Bryce, have you not?"

Chesterfield gave her a half smile and shook his head, almost in wonder. "Yes, but that does not change the facts."

"No, but it does color them. Let us be friends. Please."

"The three of us? No. But I will not tell Hawksworth

about the money—yet. That is as friendly as I can be right now."

"Thank you. I will repay you before you feel the need to tell him. Why are you here? Is there something that I can do for you?"

Chesterfield cursed again; then he sighed, as if in resignation. "I came to make certain you were all right. You had not come around by the time he took you away the other day, and I was worried about you. I came yesterday as well."

"I am fine, but I was in shock then, I think. Anybody would be."

He stepped toward her. "Anybody except you, my strong one."

Alex stepped back. "*Can* we be friends?"

"If you find yourself in need of a friend, I would be a fool to apply for the position."

Alex pulled her jilted bridegroom away from the door, where someone might hear them, and toward the center of the room. "I do need a friend, Judson. I need one badly. I need help."

Chesterfield stepped closer and took her hand. "Tell me what I can do."

"I need to stage a seduction, and I do not have the least idea how; nor do I know anyone else I can ask."

At the reverberating slam of the door, Claudia stepped from behind the drawing room curtains with a huff of frustration.

Alex exclaimed in surprise as she did.

"Drat," Claudia said. "I thought you had both left."

The seventeen-year-old grinned. "You certainly set fire to his tail with that request."

"You were listening!" Alex charged, partly in accusation, partly in admonishment, but mostly to hide her mortification. "You are worse than your sister."

"I adore Chesterfield. He is my destiny. Of course I was listening, though I do wish he did not seem so broken by the loss of you. Do you not think that fate tore the two of you apart at the very last moment so that I may still have him?"

"I think Hawksworth's excellent recuperative powers were responsible, not to mention the little matter of our previous marriage."

"Still I wish Chesterfield had been willing to discuss seduction," Claude said dreamily. "I would dearly have liked to know how *he* would go about one." Her gaze changed from otherworldly to worldly in a questioning blink. "Why do you need to seduce Uncle Bryce, anyway? I thought he was a master of seduction."

"Who in the world told you that? Never mind, I do not wish to know."

Claudia giggled. "Do you want to know what I think you should do to seduce him?"

"Good Lord, no." Alex lowered herself to the settee and covered her face with her hands, doubly chagrined. But as Claudia sat beside her, she regarded the sagacious teen with a curious respect. "Claudia Jamieson, what do you know about seduction, anyway?"

"Not nearly as much as I would like, but . . . Does this mean that you are still untouched?"

"Claudia, really!"

"Oh, all right. I have often found that words alone can be very . . . stirring, in the right circumstances. I was thinking you could tell Uncle Bryce that I have begun to ask some, er, rather embarrassing questions, which you, in your untouched state, cannot answer."

"What good will that do?"

"Then you *are* untouched."

"Claude!"

"Sorry." The girl sighed in resignation. "Perhaps, if you can get Uncle Bryce to explain all the things every young woman wants—or at least needs—to know about dealing with the male of the species, you can, ah, ask a few more leading questions. You could even require a demonstration, which might, er, stimulate . . . things enough to let nature take its proper course."

"You devious little brat. Shame on you." Alex grinned. "But you already sound knowledgeable. What *do* you know?"

"Only what I have garnered from watching the horses."

"But horses are nothing like . . ." Alex regarded Hawk's niece rather warily. "Of course they are not."

"I do think they must be. I swam once with the Cruikshank boy—you remember little Harold—and everything on him seemed a teeny, tiny version of, er, those things on a horse."

Alex remembered Hawksworth as a child, though the word *small* had not seemed to apply even then. Then there was that growing "something" prodding her in the night, and standing as if at attention beneath his dressing gown this morning—which did seem to be very much like . . .

So much became clear to Alex of a sudden that she gasped. "But a man cannot possibly grow as long as a horse?"

"Well how the blazes would I know?" Claudia spoke with utter disgust for her ignorance. "I hoped you would tell me."

That absurdity sent Alex into peels of laughter.

"However long 'it' might become," the precocious teen said, giggling as well, "I would not know what in Hades to do with it if it were dancing before my eyes."

Alex composed herself as she straightened the pleats in her skirt. "I shall tell you when you are older," she said, which set off a further bout of merriment between them. "Gad, what an inappropriate conversation."

"Outrageous," Claudia agreed. "But nothing half so scandalous as the five thousand pounds you accepted from Chesterfield. How could you Alex? And what in heaven's name did you use it for?"

Alex sat straighter. "My reason is not your concern. That I took it, and why, is between Chesterfield and me."

Claudia narrowed her eyes and turned a becoming shade of envy green. "Besides your promise, were you forced to give Judson anything *else* in exchange?"

"In exchange for what, pray tell?"

"Uncle Bryce!"

Eleven

Alex and Claudia exclaimed in shock as Hawk walked in on their conversation about the money Alex owed Judson, Claudia shooting to her feet. "In exchange for er, ah, dancing lessons," Claudia said.

Alex released the breath she had been holding.

Hawk's jaw set and he leaned more heavily on his cane.

"I mean, you know, how to act when one dances. Chesterfield taught Alex," Claudia said. "And she was supposed to teach me—for when a man asks me to dance, if ever one does. I need to learn everything, and not just about dancing. I have just been asking questions, which Alex has been trying, and failing, to answer. Is that Bea calling?" Claudia curtsied and ran from the room.

"What was that about?" Hawk asked, seating himself opposite Alex.

"She has been asking questions is all, just as she said—things a young woman is curious about—and she was embarrassed that you walked in on us."

"I see. I see also that your swain has left."

"Do not mock him. Chesterfield was here because he was worried about me. Please remember that he would have rescued everyone in this house by marrying me, which he was very well aware of and willing to do, anyway. If you had not survived, he would have made me a good husband, as I would have made him a good wife."

"But I did survive."

"Yes you did."

"I am sorry, Alex, not so much for surviving as for every selfish thing I have ever done or said to you, including today—especially today." Hawk cringed. "Perhaps I should apologize in advance for my every half-witted remark or action of the future as well."

Alex rose and went to look out the window. "Do you feature a ride about the grounds this morning, to view the property?"

"First you must forgive me; then you must break your fast, then we will take that ride."

"You are right. I should eat something."

Hawk sighed. "Eat, then, after which we can tour the estate. He hooked his cane on his left arm and took her on his right. They went to the kitchen, where their appearance together seemed to cheer the servants.

Hawk met Mrs. Parker, who served as both cook and housekeeper.

"Welcome home, Your Grace." The woman bobbed a curtsy.

Hawk accepted a cup of coffee while Alex took toast and tea. "Have you spoken to your solicitor about your cousin and heir?" she asked. "The last I saw, Baxter was carrying on and spending money as if he might run through your fortune in a fortnight."

"I did speak to my solicitor, but not to my father's, who is the man that matters. My own agrees with you, however, that Baxter is like to squander it all. At least there is still Hawks Ridge. As far as the estate and title reverting to me, all possible petitions have been filed. It simply remains for them to be approved, signed, and sealed, which, as you know, could take years, especially with my father's solicitor having passed away as well, and his heir off in Scotland at the moment. Meanwhile, Baxter himself seems to be gallivanting in the American colonies."

"Let us hope he gets stranded there." Alex sipped her tea. "We are no worse off than we were." Her expression softened when she regarded him, almost in wonder, as if seeing him for the first time and incredibly happy about it, despite his earlier thoughtlessness. "We are, in fact, a great deal better off than we have been for some time."

Hawk remained silent, afraid she was wrong and would soon realize it. That he had saved her from a dire fate and thwarted Chesterfield into the bargain—always a pleasure—was the best that had come of his return. What he feared most was that they had not even imagined the worst. "Ready for that ride?"

Alex rode Buttercup, a sorrel mare she had raised herself, which also served double duty on the home farm. Since Hawk's Arabian now belonged to Baxter, Hawk rode one of the field horses, Bumptious, a stocky, light bay with three white stockings. A sad day for the horse set. If anyone from Tattersall's saw him, Hawk thought, he would be forced to resign his membership in the Jockey Club.

Nevertheless, it was a fine, dry day for a ride—almost sunny, in fact. Bright enough for him to spot every cracked and broken window. Clear enough to see the Gothic molding on the east tower as it fell to earth with a resounding crash, narrowly missing a mongrel who dashed away squealing, tail between its legs.

Once upon a young and selfish time, Hawk mused, he might have dashed away himself from this primitive and destitute situation in which he found himself—in name, in holdings, even in his own physical aspect.

Yet he could not look at Alex without realizing how very fortunate he would be, despite present circumstances, if he were worthy of her. In his weaker moments, Hawk wished to the devil that he had not sworn on his honor as a gentleman to set her free. But he had, and he must. He would not let her down this time, as he had let them all down when he abandoned them. He would not.

Hawk returned his attention to a perusal of the estate and pondered the ways and means by which it could be improved. For the safety of his family, the house itself needed immediate attention.

Given the clarity of the day, the damage seemed even worse. Paint peeled from molding, where molding existed. Bricks lay scattered on the ground, having fallen away in clusters. The manse looked as if a giant beast had gnawed upon it, taking several large bites from its corners.

As they rode, they saw deer feeding in flower gardens, and wild ducks swimming in the huge bowl of a broken fountain. Ivy crawled along every surface of the house, and in some places it had made its way inside.

At the bottom of the drive, near the gate, the sky shone bright upon the surprising sight of Alexandra's aunt Hildy leaving the abandoned gatehouse in the most furtive of manners.

Without words or conscious thought, he and Alex slowed their mounts and stepped within the trees until Hildy passed. When they made to exit their cover, there came his uncle Gifford, out the same door, so over-easy in his gait and manner that he, too, caused suspicion.

As one, Hawk and Alex backed their mounts farther into the trees and waited for Giff to pass as well—whistling, of all things.

Hawk saw his surprise reflected in Alex's expression. "What do you make of that?" she asked.

"Ah, I had rather not conjecture."

Her eyes widened before she shook her head, dismissing whatever notion entered it, and Hawk wordlessly followed her onto the drive.

Huntington tenants, he found, were few, but those in residence were hard workers, respectful, and protective of their mistress. Clearly, they adored Alex. Of him, however, they seemed to be reserving judgment, though most had the mistaken notion that he was some kind of war hero—another of Alexandra's tales, Hawk feared.

Still, most tenants had suggestions as to how he could alleviate his wife's burdens by taking them over as soon as may be, and they were absolutely right.

"Perhaps when we get back to the house, you will allow me to go over the accounts," Hawk said. "I may be able to find ways to improve the property and increase its yield."

"I neither know how nor do I have the time to keep accounts, so there are no books to look over."

"But Alex, you must."

"My father never did."

"Which is precisely why the lodge and estate are near ruin and have lost so much money."

"Well, there is no money now to lose," she snapped as she turned her horse. "So keeping books matters not a whit."

"Alex, wait."

She slowed her mount. "Perhaps you think you can do a better job than I have?"

Hawk slowed as well, and they trod along side by side. "Only in keeping accounts," he said. "Those I will do better, for you never did them at all. But for the rest, given your obvious monetary restrictions, I am in awe of your accomplishments."

Alex reined in her mare to overlook the property from the estate's highest vantage point.

Hawk pulled up beside her. "You deserve commendation with thanks."

Alex nodded, grudgingly acknowledging the compliment.

"There, down at the home farm," Hawk said, "who are those workers in the field?"

"Uncle Giff is collecting the last of the summer vegetables; Claudia and Beatrix are weeding."

"Good Lord. By themselves?"

"Of course not."

"Thank God."

"Aunt Hildegarde is catching the winged and multilegged insects that eat the vegetation, and Nanny is helping by eating them."

Hawk opened his mouth, but no words came forth.

Alex laughed. "They do not usually work alone. I am generally there working beside them."

Bryce regarded her as if she had turned green. "What have I done to you?"

"You have done nothing. I am grateful for our present situation."

"Grateful?"

"To the lad who rescued you."

"Ah, Gaston. A good lad, if a bit misguided."

"How old is he?"

"Ten now, I think."

"A baby? Robbing corpses?"

"A baby trying to survive. As are we all. Along that line, I have been thinking that besides keeping the accounts and managing the estate, I can also do most of the required repairs to the buildings inside and out, I believe."

"What we really need," Alex said, regarding him from the corners of her unexpectedly mischievous eyes, "is someone to repair the roof."

Hawk's bark very nearly resembled mirth. "Roof climbing is out, at least for the moment. And do not say that you will do it yourself, for I will not allow you."

"Actually, Beatrix is desirous of that position, the monkey."

"Absolutely not."

"My exact words. For the nonce, then, all leaks must simply . . . leak."

Bryce nodded. "Unfortunately. How are we set for funds, Alex? Is there any money at all?"

This would be a good time, Alex thought, to tell Bryceson that she still had more than three hundred pounds left from the five thousand she had accepted from Chesterfield—under false pretenses, as it turned out. But she could not, for the revelation was not entirely hers to own, not to mention how angry Bryce would be.

"We have some little money," she said. "With the planting, and the few animals we keep, we will not starve."

Hawk frowned. He should have done better by them all. "I will write to Gideon this very day, to ask him to put in a good word for my petition with the prince regent, as regards the return of my title and property."

"What about your military pay?" Alex asked. "Is there any of that left?"

"I can contribute the grand sum of one hundred and thirty-seven pounds, two shillings, and three. Rich, are we not?"

Alex laughed. "We are, indeed. And since we are, it is time Claudia had her season. What better time than now, for we can also reintroduce *you* to society?"

Hawk shook his head. "I hate the thought of all that blasted society fuss."

"Do you? When women were swooning at your feet, I thought you rather enjoyed the bustle and fuss."

Hawk quirked a brow. "You used to loathe it."

"I guess we have switched places, then."

The words seemed to steal the very air from Hawk's lungs. "Let us put Claude's season off for a year," he said. "Or just until the spring, until I can recover my ability to walk without the cane."

Of a sudden, Alex understood, given Hawk's lifelong yearning for perfection, acceptance, approval, what have you. But understanding his need to recover his steady gait did not alter the facts. "A season will cost too much in the spring. Claudia would need a larger and grander wardrobe then. Besides, she is very nearly a spinster already."

"Claude is a baby, certainly no spinster. And you will need a proper wardrobe, as well."

"My bride clothes should suffice."

Thunder glanced off Hawk's dark, furrowed brow. "Purchased by Chesterfield? I think not."

"I purchased some things myself."

"Good. You will discard everything Chesterfield purchased and wear only what you chose and paid for.

"Fine, then; I shall go about London in my corset and stockings."

Hawk was struck dumb by the image of Alex striding down St. James Street in nothing but her corset and stockings.

When she raised a brow, he recalled the point of their conversation. "No season," he said. "Not this year. We cannot afford one."

"I have been saving for this, Bryce. I believe that

Claude's season is among the necessities we must afford."

"At the best, we might be able to purchase her a new wardrobe, since you already have your blasted bride clothes—every item of which I despise for their purchaser. But dressed like this, I am barely fit for a gentleman farmer, never mind escorting my niece about the marriage mart."

"In regard to your clothes . . ."

"I told you," Hawk said. "These are all I have."

"But the ones you left behind may have been relegated to a trunk at Hawks Ridge. If Baxter kept any of your old retainers, one of them might be loyal enough to your family to search the attics for you."

"Even if my clothes were returned to me, we do not have the money to fire Claude off properly, I tell you. The entire family can hardly be accommodated at Stephen's Hotel, and we absolutely do not have the blunt to take a house in town, even for so short a season."

"Let us just see what time brings," Alex said enigmatically, even then turning Buttercup toward Hawks Ridge.

Shaking his head, sure there was some salient point he was missing, Bryce turned his plodding beast in the same bloody direction.

Here, Alex thought as they made their way along the poplar-lined drive of Hawk's stately family seat, the lawns were manicured and greening nicely, though the drive lacked that certain flair brought on by foot-high weeds.

As far back as she could remember, the situation had always been thus. Hawks Ridge had shone bright, Huntington Lodge appeared tarnished.

In the opposite manner, however, her own dear father had always been everything a loving and doting parent should be, while Hawksworth's critical, demanding sire had been a man given to furious wrath. Though she did not think that Hawk feared his father's wrath as much as his rejection.

They stopped beside the rose garden when Leggins, the old head gardener, straightened and tipped his hat. "Blimey," the grizzled man said, scratching his head as he regarded Bryceson. "Blimey, Guv, you ain't dead."

"Indeed not," Bryce said, his eyes nearly smiling. "I do not suppose your new master is to home?"

"He is, Your Grace."

"There is a pleasant surprise," Bryce said to Alex. "We may get this settled much sooner than we expected. Good day to you, Leggins, and thank you. Alex, shall we face the lion in his den?"

"Now we may witness that seizure you worried about last night," she said with a grin, "if Baxter does not yet know that you are alive."

But Bryce did not smile. As a matter of fact, as they climbed the front steps, his jaw set decidedly more firmly, and his lids lowered, shuttering his reaction.

When the door was opened, they saw immediately that Hawk's old footman had been replaced. The current retainer bowed politely and did not so much as quirk a brow or twitch a face muscle when Bryceson gave his name, but led them directly to the blue salon.

"Everything is the same," Bryce said with stifled longing as he gazed about the cerulean room, snowy clouds drifting upon its azure ceiling. Alex's heart nearly broke for his loss.

"Well, this is a surprise," came a familiar voice from the doorway.

"Chesterfield? What are you doing here?"

Twelve

Chesterfield raised a surprised brow. "I might ask you the same question. My man said you wanted to see me."

"No. We came to see Hawk's heir. Are you staying with Baxter?"

"I do not know where Baxter has run off to, but you must have asked to see the master of Hawks Ridge, and since Hawks Ridge is now mine . . ."

"No," Bryce said without thought. Then he regarded Alex and raised his hand in a shrug of defeat. "I know; I sound like my uncle."

"This makes no sense," Alex said. "How came you to be in possession of Hawks Ridge?"

"Hawk's cabbage-headed heir wagered and lost it to me in a card game not six weeks ago, though I do think I will be changing its name. To my ears, there is something decidedly annoying about its current appellation."

Bryce cursed.

Chesterfield nodded. "Precisely how I felt at the church the day before yesterday."

"Hawk loves his home," Alex said.

"Alexandra," Hawk warned.

Chesterfield regarded Hawk with a raised brow. "You want Hawks Ridge; I will trade you—for Alex."

"Do not be an ass," Hawk said.

"Judson, be serious. You cannot keep Hawk's home."

"Hawks Ridge was Baxter's estate to wager at the time I won it, and unless someone can pay me the fifteen thousand pounds that whelp of Satan owes me, I am bloody well going to keep it."

Hawk cursed again.

"It would be a bargain at double the price," Chesterfield said, his gaze moving between Alex—very much aware that he thought of her as his lost bride—and her bristling husband, who would as soon strike the man as look at him. "Whatever you wanted of Baxter," their unexpected host said, "is it something with which I can help you?"

"Yes," Alex said.

"No," Hawk replied as fast.

"Ah, a stalemate then. Can I offer you refreshment, or shall I have my man show you out?"

"Judson, really, there is no need to be rude."

"Is there not? Odd, I thought I was being civil to the blackguard who took my bride from me. It might interest you to know, Alexandra, that were it not for your fondness for this estate, I would not have been so anxious to acquire it. It was to be your wedding present, you see. Half the countryside kept the secret of my ownership, so I could surprise my bride on our wedding day. Otherwise, I might have called Baxter out rather than accept it."

"And done us all a favor," Hawk snapped.

"Hawksworth!"

"God's teeth, Lexy, you cannot blame me for wanting to thrash the blighter. He has run my entire fortune into the ground." Bryceson regarded Chesterfield. "Your pardon for airing our dirty linen in your home. We will bid you a good day."

"Well, I'll be dashed!" Chesterfield exclaimed. "That was damned near polite of you, Hawksworth. Will wonders never cease."

"Go to the devil!" Bryce strode from the room, barely using his cane, and gleaning a modicum of respect from Chesterfield, Alex thought, from their host's approving look.

After seeing Bryce rise from the floor this morning, she understood the likely cost to him in pain for that exit, and because of it, she too experienced a frisson of pride.

Hurrying to catch up, she passed by Chesterfield, who caught her arm and stopped her. "I will send his personal belongings over later today. He looks as if he could use them."

"Thank you, Judson. You are a good man." Alex stepped near and stood on her toes to kiss his cheek, but he turned his head and caught her lips, extending the kiss. By the time Alex got her wits about her, Chesterfield was pulling away with a grin.

Alex blushed and stepped back, and when she did, she saw that her husband stood not two feet away, straight and proud and looking fit to kill. Were she guilty of the crime for which he silently accused her, the fury in his expression might turn her to salt.

He most certainly had witnessed the kiss, if not

their discussion about his clothes, for even from here she could see that frenetic tic working in his cheek.

Chesterfield chuckled. "I am not so good a man that I cannot find amusement in this situation."

"Shame on you," Alex said. "I do believe I misjudged you."

"You did. But do you not agree that a kiss, in exchange for what is owed me, is not too much to ask?"

Alex gasped. "I most certainly do not."

Chesterfield chuckled as Bryce left the house, seeming not to care whether Alex followed or not.

Having been abandoned by her husband, Alex left shortly thereafter, but took the long, circuitous route home, hoping Bryce would wonder if she was dallying with Chesterfield.

Let the dolt be jealous, if he was fool enough to think she cared to kiss anybody but him.

When she got back to the lodge, the letter from Sabrina, which she had been anxiously awaiting, had arrived. Except that, after Alex read it, her emotions were mixed. Yes, she received the answer for which she hoped. But she also learned something that made her so angry, she wished she *had* dallied with Judson, or at the least kissed him back.

Though she would rather trounce her husband than speak to him at the moment, she marched straight to the study.

The French doors leading to the overgrown garden stood open, curtains fluttering in the early fall breeze. A light scent of roses wafted upon the air from the few remaining blooms tenacious enough to have survived death by strangulation.

Hawk stood before the hearth, resting one elegant, booted foot upon the cool grate. He twirled a raised goblet of brandy before his eyes, examining it as if it held the answer to all of life's mysteries—if only he could find a way to make it give them up.

Tall, dark, and perilously devastating, he was Hawksworth, not Bryce: imperious, rigid, in control. Here, she saw for the first time the man who had expected to be a duke: cold, arrogant, a woman-slayer.

A ledger lay open upon the desk. Atop and all around it sat boxes of assorted estate receipts, as if Hawk had attempted and failed to make some sense of the monumental task. On the instant, Alex was sorry for her lack of bookkeeping skills. Then again, it served him right for staying away so bloody long.

When he bothered to look in her direction, as if he could not care less where she had been, with whom, or for how long, he raised his secret-laden goblet higher in her direction and gave her an arrogant, brow-raised salute. Then he took a long, slow swallow.

She did not know whether he was more angry about the kiss or about losing Hawks Ridge. Though she would place her wager on the estate as being of greater import to his mind.

Despite his show of nonchalance, there was something soulful lurking in her husband's eyes that made him appear more human in his vulnerability. Grief—or sorrow—filled their topaz depths, and being allowed so much as a glimpse jarred her.

But rather than step into his arms, which she longed to do—to ease those burdens and console him—Alex crushed Sabrina's letter in her trembling hand and hardened her heart.

Damn the rogue.

He had let more than a year go by since Waterloo, with nary a word from him, and according to the information in Sabrina's letter, he could have contacted her at any time for all of the past five months—at least.

He might be her long-lost husband, and a duke of the realm when he got his title back, but he had a great deal of explaining to do.

Yes, she had some little explaining to do herself, but not on his scale. Oh, no, nothing like.

Again Alex wanted to berate him. Again she kept her peace. "I have had a letter from Sabrina," she said when the silence stretched—raging inside; Hawk, daring her with his look to let loose, almost as if he ached for a good brawl. "She sends news I think you should hear."

Hawk sighed. "Then hear it I must, I suppose." He poured another liberal brandy and slouched into a butternut leather wing chair to listen, more or less.

Annoyed by his cavalier attitude, Alex stepped closer as she perused the missive, deciding to give him every foolish bit of news, prattle and promise alike, for which he pretended indifference. "Sabrina says that Juliana is growing like a weed, and at the advanced age of ten months, she has her father even more tightly wrapped about her smallest finger."

A near-smile altered Hawk's expression for a blink.

Alex faltered but continued. "Since Gideon has been relating the story of the American Indians, as told by James Adair, and embellished upon by adventurous travelers to the American West, the twins have formed a passion for Indians and have been war-whooping about the house for weeks. Just the other day, they tied Gideon to the stake."

Alex chuckled. "Not to worry, says Sabrina, the fire they set was quickly contained and barely singed his eyebrows. Though the boys may not be able to sit for a week, nor may they leave the nursery for as long, not to mention their trip to the Royal Menagerie, which has been cancelled."

Alex took the chair across from her husband, enjoying the letter, despite her ire at his haughty arrogance. Suddenly, she could think of him as nothing less than a duke. Where had Bryceson gone? she wondered. Had he never returned from the war? Had she been deluding herself?

Only time would tell.

"Gideon is Bree's new husband, I take it, the duke of Stanthorpe? The match you made for her?" Alex asked.

Hawksworth nodded. "They are top over tail in love."

"I do not believe it. Not Sabrina."

Hawk shrugged. "I saw it for myself."

"You saw that some time ago, as I understand it. About five months, as a matter of fact."

"Ah. So that is your quarrel with me?"

"Quarrel? I have no quarrel with you, though I do wonder where we would be if I had not decided to marry and you had not been forced to stop me." Alex held up her hand. "No, do not answer that. Spare me some dignity, please," she said, using his words, gratified to see him wince.

"The reason I sought you out," Alex said, "after your rude and abrupt departure from Hawks Ridge, was to tell you that Sabrina has arranged for Stanthorpe's grandmother, the dowager duchess of Basingstoke, to sponsor Claudia in London during the coming fall season. Since now is the little season and of shorter duration than the actual spring season, the cost will be much less and, therefore, easier to manage."

Hawk sat forward. "We cannot afford either this year."

"Did you know that Claudia has formed a *tendre* for Chesterfield?"

On the instant, a maelstrom of fury darkened her duke's brow. "The devil, you say."

Alex gave a half nod, satisfied she had made her point. "The duchess is inviting us to stay with her at her town house on St. James Square, which eliminates the cost of taking a house. Sabrina arranged everything. We need only pay for Claudia's wardrobe to fire her off properly."

Hawk slammed his glass on the near table, dashing it to fragments.

Alex ducked to evade the spray of glass and brandy.

"God's teeth," Hawk snapped, coming to his feet in one furious and shocking lunge, his shout of pain at the move as piercing to Alex as one of those shards might have been. Then he pulled her up and into his arms to crush her so close that she could feel him tremble, taste his fear.

"Are you all right?" he asked. "Did you get cut?" He held her away then, examining her face, her arms, and hands; kissing her brow, her fingers; disregarding the glass shards and brandy defacing his frockcoat, the blood at the tip of his thumb. "I might have hurt you. God, forgive me. I might have hurt you."

"What is the matter with you today?" Alex asked. "You are all afidget. I have never seen you like this before."

"I am so . . . unsettled, unsure . . ."

"Of what?"

"Of . . ." He hauled her back into his arms and opened his mouth over hers, drawing a response from her even as anger boiled inside him—anger through which she could feel his power. But she did not regard it any more than he did. She simply gave and took succor at the only source from which she cared to give or receive it.

"There," he said, stepping back, leaving her breathless. "There. I am calmer now. What was the question?"

"I . . . do not remember. Oh, of what are you unsure?"

"I, who used to be certain of everything, am now uncertain of same." He ran his hand through his untamed hair, certainly not the first time in the past hour. "You ask me to accept charity when I am used to giving it. I do not care for my sake, but it is driving me daft that I cannot provide for my own niece's immediate needs. All these changes are too devilish much to swallow."

"Especially for a proud man like you," Alex said. "I know. But I am going to ask you to swallow again, because your own clothes are being packed for you as we speak." She examined his frock coat. "And with the results of your fury now mottling your coat, it seems you have no choice but to accept."

Hawk tore away from her, wavered in his balance, and grabbed up his cane as if he might break it in half. Then he smacked the thing hard against the floor, leaned against it despite himself, and made his way to the open French doors. "No and again no," he said, not looking her way. "I *will* go about in my underdrawers before I take that man's charity."

Alex went and placed her arms about him, laying her cheek against his strong, unbending back. "Ah, my prideful rogue. They are *your* clothes, purchased with your money—clothes that were relegated to the rag bag when it was thought you died. Surely your pride will allow you to wear rags?"

He turned to face her. "No."

Alex stepped nearer. "If you could bring yourself to do so, Claudia might have her season this fall."

Her final words, or her stroking the hair from his brow, appeared to snuff his ire. "I hate London society."

Alex pulled her hand away and stepped back. "I wonder you spent so much time there earlier this year, then."

He cursed. "Leave it be, Alex."

"How can I leave it be when you left us struggling

for months without caring a fig whether we were fed or sheltered?"

"Of course you were fed and sheltered. I knew you were, besides which, I had every faith in your ability to care for everyone; otherwise, I would not have left them with you in the first place."

"So I have heard."

Hawk's head snapped up at that and his eyes narrowed.

Alex shrugged away the question in his look. "Why, Bryceson? Why did you not come home to us?"

"If I knew, I would tell you. I will admit, however, that Sabrina believes I was running away."

"From us? There would be no reason. Now, if your father were alive, I would understand."

"You would understand what?"

At the fury in his tone, Alex firmed her stance. "You yourself know that your father acted the tyrant, much as you are doing right now. He would never approve of you, 'broken' as you are. Your words."

"Do not be ridiculous." Hawk said. "My father has nothing to do with any of it. The man is long since dead."

"But never buried. You scrambled for his approval your whole life, Hawk, and never received it."

Hawk's eyes narrowed at that, and the light of challenge entered them, though he remained rigid and silent.

"I do not believe you went to war for the glory, as Judson thinks," Alex said, "but for your father's approval, however posthumous. He was a hard man,

Hawk—cold and heartless, as is any father who would prefer his son dead rather than imperfect."

"We do not know that for certain," Hawk said, desperate to forgive the unforgivable, Alex feared. "I simply supposed as much."

"Where a parent is concerned," Alex said, softly, "supposition is usually based on fact. I think your reason for speculation was just."

Hawk gathered his dignity about himself like a shield, much as his father had been wont to do, but Alex did not think the son would appreciate the comparison. "You go too far," he said.

"In that case, I apologize. Let us return to our discussion of Claudia's season, then."

"Claudia is not to have a season," Hawk replied with so much icy dignity that Alex feared she had lost the man she loved. "And you will not be discussing me with Chesterfield, if you please, ever again."

"Bryce—"

"That is the last I will say on the matter."

Thirteen

When they sat down to dinner, Hawksworth looked twice into his soup bowl—belly up, soft and white, tiny little feet, spiny back, sleepy eyes. "Excuse me," he said, "but there seems to be a hedgehog in my soup."

"There you are, you naughty . . ." Beatrix's expression melted with love, and she smiled. "Oh, how cute. Nanny is having a nice, warm soak."

Hawk raised a brow and made to scoop the complacent critter from his cock-a-leekie soup. "Ouch!" Not complacent now, but a hard, spiny ball.

"Do be careful," Bea said. "You will hurt her."

"Hurt her? She pricked me. Look, I am bleeding."

Bea kissed the wounded finger Hawk held up for her inspection. "Do not feel bad. She will get used to you. Let her scent your hand and soon she will let you rub her soft little belly."

Hawk barked a laugh. "Myerson," he said as his man began to pour their drinks, "I fear there is too much meat in my soup."

Bea gasped and Hawk winked as he slid his overfull soup bowl in her direction.

After a fresh bowl of soup was placed before him, Hawk cleared his throat and looked about the table.

"I am afraid, Claudia, that I have some rather disappointing news for you."

Claudia stiffened. "What is it?"

"We must postpone your season for this year."

"Yes, Uncle Bryce," Claudia said stoically; then she wilted for half a beat. "But if a girl cannot be seen in the places where eligible men congregate, how is a she to find a husband?"

"A husband?" Hawksworth said, arrested by the notion, his fork halfway to his mouth. "I had not thought of your come-out in quite that way. You are too young, at any rate, and the marriage mart is a hornets' nest. I promise you would hate it."

"Which words can only be spoken by one who has experienced the phenomenon," Alex said.

"I am as old as Alex was when you married her," Claudia said.

"Really?" Hawk regarded Alex just then with rather too much concentration, she thought, considering the fact that they were in company. Now, if they had been alone . . .

Almost as if he read her, Hawk started and cleared his throat, looking away.

Alex thought life might get easier if he *could* read her. And she did not know who was being more stubborn here: the uncle or the niece.

What was Claudia hatching, anyway? To her willful mind, only one eligible male existed in the kingdom, and he now lived . . . "That reminds me," Alex said. "Hawk's heir has struck again. It seems that he lost Hawks Ridge in a card game."

Giff turned to Hawk in horror. "Shoot the black-guard."

"Baxter or Chesterfield, Uncle? Though I must say, the notion has merit in both cases.

"Gifford, hush," Hildy said. "Bryceson, please, the children." Then she patted Hawk's arm, negating her scold. "Forget about Hawks Ridge, dear. Huntington Lodge is as much your home as it is ours, is it not, Alexandra?"

"By law, it is entirely his, Aunt."

"Except that the lodge is not really . . ." *No. Yes. It could be,* Hawk thought. Because Alex was here, and his family, the lodge could become his home. He could try to make it so. He shook his head. "It is *ours,*" he stressed. "Every splintered plank and broken brick."

"Do not forget the leaky roof," Beatrix added.

"Thank you, Bumble Bea, but Alex has taken it upon herself, more than once, to make me that particular reminder."

Alex kicked him beneath the table.

"Ouch."

"Who won Hawks Ridge?" Giff asked.

"Oh," Hawk said. "I thought you realized. Chesterfield is the happy new owner."

"Chesterfield lives next door?" Claudia cried, coming to life. "Famous. I shall go and visit him this afternoon and welcome him to the neighborhood."

"You will not," Hawksworth snapped.

"Chesterfield, by God." Giff laughed. "Now I understand your willingness to pursue pistols at dawn."

Claudia looked chagrined. "Oh, but Uncle Hawk, visiting him is the polite and neighborly thing to do."

"If you set one foot on Hawks Ridge property, young lady, I shall have you locked in your room until you are thirty. And until that advanced age, you are not so much as to exchange greetings with the blighter."

"Why do you consider him a scoundrel? Is it because he won your estate? That was an honest wager, was it not? Or is it because he nearly married Alex? You must know that Alex does not—"

"Claudia!" Alex widened her eyes to display her plea with determined clarity. "That will be enough," she said. *"Enough."*

"Of course."

Claude bit her curving lip and gave her unappetizing plate of cold mutton and mashed turnips rather more attention than was warranted.

Within moments, however, she looked up. "Uncle Hawk, Chesterfield is our neighbor across the dyke, like you and Alex were, growing up. If I cannot go and visit him, can he not at least come to visit us?"

"Absolutely not. That man is not welcome here. You will not speak to him or look at him. You are not to wave, if he passes the gate."

"But I . . . admire Chesterfield a great deal," Claudia admitted, her face pink.

Alex leaned near Hawk to speak in confidence. "He will be a constant temptation, living so near."

"For Claude or for you?" Hawk straightened without her answer. "Claudia, there are a goodly number of better men than Judson Broderick for whom to set your cap."

"But I love him," she cried with all the drama of youth.

"You what?" Ashen-faced, Hawk placed his spoon beside his bowl as he gazed from his wife to his niece. "Do you, both of you, love the knave?"

"He is not any of the things you have called him," Claudia said. "And I do love him."

"Then you must find someone more suitable."

"How?" Claudia cried. "We live in the wilderness."

"Bryceson," Aunt Hildy said, "you will have the poor child mooning about the house, staring out windows, for the next year."

Alex nodded. "With you-know-who passing by the gate thrice a day."

"Give it up, Alexandra," Hawk said. "You win." He reached over to cover Claudia's hand with his own. "Claude, if you can be satisfied with a compromise, the duchess of Basingstoke has offered to sponsor you for the coming fall season. Sabrina and Alex arranged everything. When we reach London, however, you will be under strict orders from me to choose a more appropriate suitor."

"Yes, Uncle Hawk," she said, unable to hide the light of triumph in her eyes, making Alex wonder again what she was up to.

"Alex," Hawk said, "you will write to the duchess and accept her kind invitation first thing in the morning. We will depart for London in three weeks, and I, for one, will be glad to see the last of Chesterfield."

"I like Viscount Chesterfield," Beatrix said. "When I got sick in town that winter, he rode a great distance in the snow for a doctor. Alex said I might have died if not for him."

"Is this true?" Hawksworth asked, turning to Alex.

Alex nodded. "An inflammation of the lungs. Little Miss Mischief frightened us nearly to death."

"Alex did not sleep for fully five days," Aunt Hildegarde said. "I was afraid that she would become so weak and exhausted that she would contract the disease herself."

"I was fine."

Giff winked meaningfully at her before turning to his nephew. "You should know, Hawk, that no one could have taken better care of us all in your absence than Alex did."

"I doubt even you could have done so well," Beatrix said.

Hawk nodded. "I knew she would take superb care of you all. We owe her a great debt of gratitude."

"We do," Aunt Hildegarde agreed, sending a proud smile her way.

"Do not be silly." Alex frowned, embarrassed. "Any of you would have done as much for any of us who needed you."

"Except that you are always the one we go to when anything needs fixing or settling or deciding, dear," her aunt said.

"Now I am home," Hawk said. "You must come to me when you need anything taken care of. Together we must ease Alexandra's burdens."

Bea shook her head doubtfully. "I do not think that will work, Uncle Hawk. With a cane, you will not be able to do half the things Alex does."

Hawk sighed, rose, and dropped his napkin into his plate. "Then I shall have to throw the blasted thing away." He bent over Beatrix and pressed his lips to her little brow. "I am glad you did not die that winter, Pup. I would have missed my Bumble Bea." He straightened and cleared his throat. "Alexandra, do you care for a walk on the terrace?"

Alex was concerned that he had pushed himself too hard that day. "You perhaps did not walk or ride so much when you were in London, Hawksworth. Do you not think you have had enough exercise for one day?"

"I do not, thank you very much. I shall practice walking, with or without your arm. If you care to join me later, you will find me on the terrace." Hawk quit the room without another word, leaving them all to sit in an uncomfortable, almost palpable silence.

"He is bristling," Giff said, "to head the family again, though he is not yet physically capable."

"Are you saying that I am being too . . . . too managing?" Alex asked, certain she was.

Giff rose, kissed the top of her head, and squeezed her shoulder. "You have been a darling and a savior to all of us, lass, especially to me after the way I barked at you all in early days."

He regarded the rest of the family. "I am saying that we must be careful, when we praise Alex, that we are not disheartening Hawksworth. From my own experience, after my time in the colonies, I know that a man home from war has much to deal with that is not within sight of his family, but in his head and his heart. The demons of war can be dark and tenacious, distorting even the obvious goodness in life. Past and present become entangled with a soldier's confusion and self-reproach for living when others perished, and with his need to make life as it once was. Except that he cannot go back, because time has passed and people have changed and learned to live without him."

Giff smiled, easing the sad sobriety about the table. "Give Hawk time. Be patient with him. Let him know that he is loved and needed."

Alex saw Beatrix up to bed, helped her wash, and heard her prayers. While she sat with the child until she slept, she considered Giff's words. Not only was he correct in everything he said, but she realized that Hawksworth's burdens were worse for his having lost so much, including his heritage. No wonder he seemed unsure of "everything."

Even she must seem lost to him, if he believed she loved Chesterfield, which she had encouraged in order to gain his attention. Gad, she wished she knew how she should proceed.

After Bea fell asleep, Alex went out to the terrace to look for Hawk.

When she arrived, Giff strode her way. "Enjoy the summerlike evening. It is beautiful," he said as he made to climb the steps back into the house. "This old curmudgeon needs his beauty sleep. Good night, you two."

Acting stiff and unconcerned, perhaps somewhat upset with her for not joining him sooner, Bryceson silently laid his cane on a nearby bench and offered her his arm. Alex took it and squeezed. "Bumble Bea is all tucked up and sends good-night kisses," she said by way of apology, catching his nod of understanding or forgiveness.

They began to stroll quietly, each lost in thought.

"I will not fail them again," Bryce said, breaking the reasonably comfortable silence.

"Oh, Bryce, of course you will not. You never really did."

"Did I not?" His grimace of self-derision was more felt than seen. "Do not patronize me, Alex. I failed you royally by marrying you and leaving you to mop up my mess."

"What mess?"

"I am sorry; I misspoke. I left you as the sole support of my family, with no home or even a living to provide for you all—no mess there."

Alex smiled. "*Our* family."

"Ours, then, though you should not have needed to care for them alone." He hesitated and regarded her pointedly before walking on. "Not that you did entirely, if Bea is to be believed. Judson helped, I take it."

Alex bit her lip. "Not in the way you suppose. You know this is the first time you use his Christian name."

"I must be softening in the head. Likely because of what he did for Beatrix. Lord, it makes me sick to think of nearly losing her."

"Well, we did not lose her, and yes, in that way, Judson did help."

"Then I must be grateful to the man, and we do have a mess now—one I made myself. But I am here now to straighten everything out, though, God help me, if I had not returned, you would not be so bad off."

Alex stopped and turned to him. "If you do not stop feeling sorry for yourself, Bryceson Wakefield, I swear I will strike you."

"I am sure you would, if you were angry enough. I expect you would beat me, or toss me off the terrace in much the same way you tossed me from the bed this morning." But Alex did not laugh as Hawk intended.

He reclaimed her hand, placed it on his arm, and patted it. "I am not feeling sorry for myself, but for you, Lexy."

To his surprise, she threw off his hold and strode off in a rage before turning to face him. "Stupid, stupid man. How can you not know?"

Hawk frowned in bewilderment. "How can I not know what?"

Alex began to advance on him, and sensing the strength of purpose in her stride, he began to retreat at the same pace.

She grinned. "You are running without your cane, Bryceson. Did you realize it?"

Hawk faltered for running at all, not for lacking his cane. He needed to face his ghosts, not run from them. He should ask Alex, right out, what she owed Chesterfield, and in exchange for what.

Except that he was not yet ready to deal with her answer.

Her person, however, he was very much ready to deal with. Too ready. Eager. Hawk straightened his spine and remained in place.

"Good," Alex said as she continued advancing. "You will allow me to catch you, I take it?"

"We will see who is caught," Hawk said, reaching out and pulling his wife firmly into his arms.

Fourteen

Once Hawk had Alex well and truly captured, she raised her arms and feathered the hair at his nape with her soft, sweet fingers, kissing his scars and giving him her full, tantalizing attention. He responded by opening his mouth over hers at the first opportunity.

Her like response thrummed him to life, and he moaned and tasted a trace of mint on her lips and thought it never more delightful.

Hawk had barely acknowledged—even to himself—since his return to England, the strength and inevitability of his attachment to Alex, his overwhelming desire for her; yet suddenly the veracity of it seemed written, as if in blazing stars, across the darkening night sky above them.

She had always been his.

He wanted her more than he had ever wanted another woman in his life, and with an intensity that startled even him.

What a caper-wit he was to perceive it only now, when it was too late and he could not have her.

She loved another. And he, her husband, who knew nothing of love, who had never wanted to, was broken of body and bound to let her go.

The rogue of Devil's Dyke rides no more, he thought wryly.

Yes, the situation was laughable, but he could not laugh. For the first time in years, he was attracted to the irreverent brat who had teased and exasperated him their entire lives—to Alexandra, his wife.

The tardiness of his realization shamed Hawk, for he wanted her almost to the point of madness. He sighed and kissed her again. Belated or not, the truth remained the same. They belonged together.

If only he could make her believe it. Now he had gone quite daft, for *if* he could make her care for him, *if* he was fool enough to try, might he not risk negating the likelihood of an annulment in the attempt?

Hawk set the quandary aside, for overriding sanity, his bride was eager and his body fit and pulsing— *that* worry was settled to his relief and satisfaction. Finally, he was certain that, yes, he was physically capable of making love to his wife. Now he must simply find the strength to keep from doing so.

"Would that I could carry you up the stairs to our bed," he whispered, his arousal firm and ready between them.

His bride smiled, coy, teasing. "And what would you do with me when you got me there?"

Hawk paused, sobering. What, indeed? "Excellent question." He stepped back and ran his hand through his hair. What, indeed? Trap her in a loveless marriage with a disfigured rogue? Or set her free to choose the husband of her heart?

"Why do you not go up to bed," he suggested when

he saw her shiver. "The air has cooled and you will catch a chill. I will be up shortly."

Alex sobered as Bryce stepped away and the brisk night air encircled her like the caressing talons of an icy villain. Her heart sank when she perceived that somehow his mood had shifted and he no longer intended to make her his own, if he ever had.

Dispirited, she turned and, without a word, strode toward the house.

"I am sorry," she heard him say behind her, but what could she say to that? For she was more sorry than he.

In her bedchamber, Alex wandered aimlessly about until her surroundings came into focus. A lush bedchamber prepared to receive a bridegroom, a moonlit night, perfect for seduction. What, after all, did she have to lose for trying when a mesmerizing web of sensuality ensnared her still?

Alex set tinder to flame in the hearth, producing a blaze that reflected the inferno raging inside her. By the time she finished bathing, she needed to open the windows to cool herself and the room.

From her dresser she chose the most gossamer of her satin and lace negligees, sheer and striking. The cloth of pale jonquil shimmered, even more diaphanous and alluring with its threads of gold than the white she had worn previously.

"Shame on you," she had told Chesterfield upon opening the box wherein the jonquil set nestled, and even with her betrothed's passion-glazed eyes smoldering down on her, Alex remembered thinking that she would have liked for Bryce to see her wearing it, for him to see her as a bride bedecked for her bride-groom's pleasure.

Poor Chesterfield. He never had a chance.

Her actions had been unforgivable where he was concerned. She should not have said she would marry him, for she never stopped thinking of Bryce, not even for a moment, not even as she marched down that aisle.

The gown and wrap fit like a dream and looked as if they were made of spun sugar. Before her mirror, Alexandra brushed her hair till it shone like polished mahogany, the glow from the fire reflecting the silver lights within it.

She expended a week's candle allotment, placing lit tapers on every surface, small scattered tables, the tall dresser. She set several upon her dressing table, where the mirror reflected them double—an enchanting image.

When Bryceson still had not come up, she glanced out the window, down to the terrace, and saw that he was making his slow way toward the house at long last.

Panic set in then, and Alex wondered where he should find her when he came in. Not in the bed, for that was not romantic enough by half, not in the truest sense. On the floor before the fire would be best, she thought, but why would she be sitting *there*?

She remembered Bryce coming to her the night before, to take the pins from her hair, and she went to pin it back up, shoving in hairpins helter-skelter. Then she grabbed her hairbrush and hurried to sit on the carpet before the fire, her back to the door.

By that time she was so warm, she dropped her dressing gown from her shoulders, leaving her in the dangerously low-cut, cap-sleeved night rail.

Looking down at herself, Alex noticed with pride how she overflowed the bounds of her bodice.

Even better.

When she heard the rattle of the doorknob, she removed the first of her hairpins, brush in hand, as if she sat there half naked all the time.

The door opened and Bryce's uneven footfalls stopped.

The silence pulsed.

After a dozen or more beats, Alex turned to see what was wrong.

Hawksworth the arrogant, tension investing his splendid frame, looked as if he had been turned to stone. Stubborn and craven, he wore an expression of cold horror but heated fascination.

A quick glance proved to Alex that that *interesting* portion of his anatomy had also taken note.

Better and better.

She returned her gaze to the hearth to conceal the light of triumph that she knew must be reflected there. "Come, Hawk, sit by me. I find it relaxing to brush my hair by the fire. Is the cool air and the warm blaze not a perfect combination?"

The mild scent of roses wafted up from the garden as the curtains billowed in the night-cool breeze, and the candle flames danced. Close to the fire, Alex was so warm, she thought she might prefer no gown at all.

What a delightful notion. Except that if she threw off the gown as well, Hawk might turn tail and not look back. Her battle-scarred husband was definitely not ready for so advanced a stage of attack.

For half a beat, Alex wondered where the rogue of Devil's Dyke had got to. What else had happened to him in Belgium that he had not brought his old self home again?

Perhaps she was pushing him too far, thinking to seduce him or die in the trying, so she relaxed and vowed to take her conquest a deal more slowly.

"Come," she repeated, "sit by me." She almost thought he would leave and go back downstairs, but he did not. Instead, he came to sit on the floor facing her, despite his obvious difficulty in lowering himself so far a distance.

"I am sorry," Alex said when he winced as he did so. "I have hurt you again."

Hawk shook his head. "Stop reading my expressions and read my actions. I am here, where we both want me to be." He took the brush from her hand and set it on the carpet.

As he pulled out her hairpins, she reached over to remove his diamond stickpin, the one he had worn at their wedding then given her to take home for safe-keeping. She untied his cravat and removed it, feeling very much a wife with the simple but intimate task.

She encouraged him to shrug from his frock coat and waistcoat and tossed them on a nearby chair. He let her remove his shoes and stockings. And after she did, she stroked his long, slender feet.

He took up her brush to run it through her hair as she removed several of his shirt studs and investigated the texture of the crisp, curling mat within the exposed vee.

His heartbeat quickened beneath her fingertips.

He shuddered and stopped her from removing any more studs, so as to keep his shirt. Then he moved closer, so close Alex lost her breath. As he leaned near, to bring her wrap up to cover her shoulders, his breath kissed her neck, his eyes bearing a spark so bright, she expected his lips to curve upward at the corners, and even when they did not, she might honestly say that he smiled.

When her hair was brushed to a sheen, Bryce pulled her down with him as he reclined upon the rug, bringing her fully atop him.

What an amazing place to be, Alex thought, looking into a hawk's golden eyes, knowing they blazed with desire only for her.

As if to hold her in place, he filled his hands with her bottom, a satisfied sound rising from deep in his throat. Then he slid the skirt of her gown upward, ever so slowly, allowing the breeze to caress her ankles, her calves, her thighs, and higher. And when he cupped her, bare hand to bare bottom, Alex gasped with the pure carnality of his claim.

He arched and pressed his firm male self against the place where she ached. If he grew any larger, he *would* be as big as a stallion.

Claudia had been right. Men were just the same.

Lord, she loved her husband's hands on her. She loved this decadent, intimate embrace.

"Like contented cats before the fire," Hawk said,

his lazy drawl animating the picture he created with his words.

"Is it your intention, then, to make me purr?" she asked.

Hawk nearly laughed. His bride had just issued a challenge, pure and simple, and she did so with a full compliment of lowered lashes and tongue-moistened lips.

God's teeth, she was a natural.

He could do this, he thought. He could bring them both pleasure without consummation. How else would he know where their relationship stood? How else to make her care enough to stay—*if* he was so foolish as to try?

"Sorceress," he said as he learned her with his hands, from her bottom to her core. He took to planting kisses as he did, upon a singular brow, along her nape, the pulse at the base of her throat, her luscious and willing lips.

And when he raised a knee and slipped it between her own, she cooperated to the point that arousal darkened her eyes to midnight velvet and softened her kiss-swollen lips to a pout of sensual invitation.

Keeping a firm hold on her bottom, Hawk cupped a breast, and the seductress arched to fill his palm. He fingered the nubbin, rubbed the silk of her gown over the puckered tip, back and forth, until she was peaked to perfection, pouting and proud.

He made her moan, and he grew harder.

He slipped his hand inside her bodice, callused flesh to flesh of silk, and he grew harder.

In counterpoint to his firmness, Alex slid bonelessly to the carpet beside him, and Hawk lost not a moment in the transition. Seeking greater access, he tugged a bodice ribbon and slipped her gown off a shoulder to expose her creamy skin. He laved the crown of a breast, between the full and luscious globes, and watched her eyes smolder with sexual awakening.

He *must* be her first. He must.

Laving her and taking her into his mouth, he took to suckling, encouraged by her hands in his hair, at first pushing him away, then pulling him closer, now holding him in place with a purr of pure contentment.

He eased her to her back and rose above her.

Her mewling sounds of awe and pleasure served to arouse him further, until he was the Hawksworth of old, the rogue of Devil's Dyke once more.

And when he perceived that she would welcome him, he slipped his hand up her leg until her breathing changed to short, quick gasps, until she "wept" with anticipation for his touch. And when he breached her, her "tears" had readied her to receive him.

Only a virgin, literally untouched, could be prepared so readily. A virgin . . . whose sexual initiation should be undertaken by no one less worthy than the man she loved.

The intrusive thought struck Hawk like an ice bath. He swore and moved off her like a clumsy schoolboy, like the thoughtless cad he had proved himself to be. "I am sorry," he said. "Alex, forgive me. I did not mean to take it so far." He would not touch her again. He could not be trusted.

Struck as if with horror, she rolled to her side and curled into a ball, her back stiff, yet somehow breaking under the weight of what she had almost allowed. He would swear that if he touched her now, he would be pricked by a score of invisible spines.

"Forgive me," he said again. "You deserve better. You deserve the man you love." If he did not put some space between them, he would break every rule he had set for himself concerning this wife of his.

In London, he would begin as he meant to go on. Separate bedchambers would make it easier, which surely the duchess would afford them.

Alex said nothing as Bryce undressed and climbed into the bed.

An hour later, lying beside him, she wondered where she had gone wrong. He had almost broken her, changing his mind at such a time. But had he done so at her instigation? His words would not leave her. *You deserve the man you love.*

Had she made a calculated error in convincing him she loved Chesterfield? Had this entire debacle been her fault?

How could he not know 'twas him she had loved forever?

She supposed that they had made some progress. He did want her, if only physically, as she most assuredly wanted him; though her want was more encompassing, for it included hearts and spirits, minds, even faults and imperfections.

At the moment when he had left her aching with need, she thought she might wither and die where she lay, and yet there had been such a ridiculous amount of relief as well. But why?

Because Hawk's father believed she was not good enough for his son, and she believed it as well?

What was wrong with her that she did not even know what she feared?

Sabrina would understand about her fears. She would know how she should go about seducing Hawk, *if* she should.

Simply telling Hawksworth that she loved him, after pretending to love Chesterfield, would make him think he pitied him for his scars, especially since he thought the world saw nothing but the scars.

How could she make Hawk understand that she wanted and cared only for him? That he was worthy of love?

How could she undo a lifetime of harsh persuasion?

How could she keep from losing him forever?

Fifteen

During the night, Bryceson the rogue inevitably returned. Always, when Alex got near him as he slept, he clasped her close as if she were his long-lost love, precious and adored, and spoke her name before drifting back to sleep.

No matter how many times she approached him in the night over the next weeks, every time she did, she was taken aback with joy. Sometimes tears slipped down her cheeks unheeded as she drifted off in his strengthening arms.

If only he wanted her when he was awake in the same way he seemed to want her in sleep.

Blast it, she must spare no stratagem when it came to her seductive vengeance. Her goal was selfish, Alex knew, but she wanted everything marriage entailed, including a lesson in love for her husband.

A week before they left for London, Hawk threw his cane out a second-floor window in a fit of frustrated rage.

Beatrix had slipped on a wet stair and landed on her bruised little bottom.

Because of it, Alexandra had climbed atop an old barn ladder in the second-floor hall to replace the upper molding of a window, where rain had been driven in during another of the season's torrential storms. The rising stream had floated down the hall and ultimately down the stairs.

While Bea had laughed at her flying antics, Alex had worried aloud that Hildy or Giff might be seriously hurt. And Beatrix made the mistake of adding that Hawk, with his cane, might also be, which bruised his fragile ego to begin with.

"Of course I would not," he said. "It is for us to worry about the elderly, not the young."

"But Alex says you are in pain sometimes and your leg is weak and we should be careful, Uncle Bryce."

He raged all the while she and Beatrix dragged the ladder up to the landing. "Stop, I tell you, and go away. I will tend to it myself," he charged them, but neither of them stopped to listen or do his bidding.

"Alex, do not climb that ladder, I tell you. Do not," he shouted as he made his way up the stairs. But by the time he arrived at the base of the ladder, Alex was prying the rotted slat away and preparing to affix a fresh piece of wood to the spot. She was so preoccupied with her task, however, that when he spoke her name, she jumped and nearly fell from her perch.

That was when he swore, pushed up the sash, and tossed his cane out the window. Then he slammed it shut, climbed the ladder, cursing all the way, grasped Alex by her waist, and, with surprising strength, lifted her down to replace her himself.

After that, without the use of his cane, Hawk

walked with more discomfort and less grace, but he refused to take it up again from that day on, performing every single task that anyone mentioned needed doing, no matter how difficult.

As good as his word to secure tenants and improve the estate, Hawk advertised locally and interviewed dozens of prospects. It was not difficult to find applicants, given the soldiers and sailors seeking employment now that the war was over. There were also mill workers displaced by factory closings across the breadth of England, and farmers who lost their land because the summer rains and endless hailstones had ruined their crops, the wheat suffering worst of all.

Within two weeks, a dozen hard-working military men and their families moved onto Huntington tenant property. Some would work the home farm, completing the harvest, however sodden the crops. Two were ships' carpenters, one a millwright, and two others bricklayers. They would make immediate repairs to the buildings, working in exchange for rent and no monetary compensation, as there was no money— though Hawk gave each family a goodly-sized portion of land for their own use. Wives and children could work that for themselves and raise enough produce to feed their families and sell the excess at market for a respectable profit. St. Albans was a famous enough market town to make that effort more than worthwhile.

Hawk set himself up as Huntington's estate manager. But in preparation for the time when he would take the family to London for Claudia's season, he taught one of their long-standing tenants to take over temporary management, for a lower rent and a larger cottage.

When Hawk found a widow offering two dozen black-faced Suffolk sheep for a pittance, he bought the animals to raise for wool. He secured several cows and a bull for similarly low prices, as more farmers were daily giving up and heading for the city. These he would raise for milk and beef.

Hawk's diamond stickpin bought them a mare rumored to be in foal by Mercury, a prize-winning racehorse. The mare alone was worth more than the stickpin, for she was a prime breeder in her own right and would produce fast, healthy, hard-working carriage horses. But if Mercury had sired her offspring that infamous day he broke loose and covered half the mares in Hertfordshire, then she was worth a dozen diamond pins for her foal alone. He named her Quicksilver.

If he was skilled at one thing—other than that for which he had become quite famous with the ladies—Hawk told Alex later, it was horses. And if he could not turn a profit with good horseflesh, then no one could.

Alex thought that if she could not get him to demonstrate his other famous skill, she was going to crown her gentleman farmer with his own pitchfork.

Several days before they were to leave for London, Claudia said that perhaps she did not need a season after all. Not this year, at least, and Alex laughed. "Do not even try to pretend with me, Missy," she said. "You do not wish to go, because you have failed to talk Chesterfield into following us to town. Is that not right, or as near right as might be?"

Claudia huffed and flapped a sheet to lie flat against Bea's small bed. "Just because you are content to live without love, Alex, does not mean that I am."

The words felt like a slap, and Alex gasped, looked into Claudia's stricken eyes, and left the room at a hurried pace, only to plow into Hawksworth.

"Ho, steady, there." Still unstable on his feet, he latched onto her for balance, and Alex pretended the same need, allowing him to hold her, treasuring the embrace. Between Claudia's harsh words and Hawk's arms about her in the light of day, Alex began to weep. And, once the floodgates opened, she could not seem to close them.

Then Claudia was beside her, apologizing, except that Alex could not focus on the girl, because of the wondrous look of concern in her husband's eyes, which only made her weep the more.

Claudia attempted to pull her aside, but Alex did not wish to be disengaged from Hawksworth's embrace, and fortunately, he fought to keep her there.

Alex did squeeze Claudia's hand, however, giving her a look begging understanding, hoping the girl would realize that she could not miss this God-given opportunity with her husband.

Grateful for Claudia's dawn of understanding, Alex stepped with Hawk into the privacy of their bedchamber.

When he closed the door, shutting them alone inside, Alex fairly floated in the fixedness of his attention.

He urged her onto their bed and lay beside her, pulling her close. "Alex, sweetheart . . ." He wiped a tear with a fingertip. "Tell me what is wrong."

"Hold me, Hawk. Please hold me."

His gentleness was almost too wonderful to bear. Perhaps he did not love her, but Claudia had been wrong about one thing: Alex was not content to continue that way. Oh, she was not.

Because Hawk shushed and rocked her in his arms, she cried the more. She wept for all the years without his arms around her, and for Claudia's words, because they sliced too close to the bone to be borne.

Alex felt more alive than she had since the night they nearly made love beside the fire. She wanted more such experiences. But almost as much, she wanted to know why her husband had not come home to her. "Why, Hawk? Why did you not find us as soon as you returned from Belgium?"

He kissed her brow, her lips. He sighed and resettled them, pulling the corner of the counterpane over them as if they were a pair of Egyptian mummies.

Alex experienced heaven in his arms, but hell loomed in the weight of his silence. Her fear that he could not have borne to come home to her was so great, she wanted to weep the more for his hesitancy.

"If I could understand, myself," Hawk said, several long minutes later, "I could explain it, though my staying away had nothing to do with my father, I promise you."

Silence held sway until Alex initiated a second

kiss, which at length came to its inevitable, breath-seeking conclusion. They looked into each other's eyes, then almost into each other's souls, and she remembered how, over the years, he had a difficult time overcoming his natural reticence. And Alex understood, with sudden clarity and great relief, that his current silence might have nothing to do with her, but with who he was at heart—as perhaps did his previous silence. "Just talk and I will listen," she said.

Reluctantly Hawk nodded, understanding somehow that this may be the most important conversation of his life, though he was not certain why. "You might have noticed," he said, closing his eyes against a hoard of painful memories, "that I was badly wounded in Belgium." He looked to see if she would wince or pale.

She did not. "I had noticed."

"I thought as much." He sighed. "Blast it, this is impossible."

"Just talk."

He gave her a half nod, wishing himself anywhere but here, compelled to speak of things he'd as lief forget. "For months after Waterloo, I thought I would die at any moment. Then for a while, after I began to recover, I was sorry that I had not died."

"Oh, Hawk, no."

He crossed her lips with a finger. "Shh. You promised you would listen."

She kissed the finger, humbling him. "I apologize. Go on."

Hawk pulled her closer, settled her head upon his shoulder, and allowed himself the luxury of burying his face in her hair for a moment. Her violet scent soothed him. "I was ashamed, for one thing. Better men than I had died, you see. Braver men—smarter, stronger, worthier men, who had made something of their lives. What right had I to live, with them gone?"

Alex shook her head.

"I did not promise, Lexy, that you would approve, I simply promised that I would talk, and frankly it is deuced uncomfortable enough, without your added disapproval."

"Forgive me."

He nodded. "When I suspected I wanted to live again, I was, frankly, afraid."

Alex bristled and Hawk regarded her. "I am admitting here that Sabrina may have been right. Never tell her so."

"Never," Alex promised solemnly. "Go on."

"I *may* have used Sabrina and the boys as an excuse to linger in London. She is also family and was never as strong as you, and they *were* in trouble. Ultimately, I was glad I stayed, because I was able to help them from a situation that had been plaguing them."

"Then I am glad you stayed, as well," Alex said. "Perhaps she will tell me about it one day. Sabrina is another stubborn one, like you, who keeps her problems to herself."

"And you do not?"

"Of course n—no. Perhaps. Sometimes."

Hawk hugged her tight for a second.

Alex was uplifted by the beat of his heart at her ear, and the strength and need in his crushing, almost desperate embrace. "After you helped Sabrina and the children, why, then, did you remain in town?" she asked, prodding him to continue.

"I think—I know—that I did not want to force my wretched presence upon you all, for then you would see how damaged I was."

Hawk shook his head, for he could not even understand. "Inside, Lexy, I still feel, sometimes, as if I was broken in so many ways that I was not put back together properly, as if I . . . . live now in someone else's skin. I know it sounds fanciful, but I cannot explain any better. I am sorry."

With the same tenacity required to ignore the abiding ache in her heart when she first believed him dead, Alexandra ignored the fact that Hawk did not mention missing any of them, not even Claudia and Beatrix. That he never seemed to have worried about them.

"Even on the day Sabrina came to tell me of your wedding," Hawk continued, "I was not yet ready to face any of you."

Alex felt him shudder inwardly. "Then, without knowing how I got there, I found myself standing at the mouth of hell, inside a church, and I saw you, a bride beside your bridegroom. A woman. Beautiful. About to be joined to another." He kissed her brow and held her fiercely for several long, delicious moments.

"My first inkling that I wanted to live again slipped into my conscious mind as I began that everlasting trek up the aisle. I could not for the life of me imagine why I had been so eager to go marching off to war in the first place, or why I stayed away so long after my return. I knew only that you were mine and I must stop you from going to another."

Though they were not quite the words Alex wanted—that he had missed her, needed her, cared for her—they were a great deal more than she expected, and she whooped in happiness and tightened her arms around him, kissing him wherever she could reach.

Hawk wanted to tell Alex then how much he had missed her. He wanted so badly to tell her that, to keep from admitting it, he kissed her. Otherwise, he would commit himself to becoming her husband in every way, and that, he could not do.

He kissed her slender fingers, her wrist, the pulse at her temple, her invitingly parted lips. And just when her eyes darkened and his body came to life, a hedgehog ran across the blankets.

Alex screamed in surprise.

"What the . . . ?"

They heard a familiar giggle.

"Beatrix Ann Jamieson," Alex said, "you come out this instant."

Bea rose from the floor on the opposite side of the bed and came around to their side.

Hawk held Alex close, while little Miss Mischief, behind her, placed her elbows on the bed and rested her chin in her small hands. "What're you and Alex doing up here in the middle of the day?"

Alex's giggle was muffled against his chest, and as sanity returned, Hawk became more and more grateful to his Bumble Bea by the moment.

"We were, er, taking a nap."

"Oh, good." Beatrix scrambled up onto the bed and climbed over Alex to squeeze herself into the tight place between them, crossing her shod feet and tucking her fists, as if to warm them, beneath her chin.

Alex removed Bea's tiny kid slippers and pulled the blanket over her, tucking it up to her chin.

"Remember after Mama died, Uncle Hawk," Bea said, snuggling in, "when you used to take naps with me so I would not have bad dreams? I missed our naps when you were gone."

"I missed them too, pup."

"Alex napped with me after you left. She sleeps quieter than you do, but I like napping with you, too."

"Thank you," Hawk said, looking over at Alex, raising a brow at her chuckle.

"I like best having you *both* to nap with." Bea gave a huge yawn. "It makes me feel safe and happy, like having a mama and a papa both again." Then she sighed and closed her eyes, and before they knew it, she was snuffling like a contented hedgehog.

Hawk regarded Alex over Bea's head. Just that easily this little one had cracked the foundation of all his good intentions.

He reached over to take Alex's hand and weave their fingers together. Then Bea turned on her side and buried her face between Alex's breasts, sighing in sleepy contentment.

Lucky pup, Hawk thought, Bea's words playing in his head whether he wished them to or not. Having Alex and him both was like having two parents again—a humbling but disquieting announcement from a six-year-old who had lacked parents for more than half her life.

Alex took Bea's cue and fell asleep as well, her fingers still laced with his. And Hawk lay there and worried about them and watched over them.

His family—perhaps not wholly better off without him, after all.

Sixteen

Days later, Hawk was still worrying Bea's words like a pup with a bone. If he went ahead with his plan to set Alex free, what would losing her do to Beatrix, who had already endured the separate losses of her parents? Not to mention how she must have felt for losing him as well.

He recalled how she had wept for him when she had not quite recognized him. Now here he was, back from the dead and planning to set Alex free, which amounted to the same thing as taking away her new mother. Poor Bea.

Poor Alex. She would never allow herself to be set free, if she thought Bea might suffer for it. So how could he release her now, Chesterfield or no?

Hawk had detested Chesterfield for so long. For years they had played some silent game, vying for the same stakes: women, money, the respect of their peers. Hawk did not even know exactly when the game had begun, or why.

He knew only that he had won, hands down for the most part, until that fateful day at White's when Chesterfield and his father met by accident, apparently, and found themselves sharing a brandy and becoming fast friends. Later his father had said that Chesterfield was a good man, a man a father could be proud of.

The bitter taste of that pronouncement had lingered and festered inside Hawk until the day his father contrived to offer him pride at the last— that fateful, consequential day.

After that, their old rivalry had been forgotten in the chaos of war and pain until it flared anew, blazed, that day at the church—and worse since, until Hawk discovered that Chesterfield had practically saved Bea's life. Now he found himself trying to swallow an adjustment of his attitude toward his old nemesis.

To complicate matters, Chesterfield had come striding right up to him recently, there on Huntington property, while Hawk was trying to help one of his seasoned tenants deliver a lamb, of all things. The lambing was not only Hawk's first, but the delivery was difficult at best, and out of season, so there was some worry that the lamb would be too weak and small to withstand a prolonged birth.

Chesterfield had ignored their struggle and ripped up at Hawk for the way he was raising Claudia. "She is going to get herself into trouble visiting men at their homes without even a maid in tow, sending them notes, inviting them to woodland trysts and unchaperoned walks," he practically shouted. "If you continue your lackadaisical guardianship in this way, Hawksworth, your niece will be ruined."

"Do not presume—"

"It is one thing for her to be naturally friendly and exuberant here in the country," Chesterfield continued, ignoring Hawk's attempt to respond, "but entirely another in town. If she continues to care naught for her reputation, she will run wild in London and find herself at the mercy of some blackguard who misunderstands her and accepts the wrong invitation, with no care to her safety or good name. I trust I have made my point," Chesterfield said even as he stormed off.

"Just see that *you* stay away from her," Hawk shouted after him.

"I am bloody well trying," Chesterfield snapped.

"Wait," Hawk said, stroking the laboring ewe to calm her. "What did you give Alex, for which she owes you something in exchange?"

Chesterfield cursed. "Her freedom, damn you to perdition."

No matter that Hawk called the blighter back for his foolish answer, Chesterfield did not so much as falter or turn but kept walking.

Still, Hawk wondered which piece of the puzzle remained missing, for the ones he had garnered thus far did not fit.

Now, as their borrowed carriage carried them smoothly toward London, Hawk could not decide whether he was grateful to Chesterfield for his warning about Claudia or furious with him over his mysterious "exchange of sorts" with Alex.

He did realize, however, that Chesterfield was right about one thing: Hawk knew less about raising girls than he did about birthing sheep.

He knew even less about grown women, wives in particular. One wife. His. He needed to talk to someone with experience. Perhaps Gideon, though his fellow rogue had less experience with children than Hawk. But he did have a wife, Sabrina—Hawk's sister, since his late and villainous half-brother married her.

Not that Hawk could not speak to Alex about Claudia. He could and did, to a point, but he would rather not bring Chesterfield into any of their conversations if he could help it—no need to remind her of what she had lost.

Besides, he could ask Sabrina about Alex as well as about Claudia. Bree seemed to know instinctively what to do in most situations, and she understood him so very well, in the same way he understood her. So much so that Gideon had once imagined they were in love with each other.

Now, *that* was a story he would have to share with Alex someday.

Alex was pleased that their two-hour trip to London remained for the most part uneventful. Hawk had dressed for the first time in his own clothes a deal newer and more fashionable than the ones from his Belgian family. Getting him to agree, though, had taken a bit of cajoling and more than one satisfying kiss. He even agreed to have Weston take a few nips and tucks to bring his attire up to snuff, though he hated for the ton to become generally aware that his pockets were to let.

Claudia had pouted for days because she failed to talk Chesterfield into following them into town. And Hawk was inordinately annoyed with her for trying, after the truth came out, though Alex wasn't quite sure how he learned it.

What worried her now was that Claudia's pout had disappeared, only to be replaced by the spark of satisfaction lighting her guinea-gold eyes.

As much as she worried about Claudia, Alex had to laugh at Bea's requests to use and examine the "necessary" at every posting inn between Devil's Dyke and St. James Square, though it gave them all more than enough opportunity to stretch their legs.

"I miss Uncle Giff," Beatrix said mournfully as she climbed into Hawk's lap for what Alex hoped might be a nice, long nap.

Saying good-bye to Aunt Hildegarde and Uncle Gifford had been difficult for all of them. The older couple opted to remain behind and skip the pleasures of London. Hawk said he was glad that a male member of the family would remain at Huntington Lodge to oversee the estate. And Alex was glad, because some of London's pleasures could be too much for certain people.

"You know," Claudia said, prompted by Bea's comment, "if I did not know better, I would think that Uncle Giff and Aunt Hildy were pleased to be getting the house to themselves."

Alex recalled the gatehouse incident with speculation, and by the look of him, so did Hawk. It occurred to Alex then that she might have consulted her Aunt Hildegarde about seduction. Though since the woman had never married, she might very well have fallen into an apoplexy of embarrassment if Alex tried.

Hildy and Giff could have visited the gatehouse for a perfectly innocent reason, after all.

"They are probably looking forward to peace and quiet," Hawk said, "what with our mischievous eavesdropper safe away. What do you think, pup?" He tickled Bea until she giggled helplessly and screamed for him to be careful of Nanny.

Everyone groaned. "Where is she?" Hawk asked, stilling on the instant.

Bea took her ball of a spiny pet from her pocket. "Here she is, see?"

"Did I not tell you to leave Nanny home?"

Beatrix shook her head adamantly. "No you did not, Uncle Bryce. You said that Damon and Rafferty would like to see her. Will you take the twins with us to Astley's Royal Amphitheater? Tell me again what we will see there."

Alex knew there would be no rest for any of them this trip, and no peace either—not today or in the weeks to come.

As they approached St. James Square, Hawk thought that Basingstoke House stood out like a diamond in a tasteful cluster of lesser gems.

The dowager duchess herself appeared an exquisite in every respect: petite as a sprite, disciplined as a general, and generous to a fault. Her home seemed to run like a finely geared French clock, and one hour in her company made him imagine that the twice-widowed duchess might have been a great help to Wellington on the peninsula.

She appeared as if nothing could ruffle her, until Nanny scampered under her dress and over her slippered feet.

Upon being presented to the duchess, Claudia curtsied prettily, making the older woman beam. "Enchanting." She kissed Claudia's cheek. "I vow that you shall be wed by spring, if not sooner." And Claudia glowed.

"I made an appointment for us at Madame Suzette's this afternoon to have Claudia fitted for her new wardrobe, if that is convenient for you both?" the duchess said to Alex.

Claudia looked as if she might dance on air at the prospect, and Alex accepted with thanks for them both.

After tea, Hawk and Alex followed a maid up to their apartment. "The duchess told me that we are invited to Gideon and Sabrina's town house at Grosvenor Square for luncheon," Alex told Hawk. "Afterward, Bea can remain there with Damon and Rafferty for the afternoon while the duchess and I take Claudia for her fittings, and you and Gideon can do . . . whatever it is that London gentlemen do of an afternoon."

Hawk appeared amused by her words until they entered their apartment, which consisted of two dressing rooms, a huge sitting room, and one bedchamber. The four-poster itself was less wide, if that were possible, than the one they had shared at Huntington Lodge.

Hawk stood thunderstruck as he regarded it.

Alex stood grinning beside him. "I love it."

* * *

All the way to Grosvenor Square, Alex was in a state of excitement over seeing Sabrina again, for they had not seen each other in more than a year—not since they shared Hawk's town house right after Hawk went to war.

Months before Alex and Hawk's marriage, Sabrina had escaped the villain her first husband sold her to, and sought refuge with Hawk and his family.

After Hawk left for the war, Alex and Sabrina, along with their families, had continued to live together for nearly five months. Then Hawk was "killed" at Waterloo, and Bree received his "deathbed" letter saying he had arranged her marriage to Gideon.

When Baxter Wakefield inherited Hawk's fortune and estates and tossed them all out, Alex moved her family to Huntington Lodge, and Bree moved hers to Grosvenor Square to await her mystery groom's arrival.

Damon and Rafferty, Sabrina's twins, had become best of friends with Bea when they lived together, the boys adopting Claudia as their big sister, too. And Hawk and Gideon had served in the Guards under Wellington, so Alex knew that the entire family was as eager for the visit as she.

The dowager duchess of Basingstoke was Gideon's grandmother by blood, though Sabrina told Alex in a letter that the duchess treated Sabrina's children— from her marriage to Hawk's half brother—as beloved great-grandchildren.

Sabrina's youngest, Juliana, born shortly after her marriage to Gideon, had been named after the duchess, a fact of which the older woman was inordinately proud.

Hawk thought that their arrival at Grosvenor Square was like to rival the Vienna Congress in the rise and fervor of their voices—even after the children dashed up to the nursery. He shook Gideon's hand, pleased to see his fellow rogue again.

"Ladies, gentlemen," the duchess said to quiet the raucous company milling about the foyer, "let us have some decorum, if you please, and if we cannot, let us at least remove to the drawing room."

Sabrina giggled and hooked her arm in the formidable dowager's. "Yes, Grandmama." Together the two women led the group up the stairs.

Alex exclaimed in wonder upon entering an exquisite drawing room, complete with twin fireplaces of topaz marble.

"This is just the beginning," Sabrina said. "Wait until you see the rest of the house."

"I am in awe."

Gideon turned to Alex. "As well you should be. Hawk, present me to your beautiful bride, if you please."

Hawk took Alex's arm. "Alex, another member of the Rogues Club, Gideon St. Goddard, duke of Stanthorpe."

"Since Hawk and Sabrina are all but brother and sister," Sabrina's charming husband said, totally lacking the aristocratic air Alex expected, "and Hawk became my brother under Wellington, I shall consider you my sister."

"Thank you, Your Grace."

"Oh. Ouch. Please, may I call you Alexandra? And you must call me Gideon."

"Or Uncle Stanthorpe," Rafferty said, joining them.

"Or Uncle Papa," Damon added with a giggle.

Gideon scooped the twins off the floor to dangle them one under each arm. "Ignore the scamps, Alexandra. My name has become something of a family joke with them. And what do you call me now, you rascals?" he demanded, shaking them until they laughed.

"Papa, Papa," they chorused.

Beatrix had entered behind them carrying the ugliest cat Alex had ever seen.

"What is that?"

"That's Mincemeat," Rafe said as Gideon set him down. "Isn't she beautiful? She keeps my feet warm at night and licks my fingers, and purrs soft and happy. And she is the best mama to her kittens I ever saw."

"Then she is, indeed, beautiful," Alex said as she petted the purring cat.

"Bea's Nanny is something ripping, too," Damon said. "But her quills hurt."

"I told you to pet her in the direction they grow, not away from it," Bea said. "She doesn't know you yet, so she *will* curl in a ball and set her quills straight up to protect herself. When she knows you, she will let you tickle her silky belly."

"Drizzle likes that, too," Damon said, petting the short-legged beagle happily trailing behind.

The dowager shook her head as she regarded her grandson. "Keep this up and we will have to open our own menagerie."

Gideon raised his hands in complete guilelessness.

"Do not act the innocent with me," his grandmother continued. "If Juliana becomes enamored of an Indian tiger, you will find a way to get her one."

Gideon grinned and Hawk chuckled deep in his throat.

"Alex, you should see the baby," Beatrix said. "She looks ever so darling standing in her crib with only one tooth, and a little blue dress and bonnet, and dark curls; and she giggles when she sees the twins, and calls everybody Papa."

"Julie is a brilliant child," Gideon said. "*Papa* is her favorite word."

"*Papa* is her *only* word," his grandmother said, bursting her grandson's bubble.

Hawksworth barked a near-laugh, the first Alex had heard from him since he had come home. How relaxed he looked. How at ease, of a sudden.

This change would be good for him—for the two of them.

Seventeen

They ate *en famille,* with everyone present but the baby. "I fed Juliana earlier, so she should be settling down for her nap about now," Sabrina said. "How pleased we are that you have come to town for the little season. I can hardly wait for a comfortable coze, Alex. Can you spend the afternoon?"

"Oh, no, I am sorry, but I cannot. We have an appointment for Claude's fittings."

"Nonsense," the duchess said. "Claudia, what say you to letting *me* take you for your fittings?"

Claudia beamed and the duchess nodded regally. "It is settled, then."

Sabrina shook her head at her seventeen-year-old niece. "Claudia, I can hardly believe you are old enough to be entering the marriage mart."

"Providing we can obtain entry into all the best balls and routs," Alex said. "That is always a worry, is it not?"

The duchess waved her comment aside. "Your entry has been assured everywhere, my dears. I told you I would take care of everything. Sally Jersey is an old school chum."

After luncheon, Hawk and Gideon decided they

would go to Weston's for a fitting of their own; then, they were going to see if any news had surfaced on Hawk's father's solicitor.

"We might stop by Stephen's Hotel as well," Hawk said. "I would like to inquire as to some possible military men who need work and a place to settle. We have room at Huntington for six more tenant families."

"London is teeming with out-of-work soldiers," Gideon said. "Spitalfields has thousands who are half-starved and unemployed, never mind the number in workhouses and debtors' prisons."

"God's teeth, I had not realized the situation had grown so dire."

Gideon nodded. "It is an abomination for England's defenders to suffer so. Between the war's end and the poorest farming weather in years, I fear we are looking at bad times ahead."

"Let us take a drive through the East End, then. Perhaps we can find a few soldiers we know. By having them as my tenants, we can help each other."

"Excellent," Gideon said as they donned their many-caped greatcoats and accepted top hats and canes. "I could use a few good men on my estates as well."

They kissed their respective wives with an awkwardness, at first, for the public displays of affection, then with devilish gleams in their eyes for realizing it.

"Wickedly handsome rogues, are they not?" Alex said from the open front door beside Sabrina as they watched the carriage depart.

"They certainly are."

Alex chuckled. "My goodness, you amaze me.

You, the original man-hater—not without the best of reasons, mind. But still, it is such a turnabout."

"I am so very happy and . . . contented." Sabrina shut the door. "Though I never expected to be."

"I envy you."

"You will have your turn. Tell me what has been happening with you and Hawksworth."

"Before I can, you must answer a question that has been plaguing me."

"Gladly. Please sit. Would you like me to ring for tea?"

Alex shook her head in response to both. "Hawk said that you told him I was marrying, but why did you never write to tell me that he was alive and living in London?"

Sabrina paled and lowered herself to the settee. "Oh, Alex, it is so complicated."

"I thought we were friends, Bree. I know Hawksworth is more your brother than your brother-in-law and thinks of you as his sister. I have made peace with that, even with the fact that you received a last letter and I did not. But why did you not tell me that I was not free to marry? Would you have let me commit bigamy?"

"Of course not, which is the only reason Gideon allowed me to go that morning and tell Hawksworth—so Hawk could stop you."

"Allowed you?"

"Gideon was adamant that I not interfere, and I agreed about Hawksworth—for the most part. Oh, Alex, you should have seen Hawk when he showed himself to us, which was not until we were all nearly killed."

"Killed?"

Sabrina waved Alex's worried question away. "That is a story we will save for another time, but worry not, for the danger has passed. As for Hawk, he was in a dark place, Alex. Wounded deeply, and not simply of body, though he was that, too. He was lost, as well—almost of soul. I might fancifully say that he appeared as if he *had* died and gone to hell, but in returning was forced to bring his demons back with him, that they would not let him go."

"Oh, Bree." Alex sat as well. "Sometimes I have glimpsed such darkness in him."

"It was frightening. He was frightening. We worried about him, feared for his sanity, that he might do something rash."

Alex rose, her hands fisted. She wanted more than anything to lash out in anger at her old friend. "And you did not think I could help him?"

"Hawk is better now, which must be because of you, so I wonder if we might have been wrong to wait; but we did what we thought was best, Alex. Gideon fought beside Hawk. He held Hawk as he 'died,' and he warned me that a man home from war must make his own way through his demons—or be lost to them."

Sabrina twisted a violet grosgrain bodice-ribbon as she spoke. "I wrote twice to tell you, but I never sent either letter for fear of betraying my promise to Hawk, for fear of hurting him. After we knew he was back in London, Gideon made discreet inquiries to be certain that he was taking care of himself. We invited him here several times, but other than on the day he rescued us, Hawk never came."

Bree shook her head. "On that day, I advised him to contact you, and he promised he would. We owe him our lives, Alex, and we wanted to respect his wishes and give him the time he begged us to give him."

Despite herself, Alex wept over the things Bree revealed. She could not help herself. Hawk had suffered so much more than she imagined.

Bree handed her a handkerchief, and Alex wiped her eyes and her nose and smiled, finally, before stepping into Sabrina's waiting arms. "Thank you for being so much his friend," Alex said, "that you went against your instincts to be mine rather than hurt him."

"You love him still, even though you were about to marry Chesterfield?"

"Still, and more. Am I not the fool?"

"Hawksworth is a lovable man."

"You know that because you love him, too. I thought at one time that you and he . . ."

Bree giggled. "So did Gideon. Jealousy can be a very potent apprentice in getting a man to pay attention."

"I have tried that, but now I am afraid Hawk is staying away from me because he thinks I love Chesterfield."

"Men can be so pigheadedly noble."

Alex smiled, as did Sabrina.

"Now, tell me why your frantic note said that you

and Hawk should be given one bedchamber only at Grandmama's, no matter what." Sabrina raised a questioning brow. "I must confess it has had me imagining all sorts of intrigues."

"You did not say anything to your husband, did you, about the single bedchamber?"

"Lord, no. Besides, he would tell me not to meddle there, either, and I do so love 'helping' others, especially when it comes to romance, now that I have a romance of my own—which is certainly what your request for one bedroom seemed."

Alex sat and covered her friend's hand. "Do you, honestly, Bree? A romance? Hawk said so, and oh, I am so happy for you. I am happy, too, that you *want* to meddle, because I honestly need your help. Our family's happiness—Bea's, especially, but Claude's, Aunt Hildy's, even Uncle Giff's—is at stake."

"What about *your* happiness, and Hawksworth's?"

Unable to sit still, Alex rose to wander the room. Butter-cream damask covered the walls, with pale yellow, robin's egg blue, and soft fern green in the upholstered furniture. Beeswax and citrus freshened the air and calmed her spirit.

"My happiness must be Hawk's happiness." Alex turned to her friend. "But would it not be wonderful if they were one and the same?"

"Is that not your goal?"

Alex could only nod for the lump in her throat. She found herself having to swallow before speaking. "I . . . yes, but for that to happen . . . please, Bree, you must tell me how to seduce my husband."

Sabrina rose to go to her. "Good Lord, you are having Chesterfield's baby!"

Before Alex could answer, a hedgehog scurried across the drawing room.

Having had a great deal of practice, Alex caught the scampering critter and slipped it into her pocket. "Beatrix Jamieson, you little eavesdropper, show yourself this instant." Muffled giggles and scurrying feet on the opposite side of a second door, told them that Bea would not be showing herself anytime soon.

Shaking her head, Alex turned back to Sabrina. "Chesterfield's baby? What are you talking about?"

"Why else would it be imperative to seduce your husband, unless it was to make it appear as if he fathered another man's child—"

Alex burst into laughter and threw her arms about her friend. "Gad, Bree, I have missed you. Of course I am not carrying Judson's child. I am not carrying anyone's child. How the devil could I be?"

"Do not say that Hawk has not touched you since he returned."

Alex paled and looked away. "He has never touched me."

"What, not even on your wedding night?"

"We had no wedding night. I lied to everyone and went to the St. James Hotel alone. Bryce said good-bye at the church after we married. He left for Dover that night and shipped out the next day. Sometimes I think he still finds me an annoyance, like when we were children. Do you think he does? I think he must."

"I do not think so, not from the way he watched you during luncheon when you were not looking."

"I wish he would *touch* me when I am not looking, or even when I am. I have tried to spark his interest, but I cannot. No, perhaps that is not quite right. I have sparked it, but I cannot seem to fan it into flame. God, Bree, when it comes to being a wife, I do not know where to begin."

"In the bedroom?" Sabrina suggested.

Alex smiled. "I suspected as much."

"Oh, my." Sabrina sat again and patted the seat beside her. "This is going to be very delicate, Alex, but if you want my help, you will have to share some of the more intimate details of your marriage bed with me."

"There are no intimate details."

"What, nothing? Not even a tense moment when you thought he might devour you as if you were a cream pastry?"

"When he is asleep, he is very . . . . friendly."

"Excuse me?"

"He pulls me close and says my name."

"Better than saying another woman's name. And when he is awake?"

"There has been some interest, mostly when I am wearing one of the night rails Chesterfield purchased for our honey month."

"Does Hawk know who purchased them?"

"Good God, no!"

"Then perhaps you should tell him."

"Are you out of your mind? Hawk and Chesterfield detest each other. Hawk does not even want me to wear my bride-clothes. He would be furious; he would—"

"Tear them off you?"

Alex grinned. "Like the beast he proclaims himself."

"Exactly. It is called jealousy. Hawk might imagine Chesterfield seeing you in—or out—of one of those night rails and realize that if he does not claim you . . ."

"I . . . . may have ruined the jealousy ploy. I let Hawk believe I might love Chesterfield, and now I am afraid that he is thinking of letting me go."

"Unless he cannot keep from touching you himself . . . Once he gives in to that inclination, it will be too late to let you go."

Alex laid her head back against the cushions and closed her eyes. "Do you really think so?"

"We may have to dangle you before him for a time, however, and have you walk away when he gets close. What else has sparked his interest?"

"Sometimes the way he looks at me is very disconcerting. And there is that portion of him that . . . reacts. It happens often, but sometimes at the strangest moments."

"Like when?"

"There was the time he said he would make me listen if he had to tie me to the bed. But he stopped talking and got an arrested look on his face and . . . *that* . . . happened."

Bree squealed with delight. "Lord, I have the perfect situation in mind. But we must start small and work our way up to the ultimate seduction. Fetch a paper and pencil from my desk and let us make a list of the possible ways to catch his attention."

"I am not sure if seduction will work, you understand," Alex said opening the mahogany secretary in the corner and searching for pen and paper. "I am not even certain he is fond of me."

"Pish tosh. He is. Let me think about what you will need. . . ."

"Money could be a problem, Bree, but do not say anything. Hawk does not want anyone to know."

"Fine, you have your night rails. Do you have a lace corset in black?"

"Of course not."

"Then you may borrow mine, though Gideon might miss it. But we will have to take that chance. I can distract him with another. I will lend you some scented soaps and oils, some ribbons—black, too, I think. One for each of the bedposts in the bedchamber where I had Grandmama put you."

As Sabrina spoke, Alex began to make her list. Then she looked up. "Ribbons for the bedposts? Ah, Sabrina, will I be tying something to the bed?"

Eighteen

Hawk and Gideon followed a gangly red-haired young man into the beeswax-scented office of Mr. Warren Fitzwilliams, Esquire, nephew to Mr. Malcolm Fitzwilliams, solicitor to Hawk's father.

"Gentlemen," Fitzwilliams the younger said as he rose from a well-worn chestnut leather chair. "Won't you be seated and tell me what I can do for you on this splendid autumn afternoon?"

The young clerk interrupted to offer refreshments, and afterward, he backed, literally, from the room, shutting the door behind him with a soft click.

Hawk nodded to Fitzwilliams and turned to Gideon. "Gideon St. Goddard, Duke of Stanthorpe, may I present Mr. Warren Fitzwilliams, nephew to my father's solicitor?"

Gideon and the solicitor exchanged pleasantries until their attention shifted to the subject heavy on Hawk's mind. "Frankly, Mr. Fitzwilliams, I find myself mystified and vexed that my wife was not provided for, like all Wakefield widows before her, when it was erroneously reported that I died at Waterloo. How did this miscarriage of all that is proper come about?"

Fitzwilliams pulled at his beard for several long moments as he regarded Hawk with a furrowed brow, clearly at a loss. "I do not understand. Why *would* your wife be provided for?"

Hawk scowled. "Because I am, or was until my, er, mistaken demise, the fifth duke of Hawksworth. I should think that would be answer enough."

"Oh, but . . . Oh, my. Were neither you nor your wife present, then, for the reading of your father's will? I did not preside myself, you see, or even attend. My uncle handled everything, but I remember him apprising me, during his final days, of your father's peculiar codicil."

Gideon sat forward. "Are you saying there were stipulations to Hawksworth's inheriting, of which he knew nothing?"

Fitzwilliams regarded Hawk. "Let us allow your father's words to speak for themselves, shall we?" He rose and went to a cherrywood cabinet, opened a drawer, and shuffled through a series of yellowed and dog-eared records. "Ah, yes," he said. "Here." He withdrew a pouch of parchment, darkened with age and thick with documents.

Returning to his desk, he sat and sifted through the pouch until he came upon one sheet in particular, revealing less age than the rest, the writing upon it so spidery as to be barely legible. That sheet he slid across his desk toward Hawksworth.

Aware that he regarded the thing as if it might rise up and strike, Hawk turned to Gideon. "You first."

Gideon raised a brow. "Are you certain?" At Hawk's nod, Gideon took up the document, almost with trepidation, read it once, then again. Shaking his head, he handed it to Hawk and sat back to await his reaction.

Hawk barely finished before he barked a harsh laugh. "Disinherited, by God! The bounder died making certain I was willing to give my life for his bloody approval, handling me to the last, without honor enough to say that I would be stripped of all but my title if I chose Alexandra as my wife."

"I am sorry," Mr. Fitzwilliams said, calling for his clerk to bring in the brandy.

Hawk watched the clerk pour. "Managed from the grave, by God."

"And damned near into it." Gideon accepted a goblet, himself. "Insidiously controlled, if you ask me. Did your father never say that he took exception to Alexandra?"

Hawk took a sip, closed his eyes, opened them, and nodded. "Oh, Father said. He said daily. But he took exception to so many people, who paid attention?"

"But why?" Gideon persisted. "What did he have to gain by disinheriting you? Or, perhaps I should ask what he had to lose if you married Alex."

"Status for his name, his title, his heirs. That was all he cared about. Alexandra's family was not high enough on the social ladder to be considered worthy." Hawk shook his head. "If he had but known it, back when he first objected, Alex was no more than the pest who shadowed me. He might have put the thought in my head by forbidding it. Even when we married . . ." Hawk stopped. How he felt about his wife was immaterial, especially since he had come to care a great deal for her over the past year and a half. More than he had ever thought possible.

"As ruthlessly controlling as your father was— judging by what you told me and I have just heard," Gideon said, "the man must at least have expected you to attend the reading of his will. He could not have known that you would marry and sail to France before the week was out."

"If I did not marry Alex, I could not have gone to France. Every member of my family was the better for Alexandra's care, better even than if I had stayed. If not for her, I could not have gone to fight Boney, for I had too many responsibilities."

"It seems probable that your father had no more consideration for the members of your family than for you," Gideon said. "He must have known you could die going to war, but he was willing to send you any-way. I wonder if a place in history might not have been more important to him."

"How could my actions affect his place in his-tory?"

"Then power mattered, the power inherent in his ability to control you and the future, even after his death."

Hawk cursed. "It no longer matters, though, does it?"

"I wonder," Gideon responded, regarding him so keenly that Hawk set his goblet upon the desk and rose.

"You are in the same place, are you not?" Gideon rose also. "You would have married Alexandra, whether you knew about the will or not. What is the harm now?"

"My family's strained circumstances might have been eased in advance, had I known. I might never have gone, had I known." Hawk turned to the hovering solicitor. "The past cannot be changed. I understand that. But is there any way in which this codicil, or the results of it, can be overturned?"

"There are only two circumstances that might produce results, but none are guaranteed. We could attempt to prove your father of unsound mind at the time of the codicil. Or you might seek an annulment or a bill of divorcement."

Hawk stopped himself from laughing outright at the solicitor's words. *An annulment, by God.* If he let Alex go now, he might regain what little was left of his wealth. If he kept her, he would ruin her life, for she would certainly be destitute for the remainder of it. "My father was cunning," he said, "but never insane."

"If you do not mind my knowing, Hawksworth," Gideon said, turning to the solicitor, "were there any other disapproved brides named by the old duke?"

The solicitor turned to Hawk, seeking his permission to speak, and Hawk gave it with a nod.

"Only the bride you chose," Fitzwilliams told Hawk.

"Ah, that is rich." Hawk turned to leave.

"Oh, wait," Fitzwilliams said. "I have something for your wife, obtained during the transaction she contracted me to perform for her some time back. She was supposed to have picked this up on the day of her wed—er, ah . . ." The embarrassed solicitor coughed. "She never came for it. May I send it along with you now?"

"Of course," Hawk said, taking a sealed missive and placing it in the inside breast pocket of his frock coat. He shook the solicitor's hand, as did Gideon, and they made their way from the Leicester Square building.

At the top of the outside steps, Hawk placed his curly beaver atop his head and regarded Gideon. "Say nothing to Alex of this. I need time to think. I do not want her to know that my father disapproved of her. She will blame herself for the loss of my fortune."

"Nonsense. How could she blame anyone other than your father?" Gideon said. "But it might be kinder to let her assume that Baxter simply squandered your wealth, which he has about managed anyway."

"I would have done Alexandra a great service," Hawk said, pulling on his gloves as they made their way down the marble steps, "if I had not married her in the first place."

"When did you fall in love with her?" Gideon asked.

Hawk stopped. "In love with her?" Love? He knew nothing of love. "That is rather an impudent question, is it not?"

"We were comrades, we fought side by side. You died in my arms."

"And saw you weep when I did."

"Exactly." Gideon shook his head, denying Hawk's accusation of impudence. "I am sorry, but I shall retain the right of an insolent brother for the remainder of our days. You were fond of Alex at the time of your marriage. I know you were, but you did not care for her in the same way you do now. That is also very plain."

"What makes you think so?"

Gideon held up a hand. "Do not prevaricate. You never revealed any of it, but I believe I came to know you well enough to realize as much. In addition, today I saw the way you regard her."

"To use an old cliché," Hawk said, "I am my father's son and, therefore, incapable of love. To add another, I have learned that meeting Alexandra Huntington may have been the best luck I ever had. I simply did not know it until my life passed before me. That really happens, by the way."

Gideon shuddered. "You will forgive me if I am pleased to have no such experience."

"The problem is," Hawk said once they were settled inside Gideon's carriage, "I have been thinking for months that the best thing I can do for Alex is to let her go. But if I do, what is left of my wealth will revert to me. How is such a decision to be made?"

Gideon nodded wisely. "With the heart, my friend. With the heart."

"Look who is speaking of hearts: the man who once said he had none."

Gideon grinned. "Sabrina helped me grow one. And speaking of hearts, you offered tenancies and cottages to seventeen members of our old unit, when I distinctly heard you say you had, what, six cottages left unoccupied?"

"Right. Remind me to write to my manager today and have my carpenters begin building a dozen more."

"But half of the soldiers and families you took on are leaving for St. Albans today. You heard them. Without your inheritance, do you have the blunt to build?"

"No blunt, but Huntington is enormous. We have a huge home wood and trees aplenty, stone for fireplaces, sand for mortar. And I warned the men, while you were speaking to Stewart and Guilford, that they would be three families to a cottage for a while. Their response was that they would have roofs and hearths, both missing from their lives at the moment. I feel badly that I was forced to take only men with families, however."

"Those without have a better chance at the odd job anyway."

"True enough."

After making the rounds of their clubs, Hawk and Gideon returned to Gideon's late in the afternoon. They entered a favorite small sitting room only to find Alexandra, curled up on a chaise with Juliana sitting on her lap, so totally absorbed that she did not even hear them enter.

Alex spoke to the babe, softly questioning, while Juliana herself was so absorbed in Alex that she seemed to be trying to respond with little coos and gurgles, her hands waving excitedly in the air.

It was a sight, Hawk thought. A sight to warm the heart. It made him want . . . everything he could never hope to have.

"Do you see how Juliana loves Alex?" Beatrix asked, coming in behind the men with an infant blanket that she brought straight to Alex. "Can we have a baby, Uncle Bryce? Would you not like to have one? Alex, can you get *us* one?"

When Bea mentioned getting a babe of their own, Alex looked up, and her eyes found Hawk's, and when their gazes locked, something both deep and ephemeral seemed to pass between them.

It was uncomfortable and tight, Hawk thought, though he could not put a name to it.

Whatever it was, he wanted none of it—or more of it.

Nineteen

After dinner, Alex went upstairs to see what the duchess and Claudia had purchased in one afternoon of dedicated and relentless shopping. But Hawk had too much on his plate to linger, so he excused himself and went up to their sitting room in search of a glass of brandy and a modicum of peace.

Just thinking about his father's will enraged him. He untied his cravat and tossed it. His frock coat followed as he dropped, exhausted, into a chair.

Quick upon the heels of sitting, he saw the solicitor's missive for Alex riding a whoosh of air toward the blazing hearth. With an oath, Hawk shot to his feet to rescue the charring note. He had forgotten the thing existed, never mind giving it to Alex.

Hawk plunged his hand into the flames, grabbed it by its sizzling sealing wax, and jerked his hand away, tearing it open as he did. "Blast and damnation!"

Hawk forgot his burned finger as he found himself staring at a paid receipt for four thousand, six hundred and seventy-five pounds sterling. A note was added by Fitzwilliams to the bottom: *"All debts gathered and paid. All vouchers destroyed."*

What in the world had Alex to do with such a large debt? Vouchers? Gambling vouchers?

Had she taken to gambling? To support the family?

Nonsense. Even if she had gambled and lost, she did not have the funds to repay so high an amount. Devil it, what manner of predicament had she got herself into?

Her laughter far down the hall made Hawk scramble to hide the evidence of his knowledge. He looked about and secreted the paid receipt in his portmanteau, stuffing that into the back of the closet. Whatever trouble his wife had got herself into, he needed to understand to help.

Poor, Alex, he thought. What had he driven her to, marrying her and leaving her destitute? And to whom did she owe the great sum she had used to pay what seemed for all the world like a gambling debt?

Alex stopped laughing before she entered her room. Sabrina was right; she needed to concentrate. If Sabrina's oil was to produce the desired effect, Alex must now appear uncomfortable and in need of her husband's aid.

Her hesitation to carry out a set of instructions that seemed patently dishonest fled in the face of Hawk's appearance—handsome, deeply furrowed brow, open-necked shirt, skin-tight inexpressibles, and a goblet of brandy cupped within his long, tapered fingers.

A lady-killer. A rogue. And all hers—if she managed to seduce him.

Alex stepped forward and winced. "Oh. Ouch."

"Hawk reached for her arm with his free hand and set down his glass. "Alex? What is wrong? Are you hurt?"

"I seem to have twisted my back, somehow, when I bent to place Juliana in her crib."

Immediately, her husband's attention was focused entirely on her, just as Sabrina said it would be. Alex did not even need to ask him to rub her back, for he began all on his own. Neither did she have to fake her sigh of pleasure, for that escaped of its own volition.

"Oh, that does feel good," she said, leaning against him and wincing again, lest he think he could stop too soon.

"What can I do for you?" her concerned husband asked. "Would you like me to help you undress?"

Would she like him to ravish her? Yes to both. "Bree gave me an oily salve that she said would ease the spasm in my muscles. Do you think you could rub it on for me?"

Hawk took a step back at the request and Alex wondered if he realized that he did. "Of course," he said.

"I will need your help to undress, first, though. Even raising my arms increases the pain."

Hawk swallowed as he nodded and walked her to their bed, where she remained standing, hoping he would take over in much the same way he had done that night at the hotel.

He did, but this time when he unbuttoned her dress, she made certain to move in such a way that his hand must skim her skin, but only once or twice, not to be obvious. When Hawk reached for her garters, Alex tugged her skirt upward to allow him better access and a better view of her legs.

By the time she bade him remove her shift as well as her stays, perspiration beaded his poor, beleaguered brow. "I do not wish to get oil on the fine lawn fabric," she said. "We cannot afford to replace it; neither can we allow my undergarments to ruin my gowns."

"Of course," he said, though Alex was disappointed that he somehow managed to cover her within moments of removing the shift.

No matter. The scented oil would do its trick, Bree had promised. She said she knew from experience that the oil could work magic.

The jar that contained the waxy oil was made of a pale milky-green glass. And as Alex lay on her belly, naked beneath the covers, and watched Hawksworth pick up the jar and examine it as if it might bite, she saw that his big, capable hands were trembling.

She hid her smile with a painful sigh, all the while watching, until he finally stopped hesitating and came to stand beside the bed.

"You might wish to remove your shirt," Alex suggested, "so the cuffs do not get ruined. Getting into bed beside me might help as well. Kneading as you rub the oil into the muscles will ease the spasm, Bree said, and you will certainly not be able to soothe my aches from up there."

An understatement.

Hawk retained his shirt but rolled up his sleeves, wondering what horrible sin he might have committed in his lifetime to bring him to this abysmal pass. He had grown erect from undressing her, never mind rubbing her silken skin with oil. Never mind doing so in bed.

Still, he hurt because she did, so he removed his shoes and climbed into their bed beside her. Uncovering the jar, the scent that rose from the thick, waxen oil was like to do him in for good and all.

Spice, flowers . . . seduction.

Sex, pure and unadulterated. Raw. Lusty. Potent.

"This does not smell like medicine." Hawk cursed the tremble in his voice and the tightening in his groin. "Are you certain this is supposed to ease your pain?"

"From what I have observed, it promises to accomplish everything Sabrina said it would. I hope she is right, for the wait is exceeding torturous."

At this moment Hawk well understood torture.

Alex squeaked when he placed perhaps a little too much of the "salve" on her back. "I did not expect it would be cold," she said.

"It will warm against your skin," Hawk said. God knew he would. "Are you certain you do not have a fever?"

"I think I might. The room seems very warm, of a sudden. Lower the blanket, will you, so I can cool down and you can reach my lower back, which I believe is nearest the location of my problem."

The base of her spine was a most beautifully curvaceous and inviting location. Hawk wanted to place his lips upon the very spot, but he denied himself and turned to his wife.

He saw her in profile: the curve of her cheek, her firmly set lips, and the globe of one breast pressed against the mattress.

Would that she were pressed against him, anywhere.

Beneath his hand, her skin felt like satin, the more so for the oil easing his way.

"Mmm," she said. "I like."

Then, after a few moments. "Perhaps you could use both hands."

Inside Hawk, heat flared like a pitch torch as he placed the jar on the bedside table and extracted more of the oily cure.

"Oh, that is good," his wife said on a throaty sigh. "Yes. Right there. Oh. Mmm. Just a bit lower."

If Hawk were not already afire, he might self-combust.

"Harder," she said with a satisfied moan. "To the left. Oh, God, yes."

She sighed; she purred; she moaned. "Ahh. Yes. Mmm, more. All the way up . . . yes . . . all the way down. Again, up and down."

Hawk was like to explode. If he had ever entertained the foolish notion that he could not carry out his husbandly duties, his doubts had been set to rest.

As a matter of fact, any more of this and he would explode without sheathing himself in Alexandra's tight, silken . . . *Think of something else.* "Did you enjoy your visit with Bree?"

"Hmm?"

Hawk frowned. Was *she* not the least bit tortured? "Am I putting you to sleep? How is your back?"

"Everything feels good, as long as you are rubbing."

"I know exactly what you mean."

"Hmm?"

"I would feel the same, if you were tending me."

"Nice. But Hawk?"

"Yes, love?"

"My upper back, toward the right and somewhat beneath my arm . . . I feel a slightish . . . twinge there as well. Could you rub me there?"

Hawk threw his head back and silently cursed all twinges to perdition. "Of course." If she did not desist soon, he would show her how good a rubbing could feel.

Hawk ran his soothing, oiled touch from her shoulder to the side of her breast, almost to its tip, but not quite, garnering such a wondrous sigh of pleasure from his wife that he could almost imagine it as sexual. Not to mention what stroking her was doing to him. Her breast, he knew, would fit his cupping hand extraordinarily well.

"Alex? Would you like me to . . . ease you anywhere else?"

"Mmm-hmm." She purred like a sleepy cat.

Was that a yes? "What?"

She opened her eyes. "What?"

"You want me to rub you where?"

"On my back, as I said."

"I thought I heard you say you wanted me to rub oil on you somewhere else."

"Do you think it would help?"

"Lord, yes."

"All right. Go ahead."

Hawk sighed, feeling his frustration rise up with a need to throttle, never mind stroke. "Go ahead and rub . . . where?"

"Wherever you wish."

Hawk damned near exploded. Then he stopped, because . . .

"Alex?"

"Mmmmm . . . ?"

"Do you want me to stroke your other breast—er, shoulder? Would you like to lie on your back?"

But nothing could be heard save the ticking of the mantel clock. His wife had fallen asleep, naked, one oiled breast riding his knee, his erection somehow nestled against the small of her back, just below her tiny waist and just above her beckoning bottom.

Hawk cursed, sighed, and blew out the candle before sliding perilously down in the bed, sure he would embarrass himself in the process, though he managed not to. Then he tortured himself the more by wrapping his arms around his slick and scented bride, allowing his manhood to pulse incessantly against her as his hand cupped her beckoning bottom.

And before long, Hawk's mind was so enmeshed in the puzzle of her charred receipt that his body calmed, quite of its own accord.

The following night, to protect his sanity, Hawk "misplaced" the jar of oil, not certain which of them was more disappointed, him or his wife.

Alex appeared so downhearted that he damned

near unearthed the bloody thing from the drawer where he had hidden it, just to see her smile, never mind the splendid self-torture.

But sanity reigned, thank the heavens.

Alex curled up in the bed with a book and fell almost immediately to sleep.

Well, Hawk thought, there was still the puzzle of that paid receipt to solve—not the first conundrum concerning Alex since his return from Belgium.

He rose and went to his dressing room, and just as he was about to don his dressing gown, Alex began to whimper as if she were frightened.

Hawk ran to the bed where she was thrashing and weeping and calling his name, so he climbed in beside her to take her into his arms and calm her.

She relaxed instantly, though she seemed to be trying to climb inside him, if that were possible.

That was when Hawk realized that he was stark naked and in bed with his stark naked wife—when had that happened? He could have sworn that Alex was wearing something when he went into his dressing room.

Devil take it, she was coiled about him like the roots of a tree, and heaven above, did he love it! Hawk ordered his excited body to calm, even as perspiration formed upon his brow.

Even without perfumed oil, he knew this was going to be another long, hard night.

Alexandra smiled in her sleep.

Twenty

Two nights later, as they were preparing to attend a ball—their first—at the viscountess De Monteneiro's villa in Kensington, Alex came to his dressing room wearing the most amazing black corset Hawk had ever beheld. That, and a pair of white silk stockings and black high-heeled slippers.

Her breasts, pushed upward and outward by the man-straightening garment, looked as if they might spring, literally, free at any moment.

"One of my garters is twisted," she said, studying his open shirt, while Hawk hoped that his scars did not show.

"It is one of the garters in the back," Alex said, "and I cannot seem to fix or fasten it." She turned her back on him then and bent over to brace herself on a chair, presumably to give him better access to her wayward garter, though she afforded him a most pleasant view of her delicious bottom as well.

Did she realize it? Hawk was beginning to wonder.

Probably not. That would simply be too perfect a situation to be possible.

Nevertheless, Hawk was appalled but enticed, and

more interested than he should be in every satin inch of exposed skin and every scrap of black lace.

Unable to stoop so low, literally, he placed a chair behind her and sat down.

No doubt about it, her garter was twisted beyond anything he had ever seen—not that he had seen that many up close. So close, he wanted to kiss the inner silk of her thigh. So close, he skimmed a finger, just there, and heard her intake of breath when he did, which was nothing to his own reaction.

"I like that," she said.

Did she mean she liked him helping with her garter, or she liked his more intimate touch?

No matter, for when he finished, she toppled gently backward onto his lap. Resting her head against his shoulder, she sighed. "This is nice."

But she started to slip, and he grasped her to keep her from falling and ended up cupping her warm center, neither of them daring to breathe.

They remained that way until Hawk realized Alex was throbbing beneath his hand, as she must feel him against her bottom.

When he added pressure to his cupping palm, her sigh was real, her regretful thanks something of a mystery as she rose, straightened, and departed without looking back. "I will be ready in just a few minutes," she said.

Hawk was hard as a pikestaff. "Well I am ready now!" he shouted. Let her come back and question that statement, as she had once questioned the evidence of his physical reaction to her.

I will not be fit to be seen in company for at least ten minutes, he groused to himself.

Damn. She was asking for it.

Was she? Asking? And did she even understand for what she asked? Or know she was doing it?

Impossible.

Half an hour later, to mark Claudia's first ball ever, they stopped to see how she was doing in her preparations and found her as excited as a child at Christmas. After kissing her cheek and wishing her well, they left her to finish and went downstairs.

The duchess had invited Gideon and Sabrina, Reed Gilbride, and the old duke of Hazelthorpe to make up numbers at the dinner she was giving before they left for the ball.

As they all waited for Claudia to come down before going in to dinner, Hawk stepped away to greet Hazelthorpe, and Reed approached Alex.

"C.S.M. Gilbride, how good it is to see you again."

"Please, you must call me Reed."

"Thank you, Reed. As titles go, both *Squadron Corporal Major* and *C.S.M.* are entirely too long."

"Agreed. You are looking lovely and bright this evening. Not at all pale and peaked, as you were the first time I saw you."

"How ungallant of you to say so." Having practiced social coquetry earlier that day with Claudia, Alex tapped his hand with her fan.

Reed laughed. "I am not a gallant," the military man said, "which you will soon realize. But I do know a beautiful lady when I see one. A true lady."

"Do me the honor of treating me as a friend, rather

than a 'lady,' please, for I will never really be one of those."

Reed nodded. "My pleasure."

"Thank you. As a friend, may I ask what life was like during the war? Hawk has changed to a great degree, and I have a need to . . . I do not know—help him, or simply be his friend and confidante, perhaps."

"A wife who is a friend and a confidante." Reed nodded. "A novel thought. Oh, do not frown. I am not making sport." He took her arm to walk her toward the far end of the spacious salon. "I will tell you about Hawk, if you promise not to divulge whence you received your information, else he will have my head."

"We have a bargain."

"You must know that his father . . . taunted him, shall we say, into joining the Guards. You can imagine, then, that Hawk did not know what he was getting himself into."

Alex nodded. "I feared as much."

"When the fighting began, Hawk realized immediately that he was out of his depth."

Alex felt sick, but she firmed her spine, and Reed was gentleman enough not to mention her weak moment. "Please continue," she said.

He nodded. "Hawk rose to the occasion and distinguished himself more times than anyone realizes. I do not know if Gideon is even aware of this, but your husband is quite the hero. The volley that nearly killed him was originally aimed at Stanthorpe. I saw it happen, from too far away—and with too many of Boney's troops at hand—to make a difference. But

Hawksworth was there, and he covered Gideon's back as the enemy struck, and fought their attack himself."

Sabrina gasped. Until that moment, they had not realized she was approaching.

Gideon heard, saw her stricken look, and came to her.

Hawksworth was right behind him. "What happened?"

By then, Sabrina had stepped into her husband's embrace, but she regarded Hawk. "You saved Gideon's life?" She turned back to her husband. "Did you realize, Gideon? Reed saw Hawksworth step between you and the Frenchman who felled him; otherwise, you might have been as badly hurt as he was in your stead. Or killed." Sabrina's eyes filled and she began to kiss her husband as if she would not stop.

In his turn, Gideon pulled her tight into his arms and kissed her soundly. As this was not an embrace meant for public exhibition, the rest of the company made their way back across the room.

"Perhaps we should go on to the ball without them?" Reed suggested.

"Nonsense," the duchess said, lacking her usual aplomb, for she looked as shaken by the realization of nearly having lost her grandson as Gideon and Sabrina were.

Alex was upset too, and Hawk must have noticed, because he put his arm around her waist and turned them away from the room at large. She rested her head on his shoulder. "You never said anything," she whispered.

"What was there to say?" Hawk shrugged away her

words, though she liked the way he was looking at her, as if he were seeing her for perhaps the first time.

From behind them, Reed cleared his throat. "Ah, perhaps I had better go on to the ball alone?"

Hawk tore his gaze from her—that was the only way to describe it—and regarded Reed. "We will all go. Claude would be crushed if we did not. If she ever comes down. How long can it take one girl to don one gown?" he asked, easing the tension.

Claudia did finally come down, but during dinner Sabrina and Gideon announced their decision not to attend the ball, after all. It had been clear to everyone, and a bit uncomfortable, to see how in love they were, how badly they wanted to be alone, after learning how close Gideon had come to being wounded—or lost—at Waterloo.

During dinner, Gideon, Sabrina, and the duchess in turn thanked Hawk for saving not only Gideon but all of them, ultimately, with his battlefield heroism. Alex could see that the praise made Hawk uncomfortable, and by the time they were ready to leave, he was a bit snappish.

Wraps were donned and carriages called for in a rather brisk manner. There was nothing left to say to Gideon and Sabrina, after all, except good-bye.

Since two of the duchess's carriages had been brought around, and because Hawk felt a sudden and inexplicable need to be alone with his wife, he suggested that Claudia, Reed, the duchess, and Hazelthorpe travel in one coach, and he and Alex would take the other. Claudia, in particular embraced the idea, for Reed was a handsome rogue, and being escorted to the ball on his arm would bring a new-comer like her a deal of admiring attention.

When the carriage moved off, Hawk crossed to sit beside Alex, wanting her near. He took her hand, raised it to his lips, and wished he were worthy of her.

He also wished that he had as much faith in the institution of marriage as Gideon seemed to have.

"They are very much in love, are they not?" Alex said, gazing off into some romantic distance, likely thinking of Chesterfield. "I envy them."

"Oddly, I do, too, though I am not certain why." He and Alex had been friends forever, Hawk thought. If she did not love elsewhere, she would be the best wife for him. He liked and respected her, admired her. After everything, he cherished her. If she were will-ing, he would happily take her to his bed every night for the rest of their days and be faithful unto death.

If they were not already doomed to parting, it seemed to him, that love—if the myth existed—might enrich what they already shared. But no matter how hard he tried, Hawk could not wrap his mind around the disappointing and insubstantial concept. "Do you think it exists, really?"

"Do I think what exists?"

"Love. My parents preached it until my mother's early death, but I do not think they practiced it, as happens in every ton marriage I ever saw, until Gideon and Bree's."

"I think love does exist. My father said it did. When he was last ill, he said that he had missed my mother for the entire sixteen years of my life, and though he was sorry to be leaving me, he was happy to be going to her."

"Love beyond life?" Hawk said. "Does that not seem improbable?"

"Gideon and Sabrina appear to have such a love."

"If I had not seen those two tonight, I would say you are wrong, but I begin to believe it. Between them, the elusive emotion seems very much alive and thriving."

"With their children, the five of them epitomize what I have always supposed a family should—unity, caring, the sharing of even the smallest joys and sorrows." Alex blushed and gazed out the window. "They are fortunate."

"Yes." Hawk yearned for something like that himself: the closeness of mind and spirit that Gideon and Sabrina shared. Oh, he had always had women, but never someone so much his own that she would breathe for him if she could.

As Sabrina seemed willing to do for Gideon.

As Alex had always seemed willing to do for him.

Hawk regarded Alex anew then, as though . . .

He shied away from the thought, for the staggering power of Gideon and Sabrina's love alarmed him, as did the corresponding responsibility, which only made him feel less worthy and more determined to let Alex go.

Yet despite that, he yearned to keep her hand in his and to walk beside her, however halting his steps, as long as fate—and Alexandra Wakefield herself—would allow.

Beyond life . . . Imagine.

As if sensing his mood, Alex leaned her head against his shoulder and looked up at him, and Hawk could do nothing but open his lips over hers.

He was going to unearth that jar of oil tonight and offer to rub her back for her, just so he could remove that black lace corset himself.

The viscountess De Monteneiro's Kensington villa was everything Alexandra had supposed a villa must represent: a fortune in marble and gold, art and artifice, glitter and glut. Gaudy. Uncomfortable. Hot. Crowded.

"A veritable crush. A sweeping success," the raven-haired husband-hunting viscountess prattled effusively. Immediately they entered, she set her sights on Hawk, but when she realized he was taken, she turned her narrowed kohl-lined eyes upon the man in the scarlet tunic.

Reed winked at Alex, bowed over Claudia's hand, made an irreverent comment about the power of a uniform, and gallantly escorted the viscountess De Monteneiro into the middle of a verdant Italian marble dance floor for the most scandalous of dances, the waltz.

Hawk's injured leg would not allow him to participate in that dance, but Alex was just as happy to lend him her arm as they strolled around the perimeter of the ballroom greeting old friends and meeting new. Some of their acquaintances had already learned that Hawk survived, but were seeing him now for the first time since he went to war. Others, who had not known, were astounded and excited.

One matron fainted upon sight of him.

"It is my scars," Hawk whispered, standing back as others attempted to bring her around.

"It is your ghost," Alex responded in kind.

His friends all seemed to hold him in high regard, Alex noted, though the ones she had long ago over-heard discussing "beauty and his beast" acted rude and knowing.

"I dislike that bunch," Alex said as they moved away.

"I always knew you had excellent taste."

She stopped. "But they are your friends, are they not?"

"Not," Hawk denied with a firm shake of the head. "They are acquaintances to whom I had rather not give the time of day. Hangers on, the lot of them. They talk an impressive talk sometimes, but drivel slides off their tongues too much of the remaining time."

Twenty-one

Reed Gilbride bowed before Alex. "Alexandra, may I have the honor of this dance?"

At her husband's urging, Alex allowed his fellow rogue to lead her onto the dance floor.

"You are preoccupied," he said after a few silent minutes.

Alex nodded. "Guilty. I apologize."

"Care to tell me about it?"

"It appears as if I might have made a judgment based on flawed information."

"A common enough occurrence, and mostly harmless. Anything I can do to help?"

"Tell me more of Belgium."

"Hawk's time there, you mean? You are in love with your husband, I think. Is that not frowned upon in this society?"

"You force me to say that you are impertinent and I must deny you an answer."

"You must, because you do not want your avowal repeated, I think. I wonder why?"

"Tell me about the family who nursed him back to health? Did you ever meet them? What were they

like? Did they live in a thatched hut or a brick
manor?"

"I never went to their home, but I did meet the pa-
triarch and the boy, in fact, on the day they brought
Hawk to the ship to sail home. I had a commission to
dispatch for Wellington here in England, and we traveled home together, Hawk and I."

"When was that?"

"About eleven months ago."

Hawk had been back much longer than anyone
knew, Alex realized then, but he had not contacted
Gideon and Sabrina right away, either. The pain
around Alex's heart eased somewhat, for after speaking to Sabrina, she now understood that he had taken
the time he needed. "What did *you* think of the people who saved Hawk's life?"

"They were generous to house and nurse a man
they did not know. The family was poor—that was
apparent—though not so poor when Hawk left as
when they took him in."

"What do you mean?"

"As young Gaston accompanied Hawk on his litter,
aboard ship, the old man told me that Hawk had
given them his gold buttons, his jewelry, everything
he owned of value, including the greater portion of
his military pay. The old codger tried to give it all
back to me, so I could return it to Hawk. But I
thought if he wanted them to have his thanks, then he
would not take the gifts back, and I convinced the
Belgian to keep it. Did I do wrong, Alex?"

"No. Oh, no. I would have given them anything for
what they did," she said, aware that the only jewelry

Hawk had taken were his signet ring and his wedding band. "You have answered a question that has been plaguing me, though. I will purchase him a new signet ring for Christmas, perhaps. Do you remember if it was the set with rubies, or emeralds? I cannot seem to recall."

"Hawk never wore a ring, that I noticed, in the months we fought together. I was surprised he had any to give them."

And for Alex, that said everything. His wedding band had received no different a treatment from his signet ring.

When Reed returned Alex to her husband's side, however, the sight that met them made Alex feel as if the past five years had never happened, that they were back at the St. Albans Assembly rooms, and that she was a fool to love the Rogue of Devil's Dyke.

Women buzzed around Hawk like bees in a summer garden. Except that he looked as if he did not enjoy his popularity as much as he used to, which improved her mood somewhat. Still, she could not help disliking the beauties in his entourage for their lash-batting and simpering.

"You might have discouraged them," she told Hawk in the carriage on the way home.

"Discouraged who?" he said, taking her hand once more and cupping it upon his thigh, his atop hers, as if to keep it there. This time he had not even bothered to sit across from her, but beside her from the first.

"The women who were flirting with you."

"Flirting? Are you daft? With this face?"

"Are you blind? They were all about you."

"Reed or Claudia probably mentioned my catching the volley meant for Gideon, though I wish they had not. But there could have been no other reason, believe me, except a morbid curiosity for grisly details." Hawk's eyes lit with wisdom. "Are you jealous, Alexandra?"

Alex sighed with disgust for overplaying her hand. "Of course not."

Hawk shrugged philosophically. "I rather thought not."

"You seem to think it impossible that a woman would find you attractive."

"Alex, I am a fright. Of course it is impossible."

"I will grant you that, as opposed to your former perfectly chiseled countenance, your scars give your perfection more of a hard edge, but you . . ."

Alex thought Hawk would growl or laugh, he looked so incredulous. "There is nothing perfect about this face."

"Perhaps not, but your appearance is striking, nonetheless. I am extremely sorry to say that your scars give you an aura of danger that will draw women like moths to a flame."

"The devil, you say."

Hawk and Gideon had an appointment at Gentleman Jackson's the following day. Gideon suspected that a boxer's footwork might strengthen Hawk's leg, and Hawk thought anything worth trying.

"Listen, Hawk," Gideon said before they stepped from the carriage onto the pavement before the boxing salon. "When Bree and I use that aromatic oil, I find that only sandalwood soap removes the telltale scent of its perfume. You might take a few jests this morning for that air of the boudoir about you."

Hawk regarded his friend quizzically. "What aromatic oil?"

"The one you and Alex obviously borrowed last night. I would know that scent anywhere. It makes me randy as hell."

"Well, stay the devil away from me."

"Do not be cross. What games a man plays with his wife in the bedchamber are his business."

"Obviously not, for you know more about it than I do. Tell me, are there any healing properties to this aromatic oil?"

Sabrina introduced Alexandra to the most amazing and decadent wonder in all England, a huge bathing tub wherein one or two people could immerse themselves to their chins.

Gideon had recently had them specially made in Edinburgh for all of his houses, including his grandmother's. Sabrina said that some of her fondest memories had been created since theirs had been delivered.

Alex was afraid that, by the time her seduction was complete, she would not be able to look Sabrina's husband in the eye again.

She intended to use the tub that night and had come up to bed first, but she did not order it filled until she heard Gideon's carriage depart. He and

Hawk had been closeted together all evening discussing estate management and horse-breeding.

The last kettle of hot water was just being poured when Hawksworth entered his dressing room. "Here you are," she said. "I thought that perhaps you would like a nice, hot bath before retiring tonight. It is all ready."

Alex left her husband to keep his dignity and undress in peace while she, in her own dressing room, undressed and slipped into a peach silk dressing gown.

When she heard sounds to indicate that Hawk was settling into the tub, she waited another few minutes before returning.

Could his eyes have got any bigger, Alex wondered, than when he beheld her in the silk wrap that outlined her every curve?

"God's teeth, you are breathtaking!" Hawk seemed less appalled, for once, than fascinated, which Alexandra thought a very hopeful sign, indeed.

"Thank you. Now close your eyes."

"Why on earth would I do that?"

"So I may get in with you."

"Why would you do that?"

"I do believe you are stuttering, Hawksworth. We seem to have misplaced the oil for my back again, remember? And the hot water will ease my pain. Now close your eyes or I shall be forced to drop my wrap and offend your sensibilities."

Alex suspected from that sound deep in his throat that Hawk fought a chuckle as he closed his eyes. Then she waited one tantalizing moment, to see if he would peek, before lowering herself into the heated bliss.

Hawk sprang to vibrant and willing life as his outrageous and seductive wife tangled her naked legs with his in the stroking water.

That was when he began to believe that across the tub from him sat a seductress—formidable, determined, no matter how innocent she looked with her cinnamon hair piled atop her head, loose wisps framing her face. A siren, with the crests of her breasts skimming the top of the water. A woman. His woman.

What would she do if he claimed her now? Which he was beginning to believe she wanted. Of course, she would wonder why he had not as yet made her his wife in every way. Except that, he would have thought, if she loved another, she would be relieved, not anxious for a consummation.

Why the aromatic oil disguised as a healing salve?

Where *did* he stand with her?

Perhaps it was time to find out.

"This is heaven," Alex said, sighing and purring, her head resting against the edge of the tub, her eyes closed, a feline smile playing about her full and luscious lips.

"Much like when we were children," Hawk said, "when we swam after digging in the mud for treasure, except that the sky is not blue above us and the water is a vast deal warmer."

Alex opened her eyes and grinned—God's teeth, hers was a lethal smile. "And we cannot catch frogs or lie in the sun to dry," she said.

"How does your back feel?"

"The warm water does soothe it."

"Come, turn around and I will soothe it the more."

As he suspected, Alex was ready, with barely a surprised blink, to try anything. Hawk spread his legs and settled her between them, her facing away from him.

Kneading her torso beneath the warm water became an exercise in pure sensual pleasure, and the sounds and sighs coming from his wife only served to heighten the experience.

When Hawk brought his arms around and began to stroke her midriff, Alex relaxed against him. When he cupped her breasts, she stiffened for a moment, likely in shock, then she arched to fill his palms. But when he skimmed his hands lower, she almost stopped breathing.

He kneaded lower and lower . . . until he found her core, and she squeaked and reared back, encountered his erection, and surged forward, as if she planned all along to reclaim her original place across from him. "There," she said. "That feels better."

Hawk coughed to hide a bubble of laughter, surprised that mirth had claimed him so wholly. "How did you know this tub existed?" he asked, to alleviate her obvious chagrin. "This is not the one in which I bathed previous."

"Is it not splendid? Sabrina said that the servants will always bring the small slipper bath unless you ask specifically for this large one."

Alex must feel more adventuresome at a distance, Hawk thought, for she was calling his bluff and stroking his inner thigh with her foot. He closed his eyes then and suspended his own breathing, for she was definitely working her way higher and higher, until . . .

Hawk wanted to kill Sabrina for this fantastical notion she had put in his wife's scheming head. He could not even rise and leave the bloody tub, because if he did, then the most horrible of his scars would be visible, not to mention the size of his . . .

The moan of pleasure he heard must be his own, Hawk realized, which shocked him to the point that he opened his eyes—and met Alexandra's very surprised ones. "What did I do?" she asked. "Did you like it? Or hate it?"

"Liked it," he said. "But do not expect me to run, as you just did."

"Did you feel as I did, before I ran?"

"I think it highly possible."

"But you will let me do as I wish?"

Hawk nodded, trepidation skittering along his nerves. "No more running for me," he said, reminding himself as well as her. "Do what you will. I am staying where I am."

He expected she would rise on the instant, like a nymph from the sea, and make a startling exit from the tub. As a matter of fact, he looked forward to the sight.

But though she did rise like a pearl-glistening sea nymph, she did not leave the tub but stood, perfect in every way. Then she took two steps in his direction and looked down on him, smiling, full and deadly, and lowered herself to straddle him, luscious breasts to hairy chest, and pulsing core to rod of steel.

All Hawk's fight left him as he surged to heartier life. He could do nothing but gape, and throb, and devour her mouth when she set her lips to his.

He kissed his brazen wife with the appetite of a man starved for nothing resembling food. He skimmed her every curve and hollow in the same way she grazed every inch of him.

Every throbbing inch.

When she closed her talented hand around him, her instincts were flawless.

A year of celibacy and a week of hard torture . . . and Hawk lost control on the instant.

"Bloody hell!"

"Good Lord, did I break it?"

Twenty-two

Baxter Wakefield came back to town on the thirteenth of November, and the first thing he did was show himself at Basingstoke House to pay his respects to his no-longer-deceased cousin "Bry."

Hawk would rather the blighter had stayed in America as enter polite society, but what could he do but allow his cousin to be admitted to the library, at least, wherein the duchess kindly allowed them some privacy.

"Dissipation looks to sit heavy on your shoulders, Cousin," Hawk observed. "Or should I say that it sits dark beneath your eyes and 'heavy' upon your person? Hard work depleting a fortune, is it not?" Hawk raised the decanter his way. "Brandy?"

Baxter laughed. "I may not have gotten the title, Bry, but the money's a good sight more fun."

"I daresay." Hawk knew he could not ask his cousin to keep the conditions of his father's codicil to himself, for if Baxter even suspected that Hawk wanted it kept from Alex, there would surely be a price for his silence. A price Hawk could not afford to pay—any more than he could afford not to.

"What do you want?" Hawk asked.

The blackguard fingered a Bristol Glass brandy decanter and a French silver salver before going on to examine the Rubens and the Canaletto on the wall. "Believe it or not, I want to make peace with my family," he said, though Hawk noticed that he did not say it while looking him full in the eye.

Hawk frowned. "Out of money already, are we?"

"You are, and though I have spent more than you will see in your lifetime, I am still a rich man."

Bully for you, Hawk thought as he considered the ramifications of one good, hard right to the solar plexus.

Baxter grinned as if he could read Hawk's thoughts. "Since I am ready to settle down, however, I yearn to have my family about me."

"You yearn for their respectability to net you a rich bride."

The library door opened. "Oh, I am sorry. I did not know you had a guest." Alex made to back out, and Hawk was grateful.

"No, wait," Baxter said. "Present me, Cousin, to this luscious wench."

Alex stiffened.

Hawk set his goblet firmly down, lest he pour the contents over his cousin's bumble head. "Alex, allow me to present my scapegrace cousin, Baxter Wakefield. Baxter, my wife, Alexandra, the woman you tossed out when you inherited."

Baxter grinned and took her hand. "If only I had known, we might have come to a . . . satisfactory arrangement."

Hawk stepped forward.

Alex scowled and retrieved her hand. "Your Grace."

"What?" Baxter said with a laugh. "'Twas not me who got the title. That's all Hawk's and welcome to it. Much good it'll do either of you without the blunt to make it sparkle."

Alex looked from Hawk to his cousin and back. "Hawksworth?"

Already Hawk wanted to flatten his cousin, and he hated when Alex used his full title. It could only mean he was in trouble.

Baxter laughed at the obvious awkwardness of the moment and made his whistling way to the door. "Invite me to dinner," he said, "and I will leave you to settle your differences in peace."

"Not to dinner," Hawk said. "Other plans. But to the Winkley ball tomorrow evening. You will accompany us?"

Baxter bowed. "My pleasure."

When the door clicked behind him, Alexandra rounded on Hawk. "What was that about?"

"It was better than having to eat with him."

She stamped her foot, a measure of her frustration, for she never had done it, even as a child. "What did he mean by saying that you got the title?"

"Father played me dirty, Alex. The title has always been mine, but Baxter got the money, the houses, everything else."

"How long have you known?"

Hawk picked up his brandy and stepped toward a shelf of gold-leafed books, as if he might examine them at length, but he took a sip of his drink instead, and when he finished, he turned to her. "Since we got to town. The day Gideon and I went to do 'whatever it is that gentlemen do of an afternoon,' we saw the solicitor."

"And you did not tell me?"

"Fitzwilliams is looking into ways to break the will. I did not say anything, because I had hoped I would not have to give you the bad news about our poverty." Half-truths again. How he hated the need for them. Damn his father.

"Poverty is nothing new to me."

Hawk stepped up to her and grazed her cheek. "I have proved to be a sorry provider, have I not?"

"No, it is not that. It is simply . . ." She sighed. "I thought husbands and wives were supposed to share the good and the bad. Instead, you and I seem to do nothing but keep secrets."

"What? Are you keeping secrets from me as well?"

Alex examined his face, his eyes. "Keeping secrets, plural? *As well,* meaning: in the same way that you are keeping them from me? Do you have more?"

"I asked you first."

"You asked me nothing."

"How does your back feel?"

"There is a good question. Why?" Alex reached for his cravat. "Did you find the oil?"

"I did."

She nodded as if everything was settled, and it was, in a way. They had silently agreed to hold their secrets, or at least the discussion of them, for the nonce, while they compromised to play this dangerous teasing game they both seemed to enjoy.

Perhaps it was a start, Hawk thought, his body tightening in anticipation of her sweet, sweet torture, as he followed her up the stairs.

Claudia and Baxter became great friends, in the same way that Beatrix and the twins were friends. They joked and laughed and shared secrets. Hawksworth relaxed his panicked guard, for they *were* cousins, however distant, and they acted like brother and sister.

When Claudia had no escort, Baxter accompanied her wherever she needed one, always under Hawk's or Alexandra's or the duchess's watchful eyes, of course.

Baxter had either turned over a new leaf, Hawk surmised, or was on his best behavior. Or he truly did seek the approval of his relatives, for he had not so much as committed a social blunder or gambled a single farthing since returning to the bosom of his family.

To Claudia, Baxter confessed his want of a wife, after much prompting by her and after extracting her promise to keep his secret. He also confessed his want of an introduction to a certain Miss Phyllida Middlemarch, who just happened to be Claudia's new bosom companion.

"Did you know that Phyllida is the heiress to the vast Middlemarch fortune?" Claudia asked.

"Really? No, I did not. Forget the introduction, then. I am sure that I am not good enough for her."

"Nonsense. You are a prize catch."

Baxter bowed. "I am humbled that you should think so."

In her turn, Claudia confessed her wish to make Judson Broderick, Viscount Chesterfield, so jealous that he would lay himself at her feet and beg her to marry him.

"Perhaps," Baxter said, "we could help each other."

The following day, Claudia wrote a letter to Chesterfield, in St. Albans, which she handed to Baxter for his approval. "*My Dear Chesterfield*," Baxter read aloud,

> *"You must not worry about me any longer, neither must you imagine that I will importune you further with my silly childhood infatuation."*

"Oh, not silly," Baxter said. "Call it naive. He will be charmed by the notion and less likely offended."

"Lord, you are a sly one," Claudia said, pulling a fresh sheet of stationery her way for a new draft.

Baxter grinned. "Thank you." He continued reading.

> *"London, it turns out, is great fun without you, as my cousin, Baxter Wakefield, has returned to the family fold and escorts me everywhere I wish to go. He is not only my escort, but my confidant and friend, perhaps even my knight in shining armor. He will play a key roll in my choice of husband, make no mistake, which role I had originally offered you, if you will remember. Consider yourself crossed off my*

list of matrimonial prospects, and thank you for refusing."

Baxter barked a laugh. "Nice touch that. It will lie in his belly like a summer apple. And your vague wording is masterful."

Claudia grinned.

Baxter read Claude's closing paragraph.

"Enjoy your country solitude. By the time you hear from me again, my name may have changed. Wish me luck. Your friend, Claudia Jamieson."

A week later, Chesterfield appeared at the Wellbank affair, a fine specimen of a man in a black-tailed frock coat and snow-white linen. Claudia hoped she was not drooling as she marked his approach.

"Miss Jamieson." He bowed before her even as she noted her uncle, not too far distant, and hoped that he would not clamp eyes on her companion any time soon.

Calling upon every inch of sophistication she could muster, Claudia offered Chesterfield her hand, which he raised to his lips, shivering her to her marrow.

"Dance with me," he said in his own arrogant way. "Now, or your uncle will have you over his knee, and me meeting him at dawn."

Claudia looked up and saw Alex, Uncle Bryce in tow, heading their way, so she stopped playing coy and took Chesterfield's arm to accompany him onto the dance floor for the set forming.

"Just in time," she said as she and Chesterfield clasped hands and turned to begin the dance. "Uncle Bryce is fuming. I can see the smoke from here. Oh, Lord, he and Alex are joining the set. He will hurt his leg."

"*He* is fine. What did *you* mean by saying you were considering Baxter's suit?"

"Why? Do you not think us a good match?" Claudia laughed at the appalled look on Chesterfield's face as the dance separated them and they went off in opposite directions.

As Alex passed, she suggested that Claudia leave Chesterfield to the older ladies. Her uncle simply leaned over to growl in her ear.

Claudia giggled.

As she awaited her turn to be accompanied down the strolling length of the dance line, Claudia gave her resistant suitor her undivided attention. "What I actually meant was that you need no longer worry about me, as Baxter has taken it upon himself to escort me wherever I would like to go."

"What makes you think I was worried about you?"

"You spoke to my uncle and gave me away."

"He should know better than to allow—" Chesterfield danced off on someone else's arm, his eyes smoldering as, of necessity, he turned away.

"I like Baxter," Claudia said when she passed Chesterfield.

When her uncle passed, she growled back. "I like Chesterfield."

"You cannot possibly care for the swine," Chesterfield said less than a beat later.

Claudia laughed and danced off with a soldier of the Royal Horse Guards, a handsome rake in a blue tunic.

"About Baxter," Chesterfield snapped when they were partnered again.

"He makes me laugh and has taken me to shops and museums and introduced me to his friends, as I am introducing him to mine."

"You do not want to meet the kind of 'friend' that blackguard will introduce you to. And the parents of *your* friends will certainly not appreciate the kind of—"

"How else am I to find a proper husband?"

"There is nothing proper about Baxter Wakefield. What can your uncle be thinking?"

"He is thinking to marry me off and be shed of me."

Chesterfield laughed aloud, catching the attention and the admiring glances of scores of women. "Do not pretend that giving you a season was Hawksworth's idea. He would likely rather keep you chained to the schoolroom, as would I if you were my—"

"If I were your what?" Claudia examined the look upon Chesterfield's face with a great deal of hope. He appeared . . . arrested . . . uncomfortable, and very warm. "Why did you stop speaking?"

"Pay attention to the steps; you will trip me up."

"When are you going back to St. Albans?"

"Tonight. Sooner."

"The duchess is giving a ball in my honor the day after Christmas. We are hoping to announce my betrothal that night."

Chesterfield missed a step. "To whom?"

"I do not yet know. If I send you an invitation, will you come?"

"Probably not."

"Will we see you at the Sefton ball this Saturday, then?"

"Certainly not."

Alex approached Chesterfield as he returned a glowering Claudia to the duchess of Basingstoke's side.

"Stay away from her, Judson," Alex said after Claudia was carted off by a group of young people. "You are too old for her."

"I am not too old for you, and look where that got me. Dance with me." Before Alex could protest, she was waltzed onto the floor with the man she had nearly married. "Believe me when I tell you that I am not old."

"You are right, thirty is not old, but it is nearly double Claudia's age. Claude will not be eighteen for three more weeks. She is too young for you."

"Do you suppose I might corrupt her in ways that Baxter will not?"

"Keep your voice down. We are on the dance floor, for heaven's sake."

"Then let us get off the dance floor, by all means." He waltzed her out the door and onto the terrace, but once he had her there, he simply tightened his hold and waltzed her closer and faster.

Alex pulled from his arms and stepped back to catch her breath.

"Let us have this out once and for all," Chesterfield snapped. "I was good enough to marry you, if I would buy your way out of poverty, but not good enough to marry your niece? Is that not a double standard, Alex? I am disappointed, for I expected better of you."

Alex held her hand to her hard-beating heart. "You are a good man, Judson. I know you are, but her uncle does not yet realize it. Besides, you are only giving the child your attention to annoy Hawksworth. I am more your age than Claudia."

"And well I know it, but I thought we had already concluded that anything between us was impossible."

"It *was*. It is," she said, looking away. "I should never have said yes."

"There is something you should know, Alex."

She looked sharply up. "What?"

"I am not pining for you. I simply do not want to see her hurt."

"Who?"

"Claudia. She is like the sunshine, that one, and she has the ability to slide beneath your defenses when you least expect it. She makes me want to make a pet of her one minute and throttle her the next."

"Did you never experience that wild urge to beat me?"

Chesterfield shook his head. "Never."

"You are in love with Claudia."

"Do you suppose that wanting to beat someone is love? I had rather suspected not."

Alex nodded. "I think any strong emotion is certainly a sign."

"So of course you wish Hawksworth would become so enraged as to want to beat you?"

Alex turned away.

"Even in moonlight, I can see the glint of tears in your eyes. Are you that unhappy with the sorry state of your marriage?"

"The state of my marriage is not your business."

"It is my business when you cannot repay me the money you owe me. Some marriage, if you must keep such things from your husband."

Alex bit her lip in shame because he was right.

Chesterfield took her into his arms. "Ah, my poor Alexandra." He removed his handkerchief from his pocket and wiped her eyes; then he kissed her, but more like a brother than a lover.

Yes, he cared for Claudia, Alex thought, regarding him fixedly, but no good would come of it.

"Do not think that your pretty tears will get me to forgive the five thousand pounds you owe me," he said.

As if she had been slapped, Alex stepped from his embrace.

"A good thing you let her go, Chesterfield, else I might have had to remove her by force."

Alex shivered. "Hawksworth!"

Twenty-three

Hawk raised a brow. "Chesterfield, you seem to make a habit of kissing my wife."

"I grew fond of the custom during the months before our wedding."

Jaw set, Hawk took Alexandra's arm and led her toward the garden, glad the duchess chaperoned Claudia in the ballroom. His mind held no doubt now that Alex was jealous of Chesterfield's attention to Claudia, and if he was forced to go back inside at this moment and had to be civil—even once—he might do something rash.

Having also just learned that his wife had borrowed five thousand pounds from her lover did not improve Hawk's mood any, though he supposed he should not be surprised. Whether the borrowed money had paid the mysterious vouchers was another matter, though Hawk was willing to make an educated guess that it did.

The funds to repay Chesterfield would be hard to find, Hawk thought, though find them, he would. Why had Alex taken the blackguard's blunt in the first place? And why did she not trust her own husband enough to confide in him?

He just might have to beat her later, Hawk thought, *after* he removed her clothes and slathered her with oil.

From the garden, they made their way around the Wellbank mansion to the front. Hawk sent a note inside to the duchess, saying that Alex was ill and he was taking her home. Did she mind chaperoning Claudia on her own?

Her reply was prompt. She would be happy to help. As a postscript, she added, "Get Alex to bed."

Oh, he would. He certainly would.

In the carriage, Hawk pulled the curtains down before the vehicle had barely begun its trek across town. Then he pulled his wife onto his lap and took her mouth.

Hawk ran his hands through her hair, dislodging pins, holding her head still so he could ravish her mouth, suckle her tongue. "I am furious with you for nearly marrying him, for kissing him, and for taking money from him," he said when he came up for air.

She seemed to revel in his less than gentle tactics but stopped to catch her own breath. "I am furious with you for leaving me after our wedding, for not providing for us, for not telling us you survived, for—"

"Shut up and kiss me." Hawk made love to his wife with his touch, his tongue, his lips.

Alex followed suit.

Why she suddenly slipped her hand into the front flap of his inexpressibles, Hawk knew not; he knew only that she had found herself a handful of randy man, hard, pulsing, ready to spill his seed. He covered her hand to stop her. "Do not."

"But you said you needed practice to regain your staying power."

"And so I do."

"I want to help, and I want to touch and know all of you." She knelt on the floor of the carriage, no matter that he kept trying to pull her upward, and she kissed him. There.

Hawk shuddered; he called her name, but he remained in control—and improved his staying power.

The carriage slowed. "Devil take it, he must think I called for him to stop," Hawk said. Gathering his wits, he called for Myerson to go on. "Circle Hyde Park," he added, and when he felt the vehicle change direction, Hawk knew his instructions were being followed. Myerson might suspect what they were about, but he would never reveal any of it.

Hawk pulled Alex from her knees and brought her astride him. He wrapped her hand around him and gave her the rhythm. Then he played the same cadence, slow and easy, at her center.

Damn Chesterfield to hell. She is mine.

Her head went back and she pushed air from her lungs. When he could tell from her moist, swollen bud how ready she was, as swollen and ready as he— Hawk shouted for Myerson to take them home.

Alex whimpered, she was so undone, as he redressed her. She laid her cheek against his shoulder while he put himself away—something of a challenge.

"We have arrived," she said when they stopped.

"Not quite," he said; then he carried her from the carriage and up the stairs.

The black lace corset was shed in a flash, and Hawk laid Alex atop the covers, where he could devour the sight of her. Then he lay beside her to free himself and urge her astride him, but this time he rocked her and inflamed them both until they reached a modicum of satisfaction.

Alex wept. Hawk understood. It was not enough, yet it was the best he could give her.

They were doomed. Whichever direction they went with their lives, together or separate, would be the wrong direction.

For days, Hawk rose before Alex and went up to bed after her, as well. He was confused, his mind filled with either taking her to bed or murdering her lover.

Because he was thinking of returning to the country, he asked Reed and Gideon to join him in taking Beatrix, Damon, and Rafferty to Astley's Royal Amphitheater in Lambeth, as he had promised.

Although Reed did not consider taking children anywhere a good idea for any reason, Gideon thought it a splendid notion and readily agreed. Eventually, so did Reed.

Hawk had not given his niece and nephews much attention since returning from Belgium. Besides, he desperately needed to turn his thoughts to something—or someone—other than Alex.

Beatrix was the daughter he never had, and he

adored his nephews, scamps that they were. He had missed them all, and spending time with them held the promise of a certain peace all its own.

Gideon generously procured a private box on the arena level, though the children might as soon have swung from the rafters as sat on their bottoms, they were so excited, making Hawk question his notion of peace.

Damon favored the performing monkeys, but Rafe much preferred the equestrian showmanship for which Astley's was famous. Beatrix adored the be-spangled dame who performed with a broadsword, cutting and slashing her way across the arena, though later she said she saw Baxter across the way kissing that lady. Hawk stepped between Bea and the view, concerned that Baxter was slipping into his old ways.

Not even the boys were fond of the "thunder, light-ening and hail" spectacle, and when the reenactment of the Battle of Waterloo began, the three men re-garded each other with disgust and left without an-other word. Hawk was glad, however, that they attended—almost as glad as the children, though Reed ended the evening more skittish about children than ever after Bea vomited in his lap.

They got home late, and by the time Hawk got Claudia to help clean Bea up and put her to bed, he found Alex asleep, or so he thought. He had no sooner pulled the covers over himself than she came and burrowed into him.

Hawk sighed with a mixture of satisfaction and frustration, and a need to speak, as he placed his arm about her so as to pillow her head on his shoulder.

"Why did you borrow five thousand pounds from Chesterfield?" There, it was said.

Alexandra's sigh was impossible to gauge, though *bowing to the inevitable* was a good interpretation. "I did not *borrow* the money. I was never supposed to return it. We were *supposed* to be married."

"Ah. But what did you use it for?"

"I cannot tell you that."

"Why can you not be forthcoming with me?"

"I am being as forthcoming with you as you have been with me."

"We are talking again about my not contacting you upon my return, are we not?"

"*You* are."

"Imagine that." Hawk sighed and tried to curb his irritation. "Alexandra . . ."

"Yes, Hawksworth."

"Gambling . . . while seeming to be the answer to acquiring vast sums of money with little or no effort—"

"How did you guess?"

"Brilliant deductive powers . . . and a hot fire."

"What?"

"It does not matter. Simply give me your oath that you will never gamble again and I will say no further word about it."

"I can honestly say that I have not placed a wager since I asked Fitzwilliams to pay the vouchers, nor will I gamble in the future."

"Thank you, I—"

"Will say no further word about it."

"Right."

"I appreciate that."

"Why are you still awake?" he asked, barred from probing further into her gaming. "Are you unable to sleep?"

"I have been thinking."

"Come to any conclusions?"

"Not a one."

"I have," Hawk said.

Alex rose and leaned on an elbow to regard him, though the light cast by the moon shone too pale to read her.

"Tomorrow, I am going home to Huntington Lodge."

"You are leaving me?" *Again?* Alex thought.

His turn to raise himself. Had she sounded regretful? "Leaving you? Nonsense. I need to speak to the estate manager, or he needs to speak with me, I should say, judging from his letter. And I would like to check on the property, the progress of repairs, visit the new tenants, see how they get on, make certain they have enough to eat."

"You are a better man than the one who went to war."

"Balderdash. Quicksilver is due to foal any day, and if the new cottages are coming along, I thought I might start the men on enlarging the stable. Gideon has offered me the pick of his breeding stock, you know, with the excuse that I would not have lost my inheritance, if I had not 'watched his back and "died" in his place.' "

"And you are willing to accept his offer?"

"Of course not, but I am considering borrowing his

best stallion to cover Quicksilver next spring. There is a pride of honor, but there is also a point where pride becomes stubborn and foolish."

"I am pleased you finally realize it for the most part. You are going to make the estate profitable, are you not?"

"I certainly hope so. Will that please you?"

"Only if *you* are the one managing it."

What a remarkable statement, Hawk thought—disturbingly intuitive. "Go to sleep."

"How long will you be gone? Do not forget that we are invited to remain through Christmas. Gideon and Sabrina will come to stay as well."

"I shall be back in plenty of time for Christmas."

"Oh, Grandmama's birthday celebration is the week before. Perhaps you can be back in time for that?"

"We will see."

Alex wanted to weep. She wanted to beg him not to leave her again, but she could not bring herself to do so. He was sorry he had married her; she knew he must be.

His father had been right. She had never been good enough for him.

The Huntington Lodge estate might not be thriving, but it was a beehive of activity and progress. The most important repairs on the house were done, inside and out. No more roof leaks, broken stairs, or drafty windows. The house itself was still plenty ugly, but warm and dry and infinitely more livable.

Aunt Hildegarde and Uncle Gifford were not only grateful for the improvements; they were downright agreeable, so much "in complete agreement" as to make Hawk almost as suspicious as he was pleased to see them.

The new cottages stood two stories high, thatched of roof and simple of design, but warm and cozy. The former soldiers and their families worked hard— clearing land on the home farm for a larger spring planting, digging foundations for more cottages, repairing and whitewashing the old, building the new— whatever his manager set them to.

Most of the tenant cottages now housed only two instead of three families. Several of the male tenants, members of his old unit, could not seem to break the habit of saluting him, but Hawk was working on that as well.

Mrs. Parker baked bread and made soup daily to keep everyone fed, which Hawk had asked her to do, to see their tenants through the winter until they could begin to plant their personal gardens and fend for themselves.

Hawk observed the daily activity either from atop Alexandra's horse or on foot, or he got right down and worked beside his tenants. Sometimes Giff rode with him.

Hawk spoke with everyone, man, woman, and child alike, listening to their ideas to improve the estate. The fact that he was nearly as penniless as they were made them seem to want to work the harder.

One soldier's wife suggested a pottery, and Hawk thought that might be a good idea, given the clay on the land. Another suggested a weaving loom or two, given the sheep, for blankets and wraps for winter. If they kept this up, Huntington Lodge would become a community unto itself.

Four soldiers had brought horses they could barely afford to keep, so they were happy to lend them to the breeding pot, up at the stable, for winter hay and feed. Not that Hawk would use all of them, but he *would* make use of at least one.

Through all the positive progress, however, Hawk worried—about his marriage, about Alex, for he saw her everywhere. He worried about how he was going to repay her debt to Chesterfield. Five thousand pounds might as well be fifty thousand right now.

Why did she love Chesterfield?

Did she love Chesterfield?

A prosperous Huntington Estate would be an excellent gift to leave Alex. But working beside her for a lifetime, to turn it into a successful venture, would be the greatest gift of all.

But a gift for whom? Him, or her?

He wanted to make their marriage work, but he did not want to assure his happiness at the cost of Alexandra's. Except . . . how could she have gone from Chesterfield's arms that night at the ball to practically mounting Hawk ten minutes later in the carriage?

Which of them did she love? And was he an idiot for imagining he might be counted as a possibility?

His uncle approached him one day as Hawk was fretting over the problem and pacing the winter-barren orchard. "Would you like to talk about whatever is bothering you?"

Hawk shook his head. "I suppose it would be useless to say nothing is?"

Giff chuckled. "Sometimes I think you favor me in temperament more than you favor your own father."

"Thank you. That is the nicest thing you could say."

"You still ache to please him, though, do you not?"

"How did you guess?"

"I never succeeded, either, and as old as I am, a little part of me wishes I could do more than please him. Just once before I die, I would like to best him."

Hawk nodded his understanding.

"Let me just say," Giff continued, "that you did not fail your father. *He* failed you—with his inability to love. Do not make the same mistake."

Hawk faltered in his steps, then stopped altogether. "I want to do what is best for Alex."

"It seems to me that you are already doing that."

"But suppose she still loves Chesterfield."

"If you do not know who the lass loves, you are a blind man." Giff put his hand on Hawk's shoulder. "The demons of war can distort even the obvious good in life. Do not let war win, Bryce. Open your eyes and see what you have. Do not let your father win, either. You are a good and worthy man—worthy of Alexandra's love and of so much more."

Hawk swallowed, nodded, and walked on, his uncle lending his silent support beside him.

"Uncle Giff," Hawk said after a bit, stopping again, "you bested him years ago."

Giff chuckled at the jest. "How's that?"

"You have always been a better father."

Twenty-four

After nearly three weeks at Huntington Lodge, Hawk could not stay away from Alexandra one day longer. So he packed his bags, talked Hildy and Giff into coming with him for Christmas, bade his tenants farewell, and set off.

As their carriage approached London, Hawk fingered the carved acorns atop the small wooden casket Chesterfield had returned with his clothing. The casket contained Hawk's father's wedding band, signet ring, and a gaudy diamond he had acquired on his grand tour.

Hawk kept his stickpins inside, as well as a few childhood treasures, such as the Roman coin he and Alex dug up at Devil's Dyke on the day they met, and the tiny alabaster bust they found near the water meadows some time during the halcyon days of their childhood. Alex kept many more of their treasures, but Hawk had claimed only those two.

When they reached the outskirts of London, Hawk bade Myerson to take him to Bond Street, to Stedman & Vardon, Goldsmiths & Jewelers, and then to take Hildy and Giff on to St. James Street. Hawk would catch a hack home.

At the establishment of Stedman & Vardon, Hawk opened the casket and removed his father's gaudy diamond, willing to sell every piece of jewelry he owned for the five thousand pounds needed to remove Alexandra from Chesterfield's debt.

The jeweler was a jolly old man, bald of pate and cunning of brow. He popped in his jeweler's eye and remained silent for far too long, examining the ring at every angle. "It is paste," he said, tossing it Hawk's way. "I hope it did not come dear."

"It was my father's," Hawk said catching it. Perhaps the man thought to swindle him, though the establishment had a superior reputation in the ton.

Since Hawk knew what he had paid for his emerald stickpin, he offered that as a test for the man's inspection.

"Seven hundred," the jeweler said, which was honest—even generous—but not enough, and Hawk did not think the rest, together, would amount to that much again.

Nevertheless, he emptied the casket onto the glass case and pushed the jewelry forward, piece by piece. The childhood mementos he tossed back into the box, but the man gasped and began speaking so fast, Hawk could barely understand him. "May I see them at least," he begged, and Hawk saw his gaze centered on the treasures in the casket.

Hawk relinquished the miniature bust, which was lost in the man's large hand, and the jeweler regarded it with awe, examining and running his fingers over all. "I will give you eight thousand pounds," he said with nary a blink.

Hawk's breath caught in his throat as he regarded the shrewd businessman. "Twelve thousand, cash, now."

The man paled to the point that he placed the bust on a carefully laid piece of black velvet and took out his handkerchief to wipe his brow.

After a considering minute, he picked up the coin, rubbed his thumb over it, examined its surface, and narrowed his eyes. "Thirteen for both."

"Sixteen," Hawk countered, fisting his hands to keep their trembling from giving him away.

"Fourteen and a half."

"Fifteen and not a penny less."

The jeweler nodded, and Hawk followed him into his back room.

Still quaking in reaction, Hawk went directly to Child's Bank. After his business there was concluded, he went on to 46 Berkeley Square.

Chesterfield entered his town house library less than five minutes after his butler had invited Hawk inside. "To what do I owe the honor, and all that rubbish?"

"Why did you not go back to the country, as Claude said you intended?"

"Excuse me?"

Hawk shook his head. "Sorry, I digress. Something in you gets me to bristling."

"If you must know," Chesterfield said, "I decided that, for the moment, the city has more to offer in the way of entertainment."

"This should help finance your stay, then." Hawk handed Chesterfield a bank draft for five thousand pounds and a receipt for same. "Sign the receipt, and Alex will owe you nothing more."

Chesterfield nodded. "Come into some blunt, did you?"

"Just a deal of good luck. It started the day I met Alexandra."

"I once thought the same," Chesterfield said, handing him the signed receipt. "But a recent, interesting . . . diversion . . . is beginning to make me feel like a man of good fortune once more."

"I am glad to hear it. Good day to you," Hawk said. "I hope that our paths shall never cross again."

"I am sure you do." Chesterfield followed Hawk down to the foyer and watched him make his way to the front door.

Hawk turned at the last. "You will notify Alex that she owes you nothing, but under no circumstances will you reveal that I paid you."

"In that case, she will think I am being generous in forgiving the debt."

"So be it, then." Hawk tipped his hat and strode out the door, and Chesterfield's respect for him grew tenfold.

Hawk arrived at Basingstoke House while the household was still in uproar. "They are getting married," Claudia shouted from the stairs as Hawk handed Myerson his top hat, cane, and greatcoat.

"Who is getting married?"

"Aunt Hildy and Uncle Giff."

"Good God." Hawk made his way up the stairs to the drawing room and went straight to Alex. He squeezed both her hands, kissed her cheek, and ached for her lips. "They never said a word to me."

"Well, you were terribly preoccupied, dear," Hildy

said as she came and offered her cheek. "Wish us happy."

"I do. Giff, you sly old bachelor. This will change everything, you know." Hawk shook his uncle's hand.

"It certainly will." Giff coughed and leaned close. "I am too old for all this sneaking about."

"We would like to lease the dower house, if you would allow us?" Hildy looked from Alex to Hawk and back, clearly unsure which of them she should ask.

Hawk looked to Alex for Hildy's answer.

"You may have the dower house as a wedding gift."

"I shall write today to have Davis set someone to doing the necessary repairs," Hawk said. "When will you marry?"

Giff regarded Hildy. "Next Saturday?"

Hildy nodded, her smile radiant. "The day before Christmas Eve."

"*Immediate* repairs."

"A week," Alex said. "Gad, we have a lot to do."

Though the beauty of youth had long since deserted Hildy and Giff, and the years had left their mark, Hawk saw such love, such adoration, in both their gazes. Neither seemed to see anything but beauty in the other. In their own ways, they were as scarred as him, by time, but that did not seem to matter a jot to either of them.

Hawk turned to Alex then and found himself mesmerized by her smile. *I missed you,* he wanted to say. *I want to take you to bed.*

Without a word, she took his hand and led him from the room, almost as if she read his thoughts.

No one made a move to question or stop them. "Do

not forget that we have guests coming for Grandmama's birthday dinner." Claudia's words floated upon the air behind them.

Hawk allowed Alex to precede him into their apartment; then he followed her in and shut the bedchamber door.

"I told you I would be back."

Alex stepped into his arms.

Dinner was a frustrating affair to begin with, Hawk thought, for there were too many people. Besides him and Alex, Giff and Hildy, Hazelthorpe and the duchess, Gideon and Sabrina, someone had included Baxter and Miss Phyllida Middlemarch in the invitation, along with Chesterfield, of all people.

"What the bloody devil are those three doing here?" Hawk whispered to Alex as he escorted her in to dinner.

"Claudia said that they will make Grandmama's party as merry as mice in malt."

Hawk wanted to kiss her again, even though they had kissed for all of an hour. First just standing there, the door at his back, then with him sitting and her in his lap, then on the bed. And just when things began to get interesting, the bell rang and it was time to dress for dinner.

Hawk wished to the devil that Chesterfield would find a wife of his own. He wanted to be free to ask Alex the question he ached to ask—whether she would stay or go—but he did not feel safe doing so with Chesterfield available for her to go to.

Hawk now knew that he could be brave in the face of war, but in life he was still a coward.

By the time he grasped the conversation going on about him, the duchess had invited Baxter and Chesterfield to spend Christmas with them, and when Hawk realized it, he nearly swallowed his deviled kidney whole.

Claudia, the brat, smiled with satisfaction. "If you arrive on the morning before Christmas Eve," she said, "you will be here for Aunt Hildy and Uncle Giff's wedding, then for Christmas Eve, Christmas Day, and my ball the night after. Chesterfield, you will come?"

The man had the audacity to look from Hawk to Alex and grin; then he winked at Claudia. "I would be honored."

"And you, Baxter?" the duchess asked. "It has been a long time since you spent Christmas with your family."

"I look forward to it," he said, too cocky by half.

Alex had decided before coming downstairs for the birthday celebration that she had teased Hawksworth long enough. Tonight she would stage her ultimate seduction. She even wore her mother's cameo on a black silk ribbon as a signal to Sabrina.

Between them they made certain Hawk's glass was always full. Bree said that spirits would relax him so he would let down his guard, promising it was nothing like drugging him. Hawk would know what he was doing. Then she explained in great detail—from careful observation, said she—how a man would respond to each enticement.

Making love seemed to be something of a refined game with Sabrina and Gideon, besides an expression of the profound feelings they shared. Sabrina said their spirits and hearts became closer with the physical expression of their love.

More than ever, Alex wanted that experience. She wanted Hawksworth as her lover as well as her husband.

Everyone wanted to play cards after supper. Vingt-et-un or whist. A table was set up for each. Chesterfield and Claude would be partners, and Miss Middlemarch and Baxter.

Alex heard her aunt ask Giff to partner with her.

"You hate playing cards, remember?" Alex told Hildy, who laughed at her sorry memory and sat with the duchess for a comfortable coze.

Alex took Giff by the arm to be escorted about the room. "I am so pleased that you will be my real uncle now."

"And I thought I would die a lonely old bachelor."

"You were never a lonely old bachelor. You have always had Bryceson. He thinks the world of you. We all do."

Giff grinned. "Imagine that."

"Have you and Hildy had an opportunity to talk?"

"Us? We talk all the time. Hildy and I have no secrets from each other."

Alex smiled. "I am glad to hear it."

Hawksworth's and Gideon's after-dinner-brandy goblets emptied fast and often. The rogues sat across from each other, Gideon telling Hawk about his first shocked sight of the pregnant bride Hawk had secured for him.

Alex caught Sabrina's eye. Both men had imbibed enough, they agreed with a nod, especially since Sabrina seemed to have a special night planned, herself.

Alex dubbed Bree the queen of seduction then, for even as Alex watched, all Bree had to do was walk up behind her husband and skim the shell of his ear with a finger. Like a shot, she had Gideon's undivided attention, and almost that fast, they said their goodbyes and were on their way home.

Someday, I would like to be that married, Alex thought as she approached Hawksworth. She tried stroking his ear, but he batted the air as if she were a pesky fly. Then she sat on the footstool by his chair and took his hand. And while he played with her fingers, he was engrossed in a story Hazelthorpe was telling.

"It *has* been a long day," she said, and Hawk nodded. Perhaps he was too relaxed. Was that possible?

Drastic times, Alex thought. "Hawk," she said. "My back aches."

And that was all it took. They were on their way within moments, Alex feeling cherished, for she caught the possessive look Hawk tossed Chesterfield's way before escorting her from the room.

She had also caught the look Chesterfield gave Claudia then, which bore looking into—and nipping in the proverbial bud—but not tonight.

Tonight was for her and Hawk, and Alex intended that it would be spectacular.

Twenty-five

While Hawk undressed in his own dressing room, Alex undressed in hers. She set lit candles about the bed and stepped from her gown before getting in. She lay on her stomach and made sure the bedclothes were barely covering her before she hugged her pillow and closed her eyes.

But when she heard her husband approach, she opened them, for Hawksworth in his black brocade dressing gown was as gorgeous as a mythical god. And lo and behold, said myth climbed into bed with her.

He skimmed a hand down her back without the oil, as if for the simple pleasure of touching her with nothing, not even oil, between them.

He could have no idea how badly she wanted to do the same, to open his dressing gown and let her hands wander at will—which she would do before this night was over.

They kissed and kissed before even opening that pale green jar. Then the oil, or her reaction to it, or both, did its magic. Alex was not certain which of them was more ready. She did know who was more stubborn. Hawk would not give in to his need any more tonight than in the past, so when she pretended sleep, he lay beside her and throbbed against her forever until he slept.

Lord, she hoped Sabrina's theory was correct, that he would sleep deeply and be easy to seduce when she woke him.

Alex slipped carefully from the bed, to be certain Hawk did not wake. The black ribbons on her dressing table were already tied with the necessary knots. All she need do was slip the loops over the bedposts, which she did with dispatch, and then over Hawk's wrists and ankles, and pull taut.

Except that he needed to change position. *Drat.*

Whatever she tried, she could not get him to move. At length, she touched his ear, and he rolled to his back, swatted air, and let his arm fall, leaving it extended.

A good thing Sabrina had given her long and sturdy ribbons. Within minutes, Alex had her husband bound, by wrists and ankles to the bed, and what a picture he made.

She climbed in beside him, giddy as a child at Christmas, with the most marvelous black brocade package before her, just waiting to be unwrapped.

First she untied the sash on his dressing gown. Next, she opened it, one side at a time, until the beauty of her husband was fully, finally, revealed to her.

Except that beauty was not what she saw first. His wounds were, and they were hideous.

Sorrow rose in Alex, and she swallowed several hard times to overcome her need to weep for the pain he must have endured. His scars were formidable: wide, thick, ruddy. His left thigh was all one big, knotted scar narrowing to a burst of long thin scars, as if the bayonet's blade had gotten caught and must have been thrust up and down to free it.

A whimper escaped Alex as she bent to kiss the marked flesh, which must be sensitive, because Hawk moaned and tried to shift away. Alex panicked. She had barely begun, and if he woke, her seduction would be finished.

As she watched, he calmed and remained sleeping.

Alex sighed. No wonder he limped. 'Twas a wonder he was a whole man. And he was. She had seen and felt his magnificent manhood. Ah, and he was beautiful there, too, even at rest, as was his chest, which she dared not as yet touch, and his face . . . and his soul.

Alex examined everything at length—all his various and sundry man parts. The one that would become hard was soft as silk, the soft ones were squishy.

She cupped his ballocks as she fingered his length, and just like that, the little devil came to life. Hawk sighed with her every stroke.

He gasped and she jumped; then she fingered the sudden droplet that appeared and rubbed it over the tip, and Hawk moaned and grew two lengths on the instant.

Ah, yes, like a horse.

She closed her hand around him, as he taught her in the bath, and she felt his ballocks firm and tighten, felt his entire torso start and stiffen.

Prickles chased up her spine and along her nape and Alex looked up . . . and saw that he was watching her, his topaz eyes hard as flint, but bright as fire.

Her heart tripped while lust and fear fought for dominance. "Ah . . . now that I have it in my hand," Alex said, "I do not know what to do with it."

Hawk tried to move and saw that he was bound, and the fire in his eyes leaped.

Alex got scorched.

"Mount me," he said, growing impossibly larger, his voice deep and demanding. "Have your siren's way with me. But do it now, by God. I have waited too bloody long as it is."

Her heart about to pound from her breast, Alex swung a leg over Hawk, but given his current size, mounting him seemed physically impossible. "I do not think it will fit."

"If you wish to take the lead, then do so; if you wish me to lead the way and make it easier for you, free me."

"No, you have been too skittish to follow through, and I will not go one more night untouched."

Hawk groaned and Alex saw that tic working in his cheek. He seemed actually to be suffering.

"I am coming. I am coming," she said.

"So had I better be, and soon."

Alex giggled, but she nearly managed at the same time to fit him to her, except that . . . "Really, you are enormous. Is this normal?"

He grinned. Hawksworth grinned. For the first time in years, she saw his smile.

Alex grinned as well, so happy of a sudden, she

could hardly bear it. "Prepare yourself," she said, "because this is going to be wonderful."

"I expect nothing less."

"Ouch. Drat."

"Wait. Do not hurt yourself."

"Can I do that?"

Hawk sighed. "Release me so I can at least prepare you to receive me."

"Absolutely not. How would you prepare me?"

"I would make certain you were . . . fluid."

"Wet, you mean? Oh, I am. Touching you always does that to me. It is a good thing, then? I did not know."

"It is a good thing." Hawk pulled against his fetters and cursed. "Set me free so I can make you mine, once and for all, damn it."

"No. I will make you *mine*, instead."

"Be gentle with me." That spark of mirth was back in his eyes.

Oh, how wonderful it was to see. "Ah," she said, finding the right place for everything suddenly and impaling herself ever so slowly upon him. "There, that did not hurt, did it?"

Hawk hissed and bared his teeth.

"It did hurt! Do you want me to stop?"

"Good God, no!"

"What should I do now?"

"Push harder, I have not breached you yet."

"Can you not help?"

Something akin to a groan and a pained laugh escaped Hawk as he arched and impaled her in one deep thrust.

Alex screamed, but as the scream died, her shock turned to wonder, then joy, and she smiled, because . . . "You are all the way in. I am no longer a virgin! We should celebrate."

"Move from that spot and I will strangle you."

"Yes, Bryce. What would you have me do next?"

"Ride me."

"Pardon?"

Hawk used his hips and urged his wife to follow as he went, and when she did, and they began to move with more speed and greater unity, wonder struck, and she learned what men and women had known through the ages. Making love with the mate whose soul touches yours can be a most incredible experience.

Halfway to heaven when she made the discovery, Alex continued to climb toward the firmament, her wonder growing apace with her pleasure, until Hawk called her name and she answered and followed him up and over the precipice.

She dozed astride him, her face against his chest, his arms around her, until the feel of him hardening inside her alerted her to her position and his "growing" need.

Alex sat up, pushed the hair from her eyes, and smiled, and they made love again.

"When you set me free," Hawk said, "be prepared to spend a month on your back." He thrust upward, and upward, prepared to love her in whatever position she wanted. In the tub or out. At Huntington Lodge or at the bottom of Devil's Dyke—there was a thought.

Thrice more she took him, or he took her, and thrice more they rode toward the stars, until Hawk was so desperate for the freedom to love her as he wished that he all-out yanked at his tethers . . . and snapped a bedpost.

Alex screeched as it came down.

"Are you hurt? Alex?"

She was not hurt but laughing, laughing so hard that she could not catch her breath. And when he saw, and realized what they had done, Hawksworth began to laugh as well, full-bodied and throaty. It was . . . not a bad feeling.

That lump for his dead comrades still clogged his throat; but a yearning for life—for Alexandra—filled him as well, so he stepped from his bonds, the inner bonds of sorrow, first. Then, as he regarded his hysterical wife, he divested himself of the outward bonds of black satin, took her into his arms, and loved her again.

This time Hawk led the loving, slow and easy, gentle and sweet. It was everything beautiful that life could offer—touches, kisses and soft warm strokes. He was marking Alex as his when he should not, God help him . . . for he could not help himself.

Alex opened her eyes at about noon the following day and looked into the sultry, satisfied cat's eyes of her lover.

Hawk's somber expression relaxed then, and his eyes crinkled at the corners . . . and his lips . . . A smile she saw growing there. And tears filled her eyes, but good tears, of wonder and happiness.

"I . . . missed you, Lexy. I missed you so much

sometimes that I could have shouted for wanting you."

"Why did you take so long to say so? Why not make me yours?"

"I did not want to chain you to a marriage with someone you did not love. I wanted to be able to set you free, if that was your wish. For your own good, I kept from you."

"For my own good? *My* good?"

"Well, not for mine. I have been aching to have you."

"*You* have been aching? What about me? What gives you the right to decide what is right for me, to make up rules in my name? Who do you think you are?"

"Your husband."

"Oh, of course. And husbands have that right."

"They do."

"But you have decided that you might no longer be my husband. Then you would lose your right to make decisions in my name, correct?"

"Correct," he said, wavering, unsure of himself.

"Fine. Then our marriage is dissolved in all but the signed documents. You have no more rights over me."

"Wrong. We can no longer annul the marriage. You are stuck with me."

"In that case, I want a bill of divorcement."

Hawk paled and panic infused his features. "Then you shall have it."

"Good. Now I may make my own decisions. Can you guess what I have decided?"

"No, I cannot."

"Since you have no say in the matter, I have decided to take my former husband as my lover." She mounted him, and Hawk offered no resistance; as a matter of fact, that look of panic left him and color returned to his features.

"I may no longer have you tied to my bed," Alex said, "but I am going to have my wicked, seductive way with you, anyway. And you are going to—"

"Pull you into my arms and suffer the consequences."

Twenty-six

Alex barely got downstairs that afternoon before Sabrina arrived with the children to return Beatrix, who had spent the night at Stanthorpe House.

She and Sabrina watched the boys chase Bea up to the nursery; then they went into the small salon for a comfortable chat. The minute they were alone, Sabrina put a fretting Juliana to her breast to suckle and calm her. "Now, tell me what happened," Sabrina said. "Every detail."

"I will tell you my every detail if you tell me yours."

Sabrina gaped wide-eyed for a moment, then they both dissolved into laughter. Sabrina smiled. "Your seduction was . . . satisfactory, I take it? You are positively aglow."

"As are you."

"Ouch! Do not bite Mama, sweet. I wish babies did not get their teeth quite so soon."

"Is that not the time to wean a babe, then?" Alex asked, sincerely curious, since, after the night past, she could very well find herself in the family way.

Sabrina closed her bodice and sat her daughter on her lap to pat her back. "Yes, it is. I love the connection that nursing gives me and my babies, but I will have to stop soon." She smiled. "I am expecting Stanthorpe's child."

"Ah Sabrina," Alex said, rising and going to hug her friend. "I am happy for you. I hope you are pleased, since this is your fourth."

"I am thrilled, because it is Stanthorpe's first, though you would never guess it to see him with the others, would you? And still he is as excited as a schoolboy on holiday. More so. But I think you have been avoiding my question."

Alexandra rose with a dreamy smile. "In response to your question, let me ask a question of my own. What do you think the duchess of Basingstoke will say when she discovers that we broke the bed?"

Sabrina whooped. "Oh, good show! Gideon will be green with envy, for you have managed to do something that we have not."

Alex giggled.

"Ah, you *are* happy."

Alex sighed. "I am, and yet . . . Do you think I am good enough for Hawksworth? His father once told me that I would not be a fit wife for him."

"That man was a self-centered bully. He cared for none who suffered for his cause. Oh, Alex, I am so certain that you and Hawk care for each other, and yet you seem at cross-purposes the better part of the time."

"I have always loved him—you know that—but I assure you that Hawk is only making the best of a difficult situation. He would never have married me if he did not need someone to care for his family while he went to war. I know that. But he is a good man, and he will be a good husband."

Sabrina shook her head and seemed about to argue when Hawksworth came in. "I saw Damon and Rapscallion upstairs," he said, kissing Sabrina's cheek, "and knew you would be about. How is the little one?"

"Asleep, thank goodness."

"Here," Alex, said, taking Juliana, "let me take her up and put her in a crib so you two can talk."

Hawk watched Alex leave. "She looks a treat with a little one in her arms, does she not?"

Sabrina shook her head. "How long have you loved her?"

"Love? I am quite certain that I am incapable of love. Why do you ask?"

Sabrina threw her hands in the air. "Blind, the two of you."

"I do not know about blind," Hawk said, "but I must be stupid." He regarded her earnestly. "I know, because I have done a very stupid and unloving thing."

Sabrina scoffed. "What, pray, is that?"

"I have ruined Alexandra's chance for happiness."

"How?"

"I have made it impossible to give her the annulment she deserves."

"Deserves? Annulment? What nonsense is this?"

"She merits better than a broken man like me. She should have the man she loves."

"Who is . . . Chesterfield . . . whom . . . you hate."

"All right, then, she deserves the man she loves, as long as he is . . . other than Chesterfield."

"No wonder she needed to . . ."

"Needed to what?"

"Who the bloody devil *would* you consider good enough for her?" Sabrina shouted. "No one, I say."

"You are overwrought and talking nonsense."

"*I* am? Do you remember how downhearted I once was about not having Gideon's love? Remember what you told me? 'Learn to trust,' you said. 'Trust is everything.' You also knew instinctively that love must be earned and returned, if one wished to keep it."

Sabrina patted his arm. "It is past time you learned your own lessons, Hawksworth. You were running from life when you told me those things, and I am sorry to tell you, but you are running still."

On Saturday, the vicar arrived for Hildy and Giff's wedding at a quarter to one. Hildy arrived at one-fifteen. At two, Uncle Gifford was yet to be found.

While Hawk went off in search of his uncle, Baxter took Alex to one side. "I must say that I understand my cousin's determination to keep you, no matter the cost. I must also say that I very much appreciate your help."

Alex stiffened. "What are you talking about?"

"It must be grand to have so much power as to accomplish what so many men tried and failed before you."

"What have so many tried and failed?"

"To bring down the great Hawksworth, of course. Ruin him. How does it feel to have been the one to finally impoverish him and . . . bring him to his knees, so to speak?"

Baxter's tone was so filled with innuendo, and his demeanor so forward, that Alex took a step back, but he stepped closer. "You do *know* that I inherited in his stead because his father disinherited him for marrying you, do you not? That there was a codicil to the will?" Baxter shook his head in disbelief. "The funny thing is, Hawk might annul the marriage, or divorce you, and get his inheritance back, but he refuses."

Despite her horror at the revelation, Alex knew she faced the true Baxter Wakefield—a blackguard, as they once suspected. "I am afraid that I must ask you to leave."

"You have no say in this house." Baxter smiled, though his eyes did not. "Ah, there is my dear Claudia."

Not two minutes later, Hawk came for Alex and Hildy. Giff was waiting to see them in the library, and Alex would do or say nothing to spoil her aunt's wedding.

Hildy trembled as Alex and Hawk escorted her into the book-lined room. "It is all right if you have changed your mind," Hildy said to Giff as they entered.

"My dear," he said from across the room, looking quite forlorn.

"Be happy, Giff. That is all I care about. Changing your mind will not break me. I am a tough old bird, remember?"

Giff cursed and crossed to her, then she was in his arms. "*My* tough old bird." He kissed her brow. "And if I were worthy of you, I would be honored to be your husband. But Hildy, I am not. You are better off without me."

"What nonsense is this?" Hawk asked, even as he remembered Sabrina asking him the same question—even though Giff's unworthiness rang another familiar alarum.

Alex touched Hawk's hand to calm him. "Giff, what is this about? I think my aunt has a right to know, even if Hawk and I do not. Do you wish the two of us to leave?"

"No, lass," Giff said, seating Hildy and sitting to take her hand. "I want you to hear what I have to say."

Hawk and Alex sat.

"I am an old reprobate," Giff said. "A scoundrel, a rakehell, worse. Put simply, I do not deserve you, Hildegarde Huntington. While it might appear that I have put my profligate ways behind me, I have only recently laid the last to rest; and even then, I was not capable of doing so on my own."

"Giff, no," Alex said.

The old man shook his head. "Enough of protecting me, lass." Giff regarded Hawk. "You have been the son I never had, and I wanted you to be proud of me, so I have kept my counsel since you returned. But I must speak now, because Hildy and Alex deserve my candor. You deserve it."

"Giff, honestly . . ."

"I am a lousy gambler. I have always been, but it is Alex who paid the price. Your wife paid my gambling debts, Hawksworth. Your niece, Hildy, who was already responsible for the lot of us, got me out of debt. To the sum of nearly five thousand pounds. I do not know how she paid it, but I have been so afraid that the cost would break her."

Tears filled Gifford's eyes. "Forgive me, Alex, Hawk." He bent to kiss her aunt's hand, humbly bowing before her. "Forgive me, my love."

Hildy cupped his face and brought it up to hers. "There is nothing to forgive. But thank you for telling me. I have always been proud of my niece, but never more so than at this moment."

"As am I." Giff smiled. "If you care to take this old reprobate in hand, you tough old bird, I wish very much that you would do so. If you cannot, I understand."

Alex rose and led Hawksworth from the room, shutting the door behind them.

"Why did you not tell me?" he asked when they were in the hall. "Why did you let me chastise you and make you vow to stop gambling?"

"What was there to say?"

Hawk seemed surprised at her hard tone.

"Those were your words to me, remember, when I asked why you had not told me you saved Gideon. You and I talk all the time, Hawksworth, but I swear to God that we manage to do so without speaking one word of significance. And frankly, I do not think deceit, or conscious omission, is something I can live with. As to that bill of divorcement . . . I was not joking. Please seek one as quick as may be."

Alex knew she left Hawk reeling when she went to ask the vicar and the rest of the guests to be patient.

When at length Hildy and Gifford arrived, their wedding was perhaps the most beautiful Alex had ever attended. So beautiful, she could not stop weeping.

Twice Hawk tried to pull her aside to speak to her; twice she managed to rebuke him. "Fine," he whispered at the last. "Giff and Hildy's wedding is not an appropriate time or place for the conversation we need to have." The ramifications skittered up Alex's spine like a portent of doom. "But we will talk," he promised, "and before this day is done."

The house reverberated with wedding guests and Christmas guests. It rang with the whoops of two little Indian boys and a small Indian princess named Beatrix, all of them excited by the notion that in two days' time, gifts would be brought in the night by a saint named Nick.

"Baxter, stop encouraging them," Claudia said.

"Shh," Baxter whispered, pulling Claudia aside. "I am trying to create a diversion, so we can escape."

"Are you certain this is a good idea?"

"What, Claude, crying craven?" Baxter laughed at the whooping children. "That's right, Rafe, see if you can scalp that blighter by the wassail bowl."

While Rafe and Damon performed a war dance nearby, a barking beagle and an ill-favored cat chased a hedgehog beneath a table upon which rested said wassail bowl, nearly knocking the bowl and at least one guest off their respective pedestals.

Despite Claudia's consistent warning, Baxter encouraged the marauding savages, increasing their overabundance of energy.

When war inevitably broke out, very little got broken, except an iced Christmas torte and the temper of a certain vicar who did not appreciate the notion of wearing same.

To calm the guests and the bride's and groom's nerves, Hawk and Gideon were encouraged to accompany three Indians up the stairs, each savage carrying a cat, a pup, or a hedgehog.

"You will never guess, Uncle Bryce," Damon said, "but Papa tells the most amazing stories."

"A story it is, then," Gideon said.

Bea climbed into Hawk's lap to cuddle and listen to the story of a blue fairy and a handsome prince, until she got drowsy and yawned and Hawk kissed her brow.

"I love you, Uncle Bryce," she said, patting his be-whiskered cheek. "You will always be my most handsome prince."

Hawk felt a hard old knot of sorrow melt at her words, and he looked up and saw Rafferty, with the ugliest cat in the kingdom draped over his shoulder, petting it with devoted care. That boy did not see a stub tail, scarred fur the color of mud, or a torn ear. Quite simply, he loved that cat so much, he was blind to its flaws. As Bea seemed blind to his scars.

Hawk stood, nodding for Gideon to continue his story, and went to place Beatrix in her little bed. She woke when he laid her down, and asked him to take a nap with her, so he lay down beside her.

When he woke, the color of the sky outside her window had changed to smoke. As he rose, Beatrix woke as well.

"Did you have a good sleep, pup?"

She stretched and nodded. "I dreamed that instead

of having Chesterfield's baby, Alex was going to have a baby for us. Would that not be nice, Uncle Bryce?"

Hawk stopped moving when Bea's words penetrated, and now he could barely breathe. He kissed her nose. "Stay with the twins and Uncle Gideon, will you?"

Hawk went downstairs to look for Alex, his heart beating a wild tattoo.

He found not a mob of guests in the drawing room—or anywhere—but the duchess of Basingstoke pacing the gold salon, wringing her hands. Alexandra's aunt Hildegarde, with tears in her eyes, was trying to calm the woman.

"What has happened?" Hawk asked, feeling as if he had stepped into a nightmare. "Where is everyone? Where is Alex?"

Hildy began to weep. "Alex has gone off to Gretna Green with Chesterfield."

Twenty-seven

"You know, Alex, you can ride inside the carriage," Chesterfield said. "You do not need to sit up here on the driver's box and freeze, just to keep me company."

"We should have taken the horses," Alex said. "Then we could have gotten there faster."

"We could not take the horses. I told you, after we catch up with Claudia and Baxter—and after I shoot Baxter—we will need the carriage to take Claudia back. I suppose I shall have to wait to beat her until we get her home."

Alex scoffed. "Tell me again what Baxter's note said."

"That he was taking Claudia to Gretna Green to ruin her reputation, and if I did not arrive with ten thousand pounds before morning, he would ruin her in truth and separate us forever."

"Even Baxter knows you love her."

"He is a fool. A dead fool."

"Do not be rash," Alex warned.

Chesterfield laughed, hard and self-mocking. "I was not rash when it came to you, Alex. I did not want a simpering miss nor a green girl who would bore me to tears. Neither did I want a social butterfly who would spend all my money. I wanted a rational, mature, unspoiled female to give me an heir and grow old by my side. I was not rash when I chose you, and look where that got me."

"Point taken," Alex said. "But will you have the patience for a girl like Claudia?"

"Claude has more wisdom and maturity than we sometimes credit her for. She has been forced into growing up, has she not, having lost her parents and then her uncle, for a time?"

"I have seen her maturity, yes, but I have also seen the little girl, the child who wants what she wants."

"And how does that make her different from you?"

Alex laughed. "She overheard us that day, right after our near-wedding, when you came to the lodge."

"She told me."

"When did she? You have hardly had a moment to talk."

"Alex, once Claudia knew I lived at Hawks Ridge, she used to sneak over there at every opportunity. We went for walks; we played billiards. She even helped me deliver a foal. We have talked, believe me, though never more thoroughly than on the night she climbed in my bedroom window at two in the morning. That was the day you came to London."

"The little twit."

Chesterfield grinned.

"Judson Broderick, what did you do?"

"I remained on my best behavior, I assure you."

"I *know* your best behavior. I was betrothed to you."

Chesterfield cleared his throat. "She remains untouched, I promise you."

"Look at me."

He did, but he failed to infuse his look with the depth of innocence she would wish. "Hah. Just barely, I think. Drive faster."

"Hurrying now will not change anything."

Alex paled. "But you said . . ."

Chesterfield cursed. "That is not what I meant. I meant that hurrying would not change the past, and we should probably worry about what *Claude* will do to Baxter," but Chesterfield urged his matched pair on, nevertheless. "When I know she is safe, I really am going to beat her."

"Ah, Judson, you do care for her."

"Do you think Hawksworth will let me have her?"

"Not in a million years."

As Hawk began his trek through the shrouded fog of the chill December night, he knew that Alex was lost to him. He knew it, yet he could not stand aside and let her run off with Chesterfield.

He had not looked back when the duchess and Aunt Hildy called to him, but walked faster than he thought possible. Continuing to the stables, he found a guest's saddled Arabian, ready for imminent departure, which he mounted and rode hell for leather down the mews road.

He had not even slowed his pace when Myerson and the horse's owner tried to chase him down. He simply headed north toward the outskirts of London and straight for Scotland.

Where the devil had he gone wrong?

Alex, of course—she was where he went wrong. Not by marrying her, but by being so stupid as to leave her after he had been so brilliant as to marry her.

Because of that—because of his running off to war and getting himself killed—she had become desperate enough to accept Chesterfield. But had she found it necessary to seduce the man to get him to offer marriage? Was that how she got herself with child, if she *was* with child, which Hawk could not bring himself to believe.

Seduction—that was laughable, when it was exactly what he suspected her of attempt . . .

No, with him she had *succeeded* in her passionate, single-minded, effort to . . . make it appear as if the child she carried was his?

The probability hit Hawk like a blow—sharp, breath-stealing, and . . . still impossible to believe.

She had been a virgin when he breached her, or she said she was, *seemed* she was—though there must be ways to make it appear . . . Hawk cursed, nearly as muddled now as when he woke to discover that she had tied him to the bed. Even then, he wished he had not drunk so much that night—that glorious, incredible night.

Again Hawk urged his horse to greater speed.

Damn it to hell; no one was going to have Alex but him, baby or not. No one. He was certainly not going to sit idly by while she and Chesterfield lived in bloody sin together.

Hawksworth shouted a curse into the night. *He* was her husband, damn it, and he would bloody well remain so. No one could possibly love Alex more than he did.

Did he? Was he capable? Love?

Yes, by God, and he would not let her go. How could he? How did one cut out one's own heart? Which must explain why he had not finished his deathbed letter to her. Could he not bring himself to say good-bye even then?

Devil take it, had he *loved* her even then? Before then? When?

As Hawk rode neck or nothing along the Great North Road, he tried to mark the events in his life that led him to fall in love with the scourge and shadow of his growing-up years.

He looked as far back as that tiny mud-drenched urchin standing at the bottom of the dyke, looking up at him as if he were a bright silver knight, her very own.

He saw a young girl, all arms and legs and big turquoise eyes, warning other girls away from him. He saw the joyful look on her radiant face when he asked her to marry him, then her broken expression when he said good-bye after the ceremony, her chin raised despite her pain.

He saw Alex the woman, seduction-bent, who bound him and loved him in a fever of passion, with a physical abandon he had never imagined married love could embrace.

Hawk shook his head. No single event had made him love her, but all of them, everything about her—faults and strengths—had nurtured and grown his love, not to mention the sense of worth with which she had endowed him upon sight.

To Alex, from the beginning, he was everything.

To him, now and for eternity, she was everything.

He must tell her so, finally, in the event that he was the most fortunate of men and she loved him, as he had once, long ago, suspected but denied.

No more putting it off, even if, after he was finished slicing open his heart for her inspection, she chose Chesterfield after all.

If she had the courage to run off with the blighter—for whatever reason—then she damn well had the courage to leave Hawk, if that was her choice.

And if it was, he must let her go, once and for all.

Hawk did not know why it had taken him so bloody long to realize the possibility of love. He only hoped it would not take Alex as long.

He hoped beyond hope that he was not too late.

"I am no longer certain that this is a good plan," Claudia told Baxter, "pretending we are eloping so Chesterfield will be drawn into following. Perhaps he will not realize how much he loves me, but that he had much rather live without such pranks. Perhaps we should turn around."

"This is a brilliant plan," Baxter said. "Chesterfield will think so, too, once he has you in his arms."

"And you are certain we will be home by nine? Uncle Hawk insists upon it, even though I am nearly eighteen."

Claudia turned to regard the inn they had just

passed. "Oh, wait, that was the George's Inn, where you said a maid would be waiting to chaperone me. You said we would wait for Chesterfield there, and *there* is where I said, in my note, he could find me. Baxter . . . tell your man to stop the carriage."

When he remained silent, Claudia crossed the interior of the vehicle to touch her cousin's arm. "Baxter, what are you doing? We cannot leave London so late in the afternoon. It is gone past four."

Baxter looked at her as if she had sprouted horns, and for the first time Claudia saw a man she did not recognize, a stranger she began to fear.

"You are worse than a baby," he said.

"What do you mean?"

"I mean that the note I left for Chesterfield in place of yours was worded a bit different. I mean, shut up and let me think, for bloody sakes."

At about two in the morning, Hawk entered the Gretna Hall Hotel, just over the Scottish border, the second inn he'd tried since reaching Scotland. As he did at the first inn, Hawk went straight to the bedchamber the maid said was occupied by an English couple, hoping that, this time, the occupants were not positioned in the bed so as to stop his heart.

Again, Hawk pushed the door open without knocking. "Alexandra Wakefield, I do not care if you carry the cad's child; I will *not* allow you to live in sin with him."

Alexandra and Claudia gasped.

Chesterfield barked a laugh, even as he held a pistol aimed at Baxter's ballocks. Baxter sat on the floor, gagged and bound.

Everyone began speaking at once.

"Cease!" Chesterfield shouted until nothing could be heard save Baxter's muffled pleas.

"I take it I am the cad in question?" Chesterfield drawled, "and that somehow you have it in your head—"

"Do not even say it," Alex snapped. "It was Beatrix, was it not? The eavesdropping little hoyden."

Hawk felt himself go cold. "Then you are . . ."

Alex raised her chin. "Of course I am."

Again Chesterfield laughed. "Damn, I have not had this much fun in an age."

Chesterfield's words and his mirth relieved Hawk of worry. Alexandra could not be carrying the man's child.

Claudia even grinned at the comment, though Chesterfield rounded on her for it. "Do not think you are off the hook, miss, for you will be turned over my knee the minute we get home."

"What is going on here?" Hawk asked, assimilating the scene: Chesterfield standing over Baxter, the tears in Claudia's eyes, Alexandra's arms about her, Alex's worry. "Alex? Claude? Are you all right?"

"I have a bruised jaw and bloody knuckles," Chesterfield grumbled, "but do not ask if I am all right."

"Baxter kidnapped Claudia," Alex said. "Of course we are not all right."

Claudia shook her head in denial. "Not exactly *kidnapped,* Uncle Bryce, but I did not know that he planned to take me this far. I swear I did not."

"I told you, Hawksworth, to take care of her," Chesterfield said. "This is exactly what I predicted would happen otherwise."

"I suppose you think you can do better?" Hawk asked.

"I bloody well can. As a matter of fact, I expect permission to marry her for my part in this."

"She is already married to me, damn it!"

Chesterfield looked to the heavens in a bid for patience. "Stop being love-bit for a minute and listen. This is not about you and Alex but about me and Claudia."

"If I cannot think for seeing Alex, it is her own fault, for she has been single-minded—"

"Hawksworth, do not."

Claudia grinned and nodded for Chesterfield to try again.

"Hawksworth, I respectfully request your permission to marry your—"

"Permission denied. You are not half good enough for her."

"Uncle Hawk!"

"No, Claudia, your uncle is right," Chesterfield said. "I am *not* half good enough for you. And since you are not half obedient enough for—"

"I will second that," Hawk said, scowling at his niece.

Chesterfield nodded. "Good, we are in agreement."

"We are, for once."

"Fine, then. While we wait for the law to come and claim this cod-head, let us play a game of cards."

"Cards? Now? Are you out of your mind? Besides, you know I always win."

Chesterfield shrugged. "My skills improved while you were away. Let me prove it with one hand. The winner gets Hawks Ridge."

"Of course I will not play for those stakes."

"Why not?"

"Look at the way Alex is grinning. Even she knows that you are trying to give the estate back to me. You will let me win, and I do not like to be let win. I do not want my home handed back to me on a gilded platter, nor will I accept it as a bribe for my niece's hand."

"You think I am a card cheat, then?"

"Of course not. You are simply not as good a player as I am."

"You as much as said that I would throw the game, which makes me a cheat in your mind."

"I know you are not a cheat, but I believe you would—I do not know what you would do, but . . . you are not to be trusted right now. Lust will do that to a man." Hawk regarded Alex with a raised brow and stern expression. "I should know."

Chesterfield smiled. "Perhaps I am simply a good man who would like to see you have your home back."

Hawk looked annoyed. "Perhaps."

"Perhaps I am a good man who loves your niece and will take excellent care of her." Chesterfield looked pointedly at Claudia. "I will certainly keep her too busy to get into trouble."

Hawk noted the way his niece and his nemesis regarded each other. Hope—love—filled their gazes.

Was this what happened when one loved? One could recognize the emotion in others? "Damn."

Claudia screamed in victory and tore from Alexandra's arms to fly into Chesterfield's. The kiss Hawk witnessed made the uncle in him bristle and want to do harm. He went over and slapped Chesterfield on the back, hard. "We had best find a parson."

Chesterfield looked up, eyes aglaze.

"To the parson," Hawk repeated. "Now."

"What, now?"

"Either that or we take Claudia home. I will not have you kissing my unmarried niece in that unseemly manner."

Chesterfield focused on the blushing Claudia, the light of awareness entering his eyes. "Now is a very good time."

They left Baxter in the taproom to await the law, and after they did, Chesterfield stopped to face Alex. "I did not forgive the five thousand pounds as I let you believe. Hawk paid the debt, but he did not want you to know."

Hawk cursed.

Alex ignored him. "When did he pay it?"

"A few days before Giff and Hildy's wedding, the day he returned from the country."

"Thank you, Chesterfield, for telling me."

Chesterfield nodded. "Now my conscience is clear. Claudia, will you have me?"

Ian McGillivray married them in a quaint corner of the hotel, making their wedding a deal more special than the two-minute, over-the-anvil "ceremony" that might have taken place at the old thatched and white-washed blacksmith shop down the street.

By then Baxter had been carted off, and all four made their way back upstairs to spend what was left of the night. They would set off in a few short hours, so they could be home in time for Christmas Eve with the family."

"Good night, Alex," Chesterfield said, kissing her cheek and shaking Hawk's hand. "Good night, Uncle." Then he grinned, put an arm around Claudia, hugged her close, and laughed all the way to their bedchamber.

Twenty-eight

Hawk escorted Alex into their own chamber, his jaw so rigid by the time the door closed, she half expected him to hand her that bill of divorcement.

"You are *not* carrying his child," he said. The phrase, as much a query as an order, struck like a clap of thunder, echoing off the walls and shivering Alex to her roots.

"Will you raise it as your own? As your heir, if I have a son?"

Hawk paled and wavered, but firmed his stance. "I will."

That her confirmation did not bring his instant consent to a divorce infused Alex with sorrow and hope, for if she did not force him to dissolve their marriage, he would lose everything . . . as she would gain everything. If they *did* divorce, there might be enough of his inheritance left to regain Hawks Ridge. "Why?" she asked.

"I realized, on my way here, that even when I could not step from my father's control, I found a reason to marry you that was more important than him, and more important than me—Beatrix and Claudia. They needed you, so I married you despite my father."

Hawk fixed his regard on her then, with such deep concentration—or was it longing?—that Alex began to pace, for she could not stand still. She wished he had opposed his father for his own sake, for if he did that, she would know that he was free and spoke the truth from his heart.

"Bea still needs us both," he said.

Alex sighed, aching for the one who would suffer most for their parting, but even Bea would suffer if their marriage stood on so rocky a foundation. "I know she does."

Hawk nodded. "You once said that we must remain together for the sake of the family. Do you still believe it? Though it is a great deal to ask."

The dart went straight to her heart. "Is it?"

"God's teeth," Hawk said. "I mean it is too much to ask of you."

Alex saw from his appalled expression that he spoke true. "Are you certain that staying together is what you want?"

"More than anything."

That surprised her. "The rogue of Devil's Dyke for a lifetime? I do not know. Do you think you can manage me?"

"No one has ever been able to manage you." Hawk's eyes actually smiled. "But if you mean, can I bear our remaining married? I can, if you can."

They were still playing games of a sort, and Alex despised it. "I would have a promise."

"Then you shall have it. I am in your debt for at least a dozen."

She wished she could collect every one. "This is more of a demand."

"Name it."

"No more secrets."

Hawk bent to a hearth framed with delft tiles to light the fire. "What do you want to know?"

The sight of him performing the homey task made Alex want a life with him so badly that she had to swallow twice before she could speak. "Why did you not tell me that you lost your inheritance because you married me?"

Hawk set tinder to flame, then rose to face her. "I did not know about the codicil to my father's will until I saw the solicitor, and then it was too late."

"It was not too late," she said, her voice rising. "We could have gotten an annulment back then. And you are still speaking in half-truths."

"Alex, shh." Hawk stepped forward to take her by the shoulders, as if she *must* hear him. "That it was too late had nothing to do with our consummated— or unconsummated—marriage. It had to do with my unwillingness to let you go."

"Too stubborn to give up?" she asked, stepping away, for her resolve could vanish in such joy, and then she would have no strength left to let him go.

He raised a brow. "Among other things."

Alex could not bear an elaboration; she carried too many unanswered questions. "Where did you get the five thousand pounds to pay Chesterfield?"

Hawk's quick smile weakened her knees, boding ill for her cause. "Remember the tiny alabaster bust we dug up near the water meadows a hundred years ago?" he asked.

Alex could not stop her smile. "You love that piece."

"I love it even more now. I sold it for a tidy sum. My good luck, I should have realized, began the day I found you. I will tell you all about the sale later, but know that, even after paying Chesterfield, there is enough left to set the lodge and property to rights and begin breeding horses."

"How much were you able to get for it?"

Hawk grinned. "Fifteen thousand pounds."

Alex gasped. "But that was enough to buy back Hawks Ridge! Why did you not give Chesterfield the money for your estate? Why pay *my* debt?"

"It was not your debt."

"You did not know that at the time."

"Freeing you from Chesterfield was more important—no, that is wrong. *You* were more important to me."

"But Hawks Ridge is your heritage, your home."

"Alex, wherever you are is my home, whether in a mansion, or at the bottom of the dyke. Besides, I find myself looking forward to the challenge of bringing Huntington Lodge back to its former glory." He took her hand and brought it to his lips. "Which is something I want, more than my next breath, for us to do together."

Alex might rejoice at Hawk's words, if not for his father's will. "Your father warned me," she said, turning away, fingering a blue damask bed curtain. "He said I would be the worst possible wife for you." She looked up. "I should have listened, for now I have made you turn your back on your birthright."

"My father was a heartless schemer, whose machinations served only him—*his* plans, *his* power to control. *You* are the wife for me, Alex, the best wife, the only wife I want."

Beguiled by his words, Alex pulled away. "No. Listen. If I had not married you, you would not have been able to go to war, so you would not have been wounded and scarred, or lost your home and your wealth. Hawk, you have lost *everything* because of me."

"I have lost everything *only* if I have lost *you*. Why will you not believe me?" he asked, stepping once forward for each of her steps back. Catching up, he placed his hands on either side of her face. "Listen to my words, Alex. I love you, and I want to stay married to you. In so saying, I am fully cognizant that I repudiate my father, thereby burying him and his hold over me—over both of us—once and forever."

Alex nearly shouted for joy. Hawk's declaration was everything she dreamed, but it was time for her to be honest as well. "You should know," she said, stepping to the window and looking out, "that I planned to seduce you as a form of revenge."

Hawk wanted to tell her that hers was a sweet revenge, but he could see that she was serious, and this was no time for levity. "Why did you?"

"After you left for France, I heard your friends talking—though you recently said they are not your friends. Still, they knew that you married me only to care for your family. They said you could not bear to touch me, and since you had not . . . touched me, I thought they knew what they were talking about."

"Oh, Alex, I am so—"

"Do not say it. I am sick unto death of people being sorry for me. When you came home . . . No, you never did come home, did you? When you stopped my wedding and *still* you did not touch me, I vowed to seduce you until you said exactly what you just did—that you wanted me, loved me—and then I was going to walk away. And because I learned your true feelings from someone else, I was going to have someone else tell you mine." She did not say that she planned for them to go on with their marriage afterward, because now they could not.

"How could you learn my true feelings from someone else when I did not know them myself?" Hawk shook his head. "I cannot believe that you thought of vengeance as you seduced me. As we loved, Alex."

She looked away.

"So," he said, "is it finished then? Are you planning to leave me now?"

Alex looked at the door and knew she must, but before she took two steps, Hawk blocked her path. "I meant what I said. I love you, though you have never said as much to me."

"And have it thrown in my face? I think not."

"Then you do love me?"

Alex laughed, mocking them both. "Only forever. Only since I looked up from the bottom of Devil's Dyke and saw you coming to rescue me." She raised a hand at his step forward. "No, do not come any closer. My admission does not mean that I will fall at your feet. Besides, I was never good enough for the hand-some-as-sin Rogue of Devil's Dyke. Why am I now?"

"Alex, you are—"

"Is it because people say I am . . . no longer unat-tractive? Is that why you think you love me? Because, Hawk, beauty fades with time. Always."

"I have learned a great deal about beauty since my return. I have seen it firsthand in a little girl's adora-tion. In a little boy and his motley cat. An elderly cou-ple's love." He smiled. "I saw beauty every time your back ached." He touched her lips with reverence. "I see it in the way you kiss my scars."

Alex's eyes filled. Hawk wiped away a tear. When had he stepped close enough?

"Let me tell you something else. I never saw beauty in the man you termed a 'handsome-as-sin rogue.' What I saw in that man was worthlessness. My father approved of rogues, so I became a rogue— and I enjoyed the part for a time—but I am not that man. Not quite. I am the man you have encouraged me to become. The man you see before you.

"As, layer by layer, everything I once thought im-portant was stripped from me, I saw revealed to me what was truly important. You, the girls, Aunt Hildy and Uncle Giff, Gideon, Sabrina, and their children. Us, working and making a home together, caring for our family . . . together."

Alex made to speak, but Hawk stopped her with a finger to her lips. "Let me try to explain why I could not bring myself to come home to you. If I never thought the 'handsome rogue' worthy—and I did *not*—imagine how I felt about the 'beast,' who, by some foolish blunder of fate, cheated death."

Alex sobbed and stepped into his arms. "You are not a beast, you are n—"

Hawk opened his mouth over hers and kissed her with passion, with hunger and wonder, desperate to make her understand how much she meant to him. To take her love and give it back, to connect with the mate to his soul.

"Beauty," he said, looking into her eyes, "resides where gentleness and love are the most wondrous of gifts."

"And within one who would give his life for a friend."

"I fell in love with you," Hawk said, "while I was healing in Belgium, long before I saw how beautiful you had become—or so I thought. But some time during my long ride here, I traced my love as far back as that mud-spattered urchin at the bottom of the dyke."

Alex toyed with his cravat. "Perhaps you love the memory of me."

Hawk urged her toward the canopied four-poster, the fire in his eyes reminiscent of that night-stalking lion. "I am certain that is not the case, for I am in love with a hoyden," he said, "who would shoot an arrow through the roof to get her husband into her bed." He began to undo the buttons at her bodice with single-minded determination. "I am in lust with a siren who would tie said husband to her bed to seduce him . . . exquisitely." He kissed her neck and nudged aside her bodice to kiss the crown of a breast.

"I cherish the woman who gave a mother's heart to

the orphaned daughters of another." He kissed her brow. "I thank and honor the lass who kept a curmudgeon's greatest secret to give him the gift of his family's respect."

Alex bit her lip as tears blurred her vision.

"Do not go out that door, Alexandra Wakefield, for I would only follow. Do not walk away from me, please, I beg you. I could not bear to lose you." He tried to pull her down on the bed with him, and despite her attempt to resist—to do the right thing and let him go—she toppled, landing atop him, her gown's skirt settling over her head like a veil.

Hawk's eyes darkened as his hands traveled the length of her body. "Will it hurt the babe if I make love to you?" he asked, melting her to her marrow and making her his for good and all.

"Ah, Hawk, I can resist you no longer. You think yourself unworthy of love, but you are so worthy, you would raise another man's child as your own. But there is no need, my love, for no man has touched me, save you. How could you not know?"

He became endearingly sheepish. "I fear I imbibed rather a lot that night."

"Ah . . . speaking of secrets . . ."

His eyes widened. "Damn. You drugged me."

"Never, but I did make certain that your brandy glass stayed full."

"Sorceress." He nuzzled her breasts and rolled her onto her back to rise above her. "This bed is too bloody big," he said with a grin. Then he bent to her and threaded his fingers through her hair, on either side of her face and brushed her cheeks with his thumbs. "How would you feel about giving Beatrix a mama and a papa, both, for Christmas? We could adopt her, if you—"

"Oh, Hawk, yes. And we could give her the baby she wants."

"This Christmas, she will have to settle for a mama and papa." The fire in his eyes leaped, and his body surged to life. "Though, if we begin now, and try very hard, perhaps we can give her that baby next Christmas."

"Yes, yes, and ye—" He stopped her with his kiss, unable to wait a minute longer to have her mouth again.

Some while later, Alex cupped his cheek. "I love you."

Hawk was humbled and so grateful he could hardly draw breath, and neither the lump in his throat nor the speck in his eye mattered. "You will keep this wreck, that all the king's horses and all of his men failed to put together again?"

"I should beat you for doubting it."

Hawk shook his head. "I should have known that you would accept me, broken as I am, but you deserve so much better, that I had the devil of a time asking it of you."

"No need to ask."

"I do not deserve you, but God help us both, I love and want you. Please, will you forgive this unforgivable rogue for waiting so long to come home?"

"Not unforgivable, but unforgettable, for even as I walked up the aisle to marry another, I thought only of you."

"About that baby . . ."

ABOUT THE AUTHOR

Annette Blair is the development director and journalism advisor at a private New England secondary school. Married to her grammar school nemesis—and glad she didn't know what fate had in store—Annette considers romance a celebration of life.

Since she has been working on "The Rogues Club," her Regency historical series, Annette has done a lot of thinking about what makes a man a rogue, and she would like to know what you think. What do *you* consider an essential characteristic in a rogue? What do you love the most? What makes a rogue so sexy? Drop her a line and let her know.

Besides writing, Annette enjoys speaking to writers' groups, hearing from her readers, and collecting glass slippers.

Annette Blair P.O. Box 302, Manville, RI 02838 or www.AnnetteBlair.com